# MARA

# MARA

A NOVEL BY

## TOVA REICH

FARRAR STRAUS GIROUX   NEW YORK

Copyright © 1978 by Tova Reich
All rights reserved
Published simultaneously in Canada by
McGraw-Hill Ryerson Ltd., Toronto
Printed in the United States of America
Designed by Karen Watt
First edition, 1978

Library of Congress Cataloging in Publication Data
Reich, Tova. / Mara : a novel. / I. Title.
PZ4.R3598Mar  [PS3568.E4763]  813'.5'4  78–5837

*To Walter*

1 The bride wore her glasses as they steered her down the aisle. When the women lifted her veil to give her the wine, the lace snagged in the steel frame. One of the praying men wrapped a cloth around the rare crystal goblet the couple had bought for this night. He set it down on the floor. The groom raised his foot and smashed the glass to bits.

Her father, Rabbi Leon Lieb, had tapped his influence with God many times to prevent this marriage. God had tried. During the three months of engagement He had arranged for the imprisonment of the bridegroom. Not satisfied, He went on to strip the groom's story down to its bedrock of lies, until Mara herself was forced to see it. "Okay, maybe he's sick," she said. "Of course I can't leave him now." So He served up a bomb scare to cancel the flight of the bridegroom's party from Tel Aviv to New York. Then, on the wedding night itself, He brewed a storm so foul that even some of Rabbi Lieb's best sycophants never reached the hall. For weeks they would dispatch their regrets. The train they had boarded to the pink stucco hotel on Lido Beach had crashed in the rain and wind. A preposterous excuse. In fact, it was the truth. Mara herself had insisted upon making a solitary journey to her own wedding. Her mother had cried, "A bride can't go alone. Please, Mara!" Mara's was the last train to creep out of Penn Station before the ill-fated one. Her hair was still damp as she circled Sudah seven times under the canopy.

They were both eighteen. Besides the glasses there were still some pimples on her face. She had refused her sister's satin and brocade gown in favor of a long skirt and a white cotton blouse. Her veil was an old lace tablecloth with a tea stain on it. It was held in place by a wreath of daisies, which she had braided on the train and which was already drooping. Many people noticed the red ballet slippers peeping out from under her dress.

The general opinion was that Sudah looked royal. A bridegroom is compared to a king. Some likened him to the Prince of Hell. Others were reminded of how they had always pictured the false Messiah. Mara saw in him a sheik. She had devoted the two weeks between Sudah's arrival from Israel and their wedding to a quest for the perfect bridegroom's costume. Arms encircling each other's waist, they had tramped from shop to shop until they consummated their search: a suit of black velvet with wide satin lapels and a jacket tailored to display the refinement of his small body. With the silk shirt—white as milk to warm the mysterious brown of his skin—the two hundred dollars her father had handed them would not suffice. They had to stop for more at Rabbi Lieb's office, in the penthouse of one of his old-age homes on the West Side. The rabbi recounted their visit to his eldest daughter: "One of my managers was waiting in the hall. He watched them go, smooching the whole way. When he came in he said to me, 'Isn't it disgusting how the white girls go with the coloreds these days!' Rashi, you can imagine how this made me feel."

Mara also described this episode to Rashi. Their father, she said, had attempted to do business with Sudah. Three hundred dollars more for a promise to pray every morning, trim his extravagant beard, and lop off his mane of shoulder-length hair. Sudah agreed. This enabled him to afford the dazzling black cape that completed his attire. The morning of the wedding

Sudah tamed his beard with a gleaming razor. As Rabbi Lieb chanted the benedictions, the bridegroom stuffed a mischievous lock of hair back into the tight bun under his silk top hat.

Rose Lieb clutched her daughter's elbow and revolved with her around the stranger. She prayed discreetly. Experience had shown her that she would fall precisely when the thought of falling would grip and then refuse to release her. She was always pleading with God to spare her, for once, from the inevitable humiliation. Her shins were always bruised, her knees always scraped, like a child's. The spike heels of her satin slippers, which had been dyed royal blue to match her gown, kept catching in the beading at the hem. She felt pressed to the floor by the indifferent stares of the guests, row after row of politicians, clergymen, business associates of her husband. Their wives were watching, too, rating. She had intended to slim down for the wedding, but, thank God, at least she had taken the precaution of having the dressmaker fashion a long tunic to be worn over the gown. She was safe in this tunic. If she fell now, though, she could predict what they would think. How many of them knew where she had spent half of the last year? Rose had noticed how they tended to address her in an unnaturally loud voice, enunciating deliberately, the way natives speak to foreigners. They would attribute a fall to her condition, no doubt. Still, in spite of her heaviness, she could fall with wonderful grace, folding up silently, disappearing for a second. But this time her prayer was "Please, God, don't let me think about falling tonight." She had downed eleven pills before they left home to drive, brideless, to the wedding, and she was reeling, reeling. She could not rely on this fragile Mara to support her, especially at this hour, when the girl was weak with fasting. Besides, Mara was busy flirting with Sudah, bumping brazenly against his hip as they spun around him, just as if the two of them were alone. How had this invader entered their fortress? She glanced at him in his plumage. She could never stomach such a man, though in the end it was she who had sanctioned it. She had said to Leon, "We'll have to let her marry him. I think they've already done it. It's over, you know." These words were spoken in bed, just after Leon and Rose took off their glasses and turned away from each other. "And you will be nice to him, Leon," Rose said as she dipped for sleep, "or we'll lose Mara forever."

"Mommy, hold on to me," Mara was whispering to Rose. Rose grabbed Mara's shoulder and managed to remain upright. The seven revolutions around the bridegroom had come to an end, at last, just as her knees were melting. Her weaknesses were public; she was resigned to that. But when she addressed her husband in their beds that night there was that remembered power in her voice, and Leon knew he had lost. Nevertheless, this is what he said: "Don't interfere, Rose. That boy will never get Mara from me."

Leon Lieb had first learned of his troubles from an old crony, Dr. Bernard Seligman. Seligman, with bristles like a walrus and a distinguished belly, was president of the university in Israel that Rabbi Lieb supported with an annual donation of twenty-five thousand dollars. When the institution transformed Herzl Lieb, Leon's only son, from an object that seemed to be sprouting from a basketball to an appropriately serious young man, Rabbi Lieb increased the contribution to fifty thousand. Then one September he sent one hundred thousand dollars, and Mara. Four months later he received a telegram from Seligman with the information that Mara had not been seen for several weeks. "Bernie," Leon shouted over wires that stretched seven thousand miles, "why didn't you call me sooner?"

"Because I've been doing some detective work, Leon. This is the story. She climbed out of her window five weeks ago. Why? I don't know. She could have walked out the door. Her roommate says she took along an old carpetbag and a bird cage with a bird in it. That's all."

The bird cage was soon after carried by Mara down the center aisle of a concert hall in a suburb of Tel Aviv, and presented with great ceremony to the folksinger, Rav Habakuk, who kissed her with loud smacks, once on each cheek and once on her forehead. This account was delivered by Manny Fish, Mara's friend, immediately after his arrival from Israel. Reb Anschel Frankel, Leon's most faithful sexton, greeted Manny at the airport, severed him from the arms of a mother who had not embraced him for two years, and chauffeured him at top speed directly to the Lieb apartment on Riverside Drive. A pastrami sandwich had been set for Manny at the head of the long mahogany table in the dining room. The family listened stonily as Manny Fish struggled to swallow, and Leon probed. "Tell what you know, Manny."

Manny had been drained by the long flight. His head kept bobbing into his plate. For him it was already morning and he had had no sleep. All he could recall at first was the incident with the bird cage. He looked at the expectant faces around the table, but his brain was totally clogged. Then Lieb asked, "Is there a man involved?" Reb Anschel's forearms, with their rolled-up sleeves and pelt of red hair, suddenly shot forward to place a pickled-tongue sandwich before him, and Manny remembered the night in the discotheque in Jaffa. He had danced with Mara for more than two hours, and then he sat at a side table watching her dance alone. A bearded young man with heavy black hair and wearing an antique tweed coat to his ankles slid in next to him. The candlelight flashed in the stranger's bright eyes. They both watched Mara dance. Her movements seemed so oddly private that it was obvious she felt the interested eyes upon her. The stranger tapped Manny on the shoulder and indicated Mara. "American?" Manny nodded. They watched her a while longer. Then the stranger spoke again: "First, I dance her." He smiled. "Second, I marry her." That was Sudah. Perhaps he was French. Perhaps he was an artist. Certainly he was not the boy you wished for your daughter. Over the ensuing two days Manny observed them dancing together in the Lower Depths, the Pussycat, the Pope's, Candy's, Abou Hassan's, and the Marrakesh.

Leon Lieb was no longer looking at Manny. "You're a dope, Fish," he muttered. "Get out of here."

The next morning Leon found this letter on his desk. Sadie Stern, his first cousin and personal secretary, had thoughtfully placed it face down.

With the help of God, to Rabbi Leon Lieb, long may he live! You do not know me, but you are known to me. I shall forbear from revealing my name to you, for the fate of the messenger of bad tidings is well known. I shall say only that I am a contemporary of your daughter, Mara Lieb, and a son of someone whose path you have crossed in the past. Indeed, it is about Mara that I write to you today, and it grieves me to do so, believe me. I avoid the evil tongue; that is one of my principles. But what I am about to impart to you is the truth, unfortunately. Your daughter, Mara, has strayed. She has leased a room in Jerusalem, in the flat of some students of doubtful reputation. I have seen this room. It is shabby, crowded, filthy, most unfitting for a daughter of yours, and contains a mattress of some sort. Nothing else. Only a mattress. She shares this room with a young man. I have also seen the young man. He is an exotic fellow, an Eastern Jew, notorious on the streets of our land as a connoisseur of hashish and a pacifist. Our rabbis warn us not to judge our friend until we reach his place. Nevertheless, even if this arrangement is thoroughly innocent, as I hope it is, for your sake and the sake of all Israel, do not our rabbis also remind us that the appearance of wrongdoing is almost as bad as the sin itself? I advise you to make haste and investigate this matter. There is no need to thank me. If the situation exists as I have described it, my reward will be its correction.

That night, Rabbi and Mrs. Lieb boarded the 11 p.m. plane for Tel Aviv. Rose Lieb smiled childishly as the clerk set her luggage down on the scale. One hundred and ten pounds overweight. She was concentrating on the clerk's description of the penalty fees as her husband acknowledged the greetings of the airline manager. "Rabbi Dr. Lieb! *Shalom, shalom.* I noticed your name on the list." She was still listening intently as the manager ushered Leon into the lounge, and Leon dragged her away, pursued by the clerk who was flapping his chart and sweating. "Stop!" the clerk was yelling to the manager, "they're overweight! Wait! Wait!" "Jump back to your machine, Einstein," the manager replied. Einstein's arms dropped in disbelief; his documents swirled to the floor. The manager, meanwhile, was observing the route taken by Lieb's eyes. "Our newest stewardess," he offered, "Sergeant Ronit Traub, Miss Israel runner-up. She'll be on your flight, Rabbi Dr. Lieb." Leon chuckled. "What do you think, just because I'm a rabbi, my instinct is a raisin?"

A brief paragraph in the *Jerusalem Post* announced their arrival, on family business. They spent their days in a white Continental driven at head-spinning speed by a kibbutznik named Binny. They stopped at each of the places on Manny's list of Mara's haunts. They visited the café of Uncle Moloch in the Old City, where Moloch himself, in an aqua turban, his three hundred pounds swathed in a striped silk caftan, like a tent, insisted that they sip some sweet Turkish coffee with him and sign the guest registry. On the second and third lines of the page upon which Leon inscribed his own name, he noticed the signatures "Mara Lieb" and "Golda Meir," both in an unfamiliar handwriting. "We are hot on them," said Binny, and they raced off to a college in central Jerusalem. "At the college, contact Ketantan," Manny had advised. Ketantan, however, had luckily observed a policewoman following him two days earlier and had made the decision to swallow the finger of hashish he was transporting. He was still unable to engage in useful conversation, but his companion, Frumie, directed the Liebs to Aubrey Goldsmith, an Australian chemist and organist who made his home in a Jordanian tank abandoned near the Dung Gate. When Rose saw smoke pouring from the tank's gun she hesitated to approach. She tugged at Leon's black jacket. "Don't go in there," she pleaded. Leon and Binny hoisted themselves inside and were greeted by Aubrey, who was sitting cross-legged, shirtless, placidly smoking a pipe full of kef. "You needn't bother to introduce yourself," Aubrey said. "They're in Eilat."

Rose never forgot the journey down to Eilat. She had not anticipated it, and her wardrobe was utterly wrong. Still, she clung to her fur coat, even past King Solomon's Mines, maintaining that it cushioned her against the bumps in the road, against Binny's savage driving. Sand flew and an oppressive dryness coated their tongues. By the time they reached the Red Sea, all they could do was guzzle bottle after bottle of ice-cold soda pop and listen miserably to the lullaby of the air conditioner. At night they climbed over the boys and girls retiring on the beach. Many knew Mara. Some were surprised that she was no longer among them. Saba, the owner of a small café, also remembered Mara. "A thin girl. Glasses. Certainly, yes. I'll tell you the truth, these hippies are a calamity, my noble professor. Not like my darling beatniks. I am the grandpapa to all of Eilat's beatniks. Did you know who I am? But these dreadful hippies, my dear plump lady, these hippies have no sense of family. You are quite beautiful, Missus. Are you aware? You don't mind if I say this to your wife, my distinguished professor? It is a compliment to you, too. Where I come from, your lady would be selected Miss Kazakhstan. Unanimously!"

At the police station of Eilat there was also general agreement that Mara had passed through their hot town. For proof, a pockmarked officer pushed aside his bottle of black beer and got up reluctantly to hand Leon Mara's passport, which had been found among the shells on the beach. "Stupid hippies!" he mumbled. "Outcasts!" Rabbi and Mrs. Lieb gazed quietly at the photograph of their daughter. She was wearing the long scarf Rose had knitted last year, during those six months of separation, night after night in front of the television set in the patients' lounge. Mara's hair, in this picture, was still neat, short, and smooth, and her eyes, behind the glasses, were shaped like almonds. Rose and Leon were reminded of their child.

They decided to continue their search in a more systematic way, starting with a visit to Mara's college and a discussion with Seligman. This time Leon drove; Binny had chosen to remain and build a nest on the beaches of Eilat. They stopped in the marketplace of Beersheba, where an unusual thing happened to Rose as she waited for Leon to finalize his haggling with an old Bedouin over a rug. A withered Arab passed by, seized her, threw her over his donkey, and led the two away. Fortunately, a group of bystanders remarked about the strangeness of this event, for Rose herself had not uttered a sound. They gave chase and retrieved the woman, setting her down alongside her husband, who was still trading passionately with the Bedouin.

Hours later, as they drove past the open silos filled almost to the top with oranges, Rose said to Leon, "Did you know that an Arab tried to kidnap me in Beersheba?"

"Naturally," said Leon. "What would you expect from an Arab?"

"Well, there's nothing he could have done to me that hasn't already been done," Rose said. "Except maybe kill me."

Leon did not seem to hear her. She went on, "Sometimes I think you would have preferred to make this trip alone."

"Well, you know, I could have moved a lot faster. Gotten a lot more done."

"Mara's mine, too, Leon. Don't forget that. I owe her some-thing. Where was I while she was growing up? Locked up in a loony bin. Too sick to notice when it happened. Besides, you never knew how to talk to her."

Leon said, "Let me handle Seligman, you hear, honey? I'll tell it to him straight. I expected him to give me and mine some extra-loving care. Let him *pish* in his pants for next year's donation."

Seligman was bursting with some fresh information. There was a boy in the story, before Mara had fled. A penitent, with knotted fringes dangling from his rope belt. He worked as a waiter at Yash's, a favored student meeting place, but was fired for dirty fingernails, nose picking, armpit sniffing, and other unclean habits. Even the more unstable children here found him unstable. One night he lost his mind and beat Mara until both her eyes were blackened and blood ran down her face. No one could understand how such an intelligent, charming girl could get mixed up with a maniac like that.

Seligman escorted Mara's parents to their daughter's room. Girls were scurrying up and down the corridor, gossiping, hailing each other, looking agonizingly wholesome. In the room itself they were stunned by the bareness of the two beds, stripped down to the mattresses. Mara's roommate had also vanished, Seligman explained. "With a drummer in a jazz band, I hear. Her father is the Krakover Rabbi. I figured she'd be a good influence." Seligman shrugged.

The closet and dresser still contained the best of Mara's possessions. Rose and Leon left the dormitory lugging Mara's suède jacket, the fur-lined boots, tweed skirts, and cashmere sweaters exactly like the ones displayed in the magazines for coeds, the gold watch they had presented to her at her high-school graduation, a left and right sandal, each from a different pair, the scarf, the cameo that had belonged to Rose's mother for which Mara had pleaded and wept nearly two weeks, and a picture postcard from Paris, sent by Rashi to Mara, showing two sisters, naked from the waist up, one pinching the nipple of the other. On the back, in Mara's handwriting, were the directions to Yash's place.

Yash was an amiable, unusually robust Yemenite. His place consisted of a long counter and some Formica tables and chairs set on a tile floor. Behind the counter stood his wife, Shoshi, a leathery woman with a swollen neck. Shoshi signaled to Yash as the Liebs filled the doorway. Following an animated conference, Yash rushed back to greet the newcomers. "Adon Lieb, *shalom!*" he roared. Leon led his exposed wife to a table, upon which a plate of tahina garnished with hot peppers, pickles, and olives had already been placed. "One hundred percent *kasher!*" cried Yash. "Only the finest for the papa and mama of my little Mara." Leon plunged immediately into the sauce, wiping it up with slabs of pita and washing it down with orange juice. "So you know Mara?" he inquired with a full mouth. Certainly Yash knew Mara. She was like a daughter to him. He was like a father to her. Didn't he struggle with her to end her business with that crazy Jerry? *Meshugah*, completely, believe me. Thank God, it was over and done with. In fact, why did he fire Jerry? Do you care to know? For one reason only. To get him away from our Mara. "Alas, Mara has not been here for many weeks, but friends have reported that she was seen dancing night after night at the Marrakesh. Go to the Marrakesh, Adon Lieb, perhaps you will find her. But first, enjoy your food, finish eating, and then, one thing more. When your Mara's pockets were empty, at least I made sure her belly was full. She told me all about you, Adon Lieb. I said to Shoshi, this is a girl we can trust. Adon Lieb, here is a little bill for one thousand pounds. A growing girl needs to eat, after all. Now, when I add on the eight pounds for your meal today, it comes to one thousand and eight pounds. Correct? If it's all the same to you, Adon Lieb, may I have it in American dollars?"

Rose clutched Leon's sleeve as they descended the twelve stone steps to the Marrakesh. The darkness seemed total at first. Soon they could distinguish rosy faces flickering above candle flames. In the center of the floor, on a circular platform, three naked girls were dancing barbarically. "Leon," Rose whispered, "put your yarmulka in your pocket." "Never," he snapped. He placed her at a small table where her elbow immediately capsized the drink of a man absorbed in watching the dancers, who glanced at her sarcastically, as if he were comparing her to the girls on stage. Leon stepped onto the stone floor and squeezed his tall body among the dancers, feeling himself moistened by their sweat, peering into rapt eyes, intruding upon the strange rites of these couples, his nostrils quivering with their smell, his person the target of the sudden jerks of their limbs. When he could identify an ear he would bring his lips close to it and mutter, "Mara Lieb? Do you know Mara Lieb?" "Mara, Mara," he called, as he wove through the dancers, no longer moving in his chosen direction but going wherever they pushed him. A voice answered, "I am Mara." It was one of the performing dancers. He looked up and saw between her naked breasts a ribbon with the name Mara painted on it. To her left was a girl with a Sonia ribbon; to her right, a Ronit. His eyes rose to the face. It was not his Mara. Men grew irritable as Leon, in his black suit and the crocheted yarmulka into which Rose had embroidered his Hebrew name, Aryeh, stumbled up close to examine their partners a second and a third time. It ended when one bearded boy grabbed Leon by the shirt front and growled, "Run back to your Hilton, tourist'ke. Quick, quick!" Everyone laughed.

Rabbi and Mrs. Lieb returned to their hotel. Sitting on their bed, her hands folded in her lap, was Mara.

Rose's palm flew to her mouth. "Sit down, honey," Leon said, and then, to Mara, "Mommy hasn't been feeling so hot lately. You can imagine."

Mara smiled. Her glasses were taped over the bridge of her nose and on her feet were two unmatched sandals. She was wearing an unfamiliar gray jacket, quite old, padded at the shoulders, and much too large for her.

"Oh, don't worry about me," Rose said, "I'm all right. Just a little tired." She glanced at her daughter. "But you look a mess, Mara. Are you sick?"

Leon sat down on the bed beside his daughter. He placed a strong finger on her chin and twirled her face to his. "Mommy's right. You're a mess. You could be a pretty girl if only you'd dress right. It hurts us to see you like this."

Mara spoke. "I need money to fix my glasses. My passport is lost. I have to pay for a new one. I need money to go to a doctor."

"A doctor?" Leon got up and set himself firmly behind his wife's chair.

"My throat has been hurting for three weeks. We had a snowstorm in Jerusalem. I had no place to sleep."

"Why should a girl like you have no place to sleep?" Rose was moaning.

Leon dropped a comforting hand on his wife's shoulder. "Manny tells us you're keeping company with a fellow," he said, "an artist, or something. Naturally, we'd like to meet him. We want to do the proper thing. Who are his parents? Why are you hiding him?"

"Manny has a runny mouth. I have lots of friends."

"Friends are one thing, but this is no friend. I have my sources. I know plenty. If I wanted, I could pick you up right this minute. I could carry you kicking to the airport and put you on the plane with us for New York. But, you see, I'm experimenting with self-control."

"Don't threaten me, Daddy. If you threaten me I don't know what I'll do."

"Your father is not threatening you," said Rose. "This is his way of telling you how much he loves you. Do you really think we want you to be unhappy? Do you remember that Shabbos afternoon when you were a little girl, Mara sweetheart? You were punished, I forget why, and you had to stay in your room while the other children played outside. You cried, darling. You cried so hard it broke your daddy's heart. But it was important to carry out the punishment. You'll understand this, too, when you're a mother yourself, with God's help. So your father stayed with you in your room all that afternoon, telling you story after story, teaching you songs and poems. No one wanted to punish you."

Mara said, "I was nine years old. You punished me because Herzl and I switched clothing in the lobby, on the way home from *shul.* He put on my underwear, dress, and straw hat, with the plastic fruits and the long velvet ribbon, and I put on his underwear, suit, shirt, tie, and the yarmulka you crocheted, Ma. We did this every week. You always laughed. Then, suddenly, you cracked down. We didn't expect it. We thought we'd been entertaining you. I'm eighteen years old now, Mother. It's time you stopped punishing me for my own good."

Leon placed himself in front of his daughter, his hands on his hips. "But you are not yet twenty-one, Mara," he said. "I still have my rights. Everything you have I've given you. You own nothing. It's all mine. What do you want? Tell me what the hell you want! Tell me immediately! Which school do you want? Where did you pick up such an ugly jacket?"

"I'm getting out of here," said Mara.

He shoved her back down onto the bed. "We have driven up and down the Holy Land, from top to bottom, searching for you. We saw plenty of low life, believe me. You're not getting away now, I promise you. You will just sit here and think things over. Maybe you can think a bit more clearly in the bathtub. You know, you don't smell so good. By the time

Mommy and I get back from supper, maybe we can talk business." He left with Rose and the key.

Mara glanced with interest at her own face, sobbing in the mirror. She held her breath a moment to listen to the scratching of the key in the hole. It was a skeleton-type key, used to lock the door from both inside and out. A fire could shoot up suddenly, or Egyptian planes could swoop down from overhead. They would return to find a small heap of ashes leaning against the door. She heard her parents treading heavily, then lightly, down the corridor.

Sudah crawled out from under the bed, brushing off his paint-stippled jeans. He pinched his nostrils. "Ooh ah! That mattress hold in every stink from every rich people what sleep on him." He insisted upon conversing in English with Mara, and was making good progress. Mara's weeping grew more intense. Sudah bolted the chain across the inside of the door and drew Mara into his embrace. Thus they stood for a long while, he only slightly taller and broader than she, his dark hand tracing slow circles upon her heaving back, his full lips at her earlobe murmuring, "Mara, Mara, Mara, do not cry, Mara."

They walked to the bed and lay down on it. He unfastened her jeans and she his. They kicked their pants into a pile at the foot of the bed. Neither wore underwear. Each placed hands on the buttocks of the other, and in this way they loved, Mara's face pressing into Sudah's neck, and Sudah whispering throughout, "Your father is big bullshit. Your father is great big bullshit." When it was over Sudah stroked her hair. "I have finished," he said. "You?" Mara said it was very good. He was so magnificent, she said. Still stretched out upon the bed, they wiggled into each other's jeans. "You must needs to get free from your father," said Sudah, "for the good of growing up." Mara agreed. They filled their rucksacks with whatever money and jewelry they could locate in the room and left through the balcony, climbing over onto the adjacent balcony and out through the neighboring room, which happened to have been left open, and in which they paused to collect some German marks and a necklace of black pearls. Mara's parents, when they returned, doubly regretted having gone down to dine on fare that had already left them sick to their stomachs.

Before he left Israel, Leon scheduled meetings with representatives of certain branches of government. Lieutenant Raphael Mizrahi, who had been assigned by his superior to listen to Leon's petition with special consideration, tugged at his mustache, chuckled, and had this comment: "So I see you want to do a David for the sake of your Bathsheba." Leon thought, Here is your typical sabra, a Bible amateur, a *pruste ying,* as coarse as manure. Their discussion was inconclusive, as were most of the others, primarily because Leon had not been able to ascertain Sudah's last name. However, as they were parting, Lieutenant Mizrahi engulfed their joined hands with his own massive left paw and observed, "You say he is eighteen? All eighteen-year-olds are drafted anyway, even without outside intervention. Don't worry, my friend. It will be okay."

Leon's best hope rested in the Ministry of Religion, where several dear friends sat. A close aide to the minister himself reassured him that no marriage could be performed in the land without their office's sanction. Of course, the moment these two babies came into his office *kvetching* for a license, a telegram would be dispatched to Rabbi Leon Lieb, in New York City, in the United States of America.

The telegram arrived the day after Rashi set off for Israel with the cold order to bring Mara home, by any means. "You're the only one she'll talk to," Leon said. "Do this thing for me." Two weeks earlier, Manny Fish had passed the rumor that a splendid wedding uniting Sudah and Mara had taken place on the beach of Ashkelon. The bride and groom, with sand between their toes, stood before their chanting friends and before several political radicals, for whom this occasion served to mark their defiance of the Ministry of Religion's absolute hold over marriage. All night they danced by moon and tide. A week later Manny conceded that this event had probably never happened. However, the family must believe that Sudah and Mara were about to fly to Cyprus, where refused Israelis journey for civil ceremonies. Leon said, "Try your best not to be such a jackass, Fish. He's eighteen. He's draft-age. They'll never let him out of the country. As for Mara, she has no passport." At the airport Leon placed the passport in Rashi's hand. He said, "We must put an end to this torture. Bring her home."

Rashi did, in fact, bring Mara home. They sat side by side on the plane to New York, white-knuckled from clutching the arms of their seats, for neither had any faith in aircraft. During the flight, Mara composed a letter recalling to Sudah the kisses and tears of their parting, and the toothbrush he stuck in his shirt pocket to symbolize the trip he would soon take to join her. A perfumed man, his silver hair sparkling with lotion, bought drinks for both of them. Mara let her head rest on Rashi's shoulder and slept over the Atlantic. She was weary. With Sudah, they had roamed the streets of Tel Aviv until late the night before, witnessing the Purim festivities. Their evening began after Rashi returned from the Great Synagogue, where she had gone to hear the reading of the Book of Esther. As she walked back to their hotel along Allenby Street, inspecting shop windows to prolong her absence in order to avoid embarrassing herself by intruding on her sister and Sudah in their last hours together, she was struck sharply on the head by a boy with a plastic hammer. "In this way the barbarics make Purim holiday," Sudah later explained, and they passed most of that night, as they wandered, dodging the blows, Rashi sometimes swinging her pocketbook furiously at the assaulters,

Sudah menacing them with a display of karate slices. In the first hours of the new day, they stopped to greet some musician friends slouched around a table in front of a café on Dizengoff Street. Mara said to Rashi, "Meet my friend Jack, the pianist. Doesn't he have beautiful hands?" Jack placed his beautiful hands squarely between Mara's legs, squeezing her soft mons. Uncomprehending, Mara brushed him off like a maggot. Then she gritted her teeth and raised her fist, continuing to shake it at Jack as Sudah took her away. Now, as she slept on Rashi's shoulder, Mara's hands were again clamped into little fists, the thumbs buried inside. They were really very small fists, Rashi thought, as she guarded her sister's sleep.

A large delegation of welcomers peered through the glass partition and into Mara's open suitcases, which a customs official was inspecting single-mindedly, every so often glancing at Mara, clad in her ancient gray jacket. Again and again he shook his head. "Just gifts," Mara was saying, "for my family and my friends. See them up there?" She pointed to her father, his black hat pushed back on his head, huddling with Herzl and Reb Anschel Frankel. The agent unfolded a lavishly embroidered caftan and shook it out vigorously. "That's a present for my mother," Mara said, and she sought, through emphatic gestures between Rose and the robe, to relay the good news to her fur-encased mother, who was leaning against Sadie Stern's arm, the one with the blue number, 57754, branded into it. When the agent completed his explorations under the long skirt of a cloth doll, Mara raised it up high to demonstrate its properties to Naomi, Rashi's child, who laughed openly in the arms of her father, Victor Asher, as Mara turned the doll upside down, causing the skirt to flop over the blond ringlets and exposing, in this way, another doll with a shiny black face and a scarlet turban. Those ivory pipes inlaid with scenes from a Persian garden were for Mara's friends—Manny Fish, standing up there making farting noises with his hand in his armpit to entertain Mark Bavli, Mara's old romance and author of a short story, and Reuben Kalb and his wife, Cookie, whose glossy black hair had been molded for the occasion into a hollow edifice by her hairdresser-lover. Every once in a while a gust of energy would set them into motion and they would wave their WELCOME HOME, MARA LIEB banner.

The agent looked at this group and proceeded to insert his finger into the bowl of each pipe and hold it up to the light for a more thorough examination. Then, at last, he unwrapped layer after layer of Mara's laundry and exposed a shofar, almost transparent in texture, almost gold in color, long and splendidly coiled. "For my father," Mara whispered. The agent placed his hand deep into the scalloped opening, felt along the insides, and handed it back to Mara with these words, "Pass. She's clean." Mara wiped off the shofar tenderly and raised it to her lips. She blew a terrific *tekiah gedolah*, which she held for fifty-eight seconds, or one second longer than at the shop in Mea She'arim where she had tested its resonance before handing her dollars over to the red-bearded Hasid, who laughed and laughed at this strange, presumptuous girl, wiping away tears with a twisted, maroon-bordered handkerchief he had pulled from the loops of his belt.

Upstairs, as Mara was swallowed by her friends, and as Naomi howled miserably, seeking refuge in her father whenever her mother drew near, Leon motioned to Rashi. "She will not marry that *momzer*," said Leon. He was jabbing his right fist into his left palm.

"But that was the deal," said Rashi, "you agreed. That's why she came home."

"Where is it written down? Did I promise in black and white? Show me! Were you recording our conversation over the telephone? There are always misunderstandings when people speak over such long distances, right? Many thanks, Rashi. You have done your job. Now go home."

Rashi sobbed hoarsely the whole way home. She had done Mara a disservice by assenting to her conditions. She should have let her remain in Israel, where it would have been impossible to marry in any case. Now she would be obliged to insist that Mara's terms be honored.

It had been remarkably easy. Why had it eluded everyone else? Twelve hours after Rashi's arrival in Tel Aviv, Mara had agreed to return. Just like that. They crouched by the telephone and spoke to their father in New York. First, Mara would fly back with Rashi. Later, Sudah would come and they would be married. That was the plan. Even Sudah said a few words to Leon. For the sake of Mara, he would become an observant Jew. He promised. *"Shalom, Aba,"* said Sudah, "see you soon." He handed the receiver back to Rashi, who reassured her parents that Sudah was worthy. "The main thing is to get her home," Rashi declared. As she murmured her closing consolations, she watched Sudah nuzzling Mara in the corner, unbuttoning his oversize tweed coat, the pockets bulging with the sum of his possessions, and drawing her into it.

This was the same coat he had worn when he had accompanied Mara to the airport the night before to meet Rashi's plane. Rashi later learned from Mara that it had belonged to Sudah's father, an Egyptian sculptor, who had been killed when the car in which he and Sudah's mother were conversing dropped into the sea. As quietly as that. This occurred in the south of France, in the city of Tarbes, where Sudah was born. Orphaned at the age of three, Sudah was brought to Israel and reared in Tel Aviv by an aunt and uncle he despised. The gray jacket Mara wore had often warmed the naked body of Sudah's mother, her husband's favorite model, during the breaks in those long sittings in his icy studio.

"Sudah is an artist, too, obviously," Mara said. "He studies with the painter Yishai Ben Yishai. Yishai is a well-known plagiarist. He'll get his reward some day. Sudah is also Yishai's model."

It was after midnight and they lay on the bed of their hotel room, with the glass doors flung open to the terrace and to the sea pounding below. Sudah had clasped Mara fiercely and finally retired to a room down the hall with a less spectacular view, which Rashi had also leased. Between the sisters on the bed was a carton of cigarettes, purchased by Rashi in flight, and a stuffed ashtray.

"He wants you to like him, Rashi," Mara said. "That's what he's hoping for. Without compromising himself, of course." She glanced sharply at Rashi and looked away.

"Well, tell him not to work so hard. I like him already. Why not?" That's what Rashi said, but she was not so sure. She was overwhelmed with a sense of incompleteness. She had just rummaged through her suitcase for her radio and it was gone.

Mara continued. "I prepared him for you, you know, but he sized you up immediately. Well, I really didn't need him to tell me I was completely off about you. I could see that for myself, the minute you stepped off the plane. You're simply an ordinary woman, and that's fine. Daddy just kept on creating you to terrorize me."

"That takes a burden off me, I suppose," said Rashi. She was tearing apart the strands of a cigarette filter.

"Really, Rashi, Sudah helped me a lot as far as you're concerned. He freed me of you. Now I can be myself. Why should I continue to imitate you just because they expect it of me? You remember Mark Bavli? When he split with me after a year, he told me that at last he had gotten over you. Well, Sudah never even knew you."

Dull brown hair, straight and flapping like a patch over one eye. A boy too young to charm. That was Rashi's memory of Mark Bavli. "I'm sorry about Mark," she said, "it wasn't my fault. It had nothing to do with me. He probably also had the wrong impression of me. Still, I'm sorry."

"Forget it, Rashi. I've already forgiven you. Sudah got the whole picture, though, at once. It's really amazing."

"Sudah's a good friend, that's obvious." Rashi paused. "You're sleeping with him, of course."

Mara said, yes, of course. For a moment Rashi felt as if she were being strangled. Her arm reached out limply, gripping Mara's thin shoulder. "Oh, Mara," she whispered. Sudah's triumph floated disembodied down the hall, into their room, and hovered over them. So that's that, thought Rashi.

"How often?" Rashi wanted to know. Mara estimated about thirty times. Mostly in a sleeping bag. Once, however, on a bed, though the linen was not fresh.

"Thirty times?" Rashi repeated. "Well, that's not too bad." Mara explained how difficult it was, after all. They hardly had any privacy, even in the room they had shared for a short period. Full of delight, they had spread their sleeping bag out on the floor, filled a drinking glass with purple and red anemones, and placed it on the windowsill. But the students who leased the house would make great sport out of stationing themselves in front of the closed door and shouting continuously, "Shut up! Shut up! They're fucking again!" Sometimes these heralds would open the door a crack, poke their heads in, and inquire, "Well, are you through? What's taking so long?" So they slept in each other's arms on the beach. On every side boys and girls were coupling. Thus they were alone. But their bag was ripping. It was shrinking from the rain. And Mara's throat had been rough and painful for many weeks.

In answer to Rashi's next question, Mara produced from her jacket pocket a crumbling envelope in which some brown pills rattled. They had been given to her by a friend who said they were manufactured by a German company specifically for distribution in Israel. They were guaranteed to be the surest birth-control equipment in the Middle East.

Rashi stared glumly at the liver-colored pills. "Promise me one thing, Mara," she said. Mara waited. "That you won't have intercourse with Sudah while I'm here."

"Sure," said Mara, "it's a deal." She walked to the balcony and tossed the pills into the Mediterranean. Rashi heard a deafening splash. Pausing in the doorway against the early-morning sky, Mara said, "I'm also ready to go home with you, Rashi. I know that's what you want. Sudah and I have discussed it. You can call Daddy and tell him. I'll come home on the condition that Sudah joins me in June and we can be married."

"Okay."

"Will Daddy agree, do you think?"

"I'll convince him it's for the best."

Mara lay down beside Rashi and kissed her on the temple. She said, "Sudah was very surprised that we didn't embrace when we first saw each other after such a long separation."

"You should have told him we're typically cold Westerners."

"In fact, I did explain it."

"What did you say?"

"I told him we're strangers, actually," Mara said. "I told him you're very formal. Self-conscious."

Rashi slowly stroked Mara's forehead, pushing the hair back and exposing scattered clumps of pimples. "I dread hurting them, you know," Rashi whispered. "Daddy and Mommy, I mean. Over the years they've somehow created the impression that they couldn't take it. What do you plan to do about religion?"

"Oh, don't worry, Rashi. Sudah will put on a good show. He knows how to fake it."

"I hope he won't think I'm asking him to compromise his principles."

"He's very practical," Mara said. "And he has his priorities. Sometimes it's necessary to pretend a little. Besides, he wouldn't want to wound them, either. He thinks they're probably rather fragile."

Rashi's hand caressed her sister's cheek. "You know, Mara," she said, "you've been in this hot country for nearly six months, yet I think the sun hasn't once touched your face. You must have been very preoccupied." Mara curled up, folded the pillow around her head, and made no answer.

"Do you have orgasms with him?" Rashi asked at last. The girl turned her wet face to her sister. "Yes," she cried. "Yes, I do. Yes, yes, I do!" She seemed to be retching sobs, and her grief now came out loud and raw.

Sudah dispatched a number of letters to Leon Lieb, in which he outlined, in Hebrew, his program of preparations for the marriage. He wrote: "As you know, *Aba,* I have had an unfortunate background. I blame my sins on ignorance. But even Rabbi Akiva did not know aleph from bet until he met his beloved, Rachel. He was forty years old at the time. I am still only eighteen, which, our sages tell us, is the proper age for a young man to be led under the canopy. Mara is my Rachel. Thus, you may be compared to Rachel's father, Kalbah Savuah, who was won over and became Akiva's greatest benefactor in time. You see, I have already begun my education. Every day I set aside some time to study the Song of Songs and the Zohar." And: "Rest assured, Mara and I shall establish a worthy household. I shall put on *tefilin,* morning and night." And this: "We hope to have many sons who will be a light in Israel. I plan to name our first-born for my own father, Azriel Mizrahi, may his memory be a blessing. My second will be named in your honor."

Leon would read these letters with painstaking attention, his body rigid, his head shaking morosely. He would then pass them to Rose, who would grope for the wing-shaped glasses with the rhinestones at the tips that dangled from a gold chain around her neck. "Well, he's trying, Leon," she would mutter, "at least he's trying. If it doesn't work out, they can always get a divorce." Each of these documents would then be stuffed into the pocket of Leon's black overcoat with the Persian lamb collar. During his trips to his office he would squeeze the latest letter until it became a compact ball, which he would then toss on the desk of Sadie Stern, who would patiently unfold it and place it under the cushion of her chair. She would sit on it all day until it became reasonably straight and manageable. Before leaving in the evening, she would go clattering on her high heels down the long hallway to the back room where the confidential papers were filed in locked cabinets, and she would slip Sudah's warmed letter into a crisp new folder labeled s.m.

To Mara, Sudah wrote: "My tongue in your noses, Mara'ka." And: "I'm painting you by the memory. Is the little red mole on the left tit or the right titty? Telegram answer quick. My brush gets stiff in waiting." Another contained a self-portrait: Sudah at table, clad in jacket, shirt, and tie, and on his head a very full yarmulka. Under the table you could see his naked legs covered with black hair, and his blue-tipped erection. In his hands a knife and fork are poised politely over the large gray turd upon which he is dining. These letters would arrive unsealed at Rashi's house. Rashi would hold them up against the light, twisting and flattening them to decipher their message, but she would never simply unfold and read them, perhaps fearing that, were she to do so, she could not then convincingly deny a charge, however false, of having unsealed them in the first place. Weeks would pass before Mara would be inspired to come and collect them. Rashi had to avert her eyes from the growing mound on the desk, and from Sudah's presence, which seemed to grin there. A day would then arrive when Mara would burst urgently through the door, followed by Manny Fish, or Mark Bavli, and once even by the toothless, fifty-year-old poet, Luke Alfasi. She would skim through a letter, laughing, commenting, reading passages aloud, and then hand it over to her companion or to Rashi. Almost always she would forget to take the letters when she left.

Rashi had heard a great deal about Luke, for Mara and some of her friends were among his most steadfast admirers. At least once a week they would take the subway down to the tenement on Second Street where Luke lived with his mother. They would cluster around the kitchen table, next to the bathtub in which Luke fattened a fish named Eliot, upon whom all of Luke's sins would fall at year's end, to be slaughtered in his stead on the eve of Yom Kippur. The children would read their newest stories and poems to Luke and await his comment. He would always say, "First draft, first draft! Write and rewrite! Polish and repolish!" He himself had published a poem more than a quarter of a century before, which had been praised by Mr. Prufrock. Luke spent his days perfecting this poem and his nights studying the Jerusalem Talmud. Although he seldom left home because he had no shoes, on this occasion he shuffled out in his carpet slippers and accompanied Mara to Rashi's house to seek the help of Victor Asher, who was a psychiatrist. It seemed that the day before, Luke's mother, dressed only in her nightgown, had run down the four flights of stairs into the street to inform the passers-by that she was the long-awaited Our Lady of Mental Health. One old woman, also in a nightgown, knelt down and kissed the hem of her garment. A man threw some coins at her feet. She continued to reveal her true identity all that morning and afternoon, until a white van pulled up and two solemn orderlies and the girlfriend of one of them climbed out, caught her in a large butterfly net, and carted her, writhing and struggling, to Bellevue Hospital, where she was confined against her will. Luke wanted Victor's help in obtaining the release of his mother. Unfortunately, Victor was out of town and would not return until after the legal period for involuntary commitment elapsed. Meanwhile, Luke sat on the couch next to Mara, nodding as he read one letter after another. Rashi, too, read each of the letters, her face composed in a look of unrevealed depth, which was reinforced by her wise silence. Luke, for his part, was always sparing with words, in any situation, because the loss of his teeth made it difficult for him to articulate certain sounds, and because he did not enjoy exhibiting a soft pink mouth. The silence in the room was only occasionally broken by an exclamation from Mara, or a remark, such as, "Sudah's an original, isn't he, Luke?" or "Didn't I tell you he was an artist?" Rashi felt uneasy throughout their visit and was relieved when they rose at last. She said to Mara, "Well, I guess you won't be hearing from Sudah for a while now."

"Why not?"

"Didn't you read his last letter?" And she pointed out to Mara where Sudah had written that he anticipated, at any moment, the arrival of the military police to take him away for resisting the draft. For Mara this news had been eclipsed by the sentences that immediately followed it: "They cannot take away from me my finger. I don't never wash him. He is still smelly from your cunt."

Mara slumped against the door. She said, "They don't have very many pacifists in Israel, do they?" Rashi suggested they examine the postmark on the envelope. The letter, the last one to arrive, had been mailed more than two weeks earlier. "Sudah's in jail," Rashi concluded.

Mara began to speak very excitedly. "It's not the first time, you know. He can take it. He can take it, though how would they treat a pacifist there? I don't know. They'll be afraid of him, won't they, Luke? What if pacifism is contagious? What if it spreads? So now we know who has been opening all these letters. Well, he can handle it. Don't you think he can handle it, Rashi? When he was put away for hashish, even the judge got to like him. The second time around, the judge called him 'Sudah Messiah' and pinched his cheek. Not hard. Affectionately. Sudah was just sixteen then. He still has red cheeks. The soldiers who guard him will get to like him, too. Don't you agree, Rashi? Or would they resent him because he had the guts to do what they always wanted to do but didn't dare? We've got to get him out of there, Rashi. We've got to do something right away, before they mutilate him. He's too beautiful. He doesn't want to be a killer. He's an artist. He's not political. I'm going to talk to Daddy. Daddy has got to do something. Daddy has lots of friends. Daddy will get him out."

Leon was relaxing in the living room, the Yiddish paper on his lap opened to the obituaries. Mara sat down on the ottoman next to her father's stockinged feet and absentmindedly began to tickle his soles, as she had often done, at his behest, on many Friday nights of her childhood. Leon tugged at his goatee as he listened to Mara's demand, and for a long time said nothing. At last he spoke: "All right, Mara'le, I'll look into it. But do me a favor, will you? Stop wearing your skirts so short. And try to be a little more affectionate with me. Give me a kiss now. I'll give you an answer in a few days."

The next morning Sadie Stern put through a call to Jerusalem. A high-placed underling in Defense confirmed the story. Sudah Mizrahi was under arrest for draft evasion and was being held at an undisclosed location. Leon thanked him and hung up. During the Sabbath dinner the following Friday night, after they had swallowed the last morsel of gefilte fish and as the black maid, Ophelia, ladled out the chicken soup glistening with sequins of fat, Leon said to Mara, "You know I don't like you to come to the Shabbos table in your bathrobe, with your hair all wet." Mara did not respond. Leon took a loud sip of soup and put his spoon down. "Well, Mara'le," he said, "I have looked into it. It's a fact. Your *boychik* is now a jailbird. *Mazel tov.* There's nothing I can do." Mara hurled her spoon across the table, upon which it bounced once before it hit a wall, and ran out of the room. Rose and Leon heard the slam of the bathroom door, and the lock turn.

It was not until well after midnight that Rabbi and Mrs. Lieb grew alarmed about Mara's prolonged self-imprisonment and the utter silence behind the door. They began to call their daughter's name, softly at first, for fear of scandalizing the neighbors around them, but when they got no answer, louder and more frantically. Very soon they were banging and kicking wildly. At 1:30 a.m., the accumulated force of their combined weight against the door ripped it from its hinges entirely, and they were launched into the bathroom. A thick mass of smoke engulfed them. As it drifted toward the gaping doorway, they could distinguish Mara, leaning placidly against the tub. Next to her, on the black and white hexagonal tiles of the floor, was an ashtray overflowing with the butts of the pack of cigarettes she had smoked methodically, one after another, on the Sabbath. Leon took in this scene, pivoted, and walked out. Rose said, "You just broke Daddy's heart," and went after her husband down the hall.

That Sunday night Mara was sitting cross-legged on the floor of her bedroom, her glasses sliding down to the tip of her nose. She was shortening her skirts. Cookie Kalb lay sprawled across the bed, her hair in disarray. Her lover, Ozzie Kahn, had finally succumbed to his wife's relentless pressure to close the beauty salon for a week and to accompany her and their six children to their country house on Lake Hopatcong, in New Jersey. Three days of the projected week-long separation had passed and Cookie was aching. She had hoped to use this period to take the first steps toward what she knew must be the inevitable break in their relationship and to become once again a faithful wife. It had been for faithfulness, after all, that she and Mara had been prepared in the religious school, the same one in which they had passed many hours in the girls' washroom smoking and embellishing their first sexual excursions. But now Cookie knew she would be powerless to resist the temptation to trot right back into Ozzie's shop the moment the pink-tasseled shades flew up. "Am I addicted to hair spray, or what?" she cried. "Why am I so weak? Why can't I break it off?" Again and again she indulged in the penance of repeating her story. The sin for which she could never forgive herself, the high point of her infidelity, was the breaking of her vow not to have her hair done on her wedding day. "On my wedding day itself!" she lamented. "Can you imagine? I had already gone to the *mikvah*. How would Reuben feel if he knew, the poor, miserable sucker! I'm a worm."

Mara only half listened. She had heard the story many times before. Besides, she had her own worries, which she mulled over quietly, since nothing she could say could ever penetrate Cookie's total self-absorption. And slowly, as Mara stitched and commiserated, a plan took shape. It was quite simple actually, lovely and obvious. Sudah was not, after all, a native Israeli. He was born in France. His aunt and uncle, who had had him declared an Israeli when he was too young to form his own allegiance, must now take themselves before the appropriate authorities and identify him as a Frenchman. Why should a foreigner, and a pacific one at that, fight a stranger's fight? Sudah could fly from Israel tomorrow. Let him pack his bag. New York would greet him with ardor.

This was the plan that Mara laid before her father. It was two o'clock in the morning when she stood in her parents' bedroom, insisting that Leon telephone Ezra Mizrahi at once, to demand that he do the honorable thing by Sudah. Rose propped herself up on two pillows, her forearm across her brow. She was frowning, and two deep furrows made their way upward from the top of her nose. Leon lay on his side. He had not spoken a word to Mara for two days and he offered no reply to her demand now.

Mara said, "Daddy, I know you're not talking to me because you caught me smoking on Shabbos. But for your own sake you'd better listen to me, because I have something important to say. Okay. I want you to do what I ask to get Sudah out, do you hear me? Because if you don't, I promise you this, I'm going to kill myself. I'll commit suicide. I'm serious. Remember."

Leon flung his legs over the side of his bed and groped for the light switch. He was wearing his green-striped pajama top and yellow boxer undershorts. He placed his black-framed glasses on his nose, picked up one of the telephones from the cluster on his nightstand, and called Tel Aviv. Ezra Mizrahi answered. It was eight o'clock in the morning for him, and he and his wife were just about to leave for their jobs as bank managers. Mara could picture them standing by the phone— Ezra, trim in his open-necked, short-sleeved white shirt, a worn briefcase in his hand, and Jacqueline, plump, dark, and beautiful, in her sleeveless chemise dress, white plastic handbag, and white high-heel shoes, like boats. Mara had observed their daily routine—their efficient toilet, their unvarying breakfast of salad, scrambled eggs, and coffee, their resolute departure— during the two days that she had been a guest in their flat. In fact, in spite of Sudah's disparaging portrayal of his aunt and uncle, she had been quite favorably impressed by the half hour that Ezra spent before dinner standing on his head, and by his urbane and liberal conversation. So on the third day of her stay she had approached Ezra and Jacqueline. "It's no secret that Sudah and I are lovers," she had reasoned with them. "I'm sure you would not object if we slept in the same room." Ezra's answer was, he regretted that that could not be, not under his roof. Sudah and Mara shook their heads at such hypocrisy, at such false enlightenment, and departed that afternoon. Mara knew that now, across an ocean and a continent, Ezra Mizrahi was growing increasingly anxious because of Leon's circuitous and repetitious way of presenting her plan. He was probably darting glances at his wristwatch, tapping his foot impatiently.

There was a long and costly silence when Leon finished. Then Ezra said, "I am glad you have concern for Sudah, Adon Lieb. You have mentioned a good plot, but for one small detail." He paused and then said, "We are not dead."

"God forbid!" Leon said. "I meant the boy's parents, of course."

"But *we* are Sudah's parents."

Leon covered the mouthpiece of the telephone and addressed the room in general. "You won't believe this. He says that they are his parents." Rose exclaimed, "What? Is he crazy or something?" Mara tore the receiver out of Leon's hand. "You're a liar and you know it, Ezra," she screamed. "You don't like me, that's why you're saying this. You're trying to sabotage us. You just want to hurt me, that's all."

"No, Mara," said Ezra. "Why should I desire to hurt a child? The truth is, I am Sudah's father. Jacqueline is his mother."

"But he told me that you are his uncle and aunt!"

"I don't understand why he said this thing to you. It is not the truth. Sudah is our son."

"Oh, tell me this isn't happening," Mara cried. "Tell me that you're dead!"

"I'm sorry, Mara."

Mara let the phone swing to the floor and left her parents' bedroom. She entered her own room and closed the door. Rose did not permit her children locks on their doors, and so, during the three days and three nights that Mara remained inside, trays of food were carried in and brought out, untouched, and people came and left after failing to elicit a response from Mara, who lay on her bed with her face to the wall.

"She can't marry him now and she knows it," Rashi said to her father. "He's a stranger. The old Sudah no longer exists. She's mourning him. She's sitting *shivah.*"

During this period Leon received this response to his wire to the records department of the city of Tarbes:

J'ai le regret de vous faire connaître que nous ne trouvons pas trace de la naissance de:
—M. Sudah ou Saadia MIZRAKA ou MIZRACHI ou MISERIE sur nos registres d'Etat Civil de 1943 à 1962.
Veuillez agréer, Monsieur, l'expression de mes respectueux hommages.

Le Maire

Leon mumbled, *"Nu,* so maybe he doesn't really exist after all," and he clipped this telegram to another, which Ezra Mizrahi had intended for Mara. Ezra's message was: "Please, not to break with my son now. He already suffers much in prison." Sadie Stern slipped these two documents into Sudah's folder. She said to Leon, "Thank God. It's the best thing that could have happened. Soon we'll close this file."

Herzl Lieb dropped in on one of those nights and sat for a while in silence at the foot of his sister's bed while Rose leaned against the doorpost, her fingers rhythmically tapping her thigh. As he prepared to leave, Herzl spoke his first words to Mara: "Judy and the kids want you to come over for a weekend." He paused, but Mara said nothing. Herzl explained: "There are some nice fellows from the yeshiva we want you to meet. One of them is really tops. A genius! Boy, what a head!"

"You could wear that white knit you bought before you went to Israel," said Rose. "The tags are still on it."

Rashi came and sat beside Mara, murmuring consolations. "I know it's hard, Mara, but we're lucky we found out now, before it's too late. He's sick, you understand that. Whatever you may think, it's not too late now, believe me. Thirty times is nothing, really. Time will heal it."

Because of the extraordinary circumstances, Rose Lieb allowed Mark Bavli to spend some minutes alone with Mara in her room. Mark expressed his gratitude, closed the door, and lit a joint. Mara sat up and took a pull. He said, "I made six hundred dollars in tips last summer as a waiter at Stoffmacher's. It's in the bank. You can have it if you need the money to go to Israel."

"I don't know what to do," Mara said.

"Well now, that all depends," Mark observed.

"On what?"

"On how much you love him, of course," said Mark.

They smoked quietly. A comfortable serenity was beginning to settle around them, like cushions, and Mara no longer felt the injury of Mark's comment. Manny Fish came apologetically through the door. "Your mother sent me in," he said to Mara. "She doesn't trust you two alone for very long."

Mark said, "I guess a *ménage à trois* would be beyond her powers of imagination." They all laughed, and Manny, who was engaged in a long struggle with his homosexuality, the loudest of all. Mark passed him a pair of tweezers, between which the butt of the joint was squeezed. Manny sucked on it. "Ah, ah, good," he moaned. Mara put on some jazz. "Have you seen Luke?" she asked Manny.

"Yes."

"What does he think?"

"He didn't seem to want to discuss it," Manny reported. "He talked about the troubles he's had trying to get his mother out of the bin. That's on his mind right now, you understand.

He said, 'People have called me crazy, too,' and he rolled those big round eyeballs of his, you know, the way he does, to scare the shit out of strangers. Then his head slumped down on his chest and he fell asleep, instantly, right there in his seat. He's really knocked out from running back and forth to the hospital in his slippers."

When Victor Asher lit the candle in Mara's room and pulled a chair up to her bed that evening, her face was again turned to the wall. Victor sat in silence, tugged at his mustache, and squinted to read and reread the titles on her bookshelf: *Confessions of Zeno*, Anne Frank's *Diary*, *Story of O*, *Life with Picasso* by Françoise Gilot. He opened this last book and slowly turned the pages, examining the photographs. For a long time he stared at the picture of the beaming Françoise, strutting with head high on the beach, behind her Pablo, openshirted, short, demonic, shielding her from the sun's glare with a giant umbrella, his mistress's menial, but, without question, her master. An invisible shackle dragged from Françoise's ankle. Half an hour passed in this way.

At first Mara attempted to smother her giggles, but then she let her head fall back on her pillow and laughed and laughed. "You shrinks!" she cried. "You goddamn shrinks!" She said this over and over again, but the words and the laughter were vying and she could hardly speak. Victor smiled. Mara wiped her eyes. The laughter made her cheekbones ache.

"You're the same," she said finally. "I told that to Rashi. You and Sudah. Oh, my God! I recognized it immediately. You're two peas in a pod. I can't believe it!"

"Well, thank you," Victor whispered.

That started Mara laughing again, and she clutched her belly as it came in long, hoarse gusts. When, at last, it ended, she sat up and said, "Okay, Victor, come on. Out with it. Speak your piece. I know what you're here to say."

"Do you?"

"Of course. You're going to tell me he's crazy. Bananas. Come on, get it over with."

Victor said, "No, Mara, I'd never say such a thing. It's different when it comes from someone in my profession. After all, I haven't even met the boy."

"Well, everyone else thinks he is. Rashi does, I know. There's a consensus. Don't you have faith in the opinion of the majority?"

"I don't know. Maybe he is, maybe he isn't. But I do know one thing."

"What?"

"That he lied to you when he was bound to get caught. Why do you think he'd do such a thing?"

"I don't know. You're the shrink, you tell me."

Victor hesitated. "It could be he wanted to be exposed. That would be one way of ending your affair. He built into your relationship a self-destruct mechanism."

"You're wrong, Victor," Mara objected, "he's not such a strategist." She paused. "Do you really want to know why he made up those things? I'll tell you. To make himself more attractive to me. More romantic, more mysterious. He sensed what I wanted to hear. He read my soul. It's my fault, actually. I was begging for it."

Victor shook his head. "Mara, Rashi says she saw her radio stuffed in the pocket of his old coat."

"Oh, God, Victor, you're really sinking low."

Victor sighed. "I don't know whether he's sick or not," he said, "but one thing is clear. You don't have to be a psychiatrist to see that you shouldn't marry this person. It would be a disaster."

"You're right about one thing," said Mara, "you don't know him. Sudah is an artist. Someday he'll be great. I despise myself for talking about him this way when I know he's sitting in jail.

As if he were a case, damn it! God knows what they're doing to him at this very moment. There's got to be a reason for this. I'm not going to cut it all off without even talking to him. I'm going to help him, Victor."

"But who will help you, Mara?"

The next morning Mara put on the old gray jacket, which her three-day fast had rendered even larger on her, and took the subway down to Mark Bavli's apartment in Brighton Beach. Mirabella, with her chubby, naked-bottomed baby, Flora, straddling her hip, opened the door. Mark had found this dark-eyed woman squatting under the boardwalk one rainy night, suckling her baby. He took them to his small, white, stucco-walled apartment, and Mirabella promptly set to work scrubbing and tidying the two rooms, gathering rocks and shells and driftwood to decorate them. She would press herself into a corner, shushing her baby energetically, her face screwed up with worry as Mark sat at the linoleum-covered table travailing over a new short story about an aged man who masturbated to the fantasy of his own death. During her first nights there, she used to appear naked at Mark's bedside, offering herself, but Mark merely sent her away with a royal gesture. All he asked of her was to draw the water for his bath, and to remain silently in the room as he soaked. It was his great delight to fart in the tub. He tried to explain to Mirabella that farting, always a pleasure for the gratification it affords to the senses of feel, smell, and hearing, was, in the water, an even greater pleasure because of the visual stimulation it provided. Her presence and acceptance enhanced it even more. However, Mark had little Spanish, and Mibi even less English, and this, after all, was a complicated thought to communicate in any language.

Mibi indicated to Mara that Mark was away at his job tutoring bar mitzvah boys. Mara stretched out on the bed as Mibi watched steadfastly from the stool, her baby in her arms.

37

When Mara awoke, Mark was beside her. "Have you left home?" he asked.

"No. I just came down here to use your phone. May I?"

Mara called Tel Aviv, authorizing the operator to bill her father. Ezra Mizrahi answered. "Mara!" he exclaimed cheerfully. "You are just at the right spot. Sudah came home yesterday. Here he is."

Sudah spoke softly, in Hebrew. "I love you, Mara," he said. "I shall be there in June for our wedding. I shall explain everything then. There are good reasons. Trust me. You have stood up to the test. Forgive me the pain I have brought upon you."

They murmured tenderly to each other and said farewell many times. Neither would be the first to hang up. When, at last, it seemed as if the final goodbye had been spoken, Sudah switched to English, talking rather loudly and hurriedly, as if he dreaded the words would be prevented. "By the way, Mara, you must to tell to Victor that I was let out of army for reasons sociological, not psychological. Socio! Not psycho! I have documents. Remember to tell this."

Mark and Mara went out for a slow walk on the beach. It was evening and Mara pulled her jacket tightly around her against the chill. They came to a pile of rocks jutting out into the ocean and lay down beside it. Mark drew Mara to him and they began to kiss familiarly, nostalgically. Mark said, "I'll bet I look pretty good to your father now." Mara laughed, remembering that mad night on a boardwalk somewhere, Leon following ten paces behind them, hour after hour, until the sky reddened with the dawn. Mark placed his hand under the scratchy wool of her jacket, upon her breast. Mara said, "Remember, I'm engaged." "I have it in mind," Mark whispered. "I see you're still wearing your old lady's cotton undershirt. In the dark it feels pink." Mara's head was tucked comfortably under Mark's chin. She said, "As soon as I get home I'm going to make the longest list you ever saw. I'm going to collect the hottest trousseau in town. Wait till my father sees the sheets, the towels, the toaster, the Mixmaster, the frying pans—the works—pile up in the house. He'll know I mean business. He'll cave in just to get the crap out of the place."

Mara spent the next weeks rushing from store to store, her eyes darting in every direction, accumulating an enviable hoard. Rose, who had resigned herself to the inevitability of this marriage and had so informed Leon, handed the charge plates to Mara each morning without a word. In the evening Mara returned lugging shopping bags stuffed with nightgowns, panties, tea kettles, potato peelers, trash cans, pots of every size and shape, quilts, dish rags—and unpacked the goods triumphantly as her mother watched and approved through a frown. This dogged shopping was a comfort, after all, for it denoted that Mara was still a normal girl who still valued the essentials her mother had taught her. Leon ignored their enterprise, however, and made no arrangement with the caterer. After Rose left, Mara would take out her pad and pencil and sprawl on her belly across her bed, amid heaps of household merchandise, to continue work on a project that Luke had praised with uncharacteristic ardor. It was a work of fiction, to be called *How I Lost My Virginity*, and would contain a series of first-person accounts of this once-in-a-lifetime event. In the period before her marriage to Sudah, Mara composed the opening chapter.

### How I Lost My Virginity: Martha

The place we had chosen was a hotel in Manhattan, one of my father's. It was called the Christina Leuvelink, in tribute to the mistress of an original Dutch settler of the island, but the neighborhood people called it the Loo. This was because it had been constructed before architects wised up enough to set the public bathrooms of hotels in back corridors and hard-to-find passageways, and at the Christina Leuvelink the local vagrants made a pastime of sitting upon the toilets throughout many a cold winter's afternoon. One of my father's first actions when he took possession of the place was to order the doors removed from the stalls. But Sonny has informed me that the bums sit there anyway, their trousers in a circlet around their ankles, their eyes staring ahead, lusterless, unseeing. I don't know if the same edict had been directed against the ladies' booths. Personally, I never used the public facilities. When the need had arisen during one of those occasions that I accompanied my father to this property, the manager had interrupted their discussion to point, in a preoccupied way, to a door off his office that led into a cubicle in which a glossy calendar displaying a fat naked Negress hung over the commode for the manager to contemplate each time he stood there and pissed.

Nevertheless, when Sonny and I used the Loo, it was still a respectable establishment. The burgundy rugs and overstuffed furniture in the lobby, while somewhat dusty and frayed, still preserved a genteel appearance. This general air of propriety was enhanced by the old ladies and gentlemen who, each morning, would ride the elevators down from their narrow rooms cluttered with pictures of children and grandchildren in gilt frames, to spend their day sitting in the lobby, reading the papers, knitting, playing cards, gossiping, and flirting. Prostitutes and their clients came and went, it is true, but not hourly or brazenly, and funds for the employment of a house detective had been authorized by my father to maintain the hotel's good name.

I had gotten myself into a situation with Sonny where it was impossible not to go through with it. It was necessary to live up to the image of myself I had constructed for his benefit. He was nineteen, and his total experience consisted of fourteen prostitutes of an average age of forty-nine years, an average weight of one hundred and sixty-two pounds, and an average fee of ten dollars, who would squat behind a screen before rendering their service, and Sonny would listen to the tinkle of their urine in the pot as he lay on the bed in his T-shirt, adjusting his condom. I was seventeen. I had read many books by the light of my night lamp, and had molded myself accordingly. Sonny would describe to me, with awe, how the prostitutes would roll his penis between their two hands and then insert it into their vagina. I knew that I, too, would be expected to perform this "womanly" rite if it ever came to it. When, in fact, the great day arrived, I recognized immediately that the purpose of this brief ceremony was to discreetly, but efficiently, check the overall quality and coverage of the rubber.

Very little can be said in praise of Sonny. He was not particularly handsome or intelligent. To be sure, he was generally acclaimed to be a nice guy, but I knew that this reputation was the result of the intrinsic weakness of his character. Indeed, it was for this very weakness that I had chosen him. I could rely upon it to protect myself; through it I could control him, manipulate him into silence, even into marriage, if necessary.

Naturally, I hid from Sonny the parameters of my inexperience. I have always been skillful at learning on the job. As he would tell his pitiful tales of sex, relishing his position as connoisseur, I would set myself to nodding and exclaiming at, I hoped, the appropriate places, letting him believe that he was narrating adventures whose nature was at least familiar to me instead of totally strange and astonishing, which, in fact, was how they actually struck me. Unfortunately, this method did not allow me sufficient time to recover from each fresh shock. For instance, the shock of his masturbation. One night on the sofa in my parents' living room he unzipped, and out popped this red and blue fish, stiff with expectation, poor thing! Although I had been conferred the honor of viewing a penis before then, I had never seen one in such a bloodthirsty state. Sonny commenced to massage it up and down, up and down. He invited me to try my hand at it, and I obliged, wanting to appear cool and experienced, though I tend, as a rule, to avoid handling, and, in truth, must always make an effort to control my fear of almost all animals. Fortunately, Sonny criticized my attempts. I was squeezing too hard; I was grabbing the skin, pinching, lacerating. So I was absolved from continuing, at least that time. Suddenly the creature quivered and spouted out some sticky white stuff with the smell of ammonia. What a big shot that little prick was! Such gaudiness, such agitation; it was funny actually. It poked itself up unsteadily, as if it were announcing how tough it was. So much seemed to be riding on my complicity. It could collapse instantly. I trembled at the savagery that might ensue. It evoked the maternal feelings in me, poor thing!

For my own part, I felt it necessary to endow myself with a past, to contribute stories of my own adventures. That's how I came to tell

Sonny about the encounters between my father and me which had occurred three years earlier. We were drinking beer at a small table in the back of a café draped all over with fishing nets when I told Sonny how Dad would slip into my room after I had showered, part my robe of terry cloth, stroke my breasts, and whisper to me that I was sensational. My father beseeched me to touch the protuberance in his pants. By then, Sonny had emptied three bottles. He stood up abruptly, sending his chair crashing against the wall, and with his fist he pounded the small table so that all it contained rattled menacingly. "I'm going to kill that bastard for messing with my girl," he screamed. An employee of the establishment pushed Sonny out from behind, and I followed with my eyes to the ground, as the sawdust-strewn floor of the restaurant became the glittering concrete of the street.

On the appointed Saturday night—it was a new spring, March—I lay in my room at home awaiting Sonny's call. Nevertheless, the ring startled me. Sonny's voice was husky. "Six thirteen," he mumbled, and hung up instantly. As I approached the entrance to the Christina Leuvelink, I was regretting that all I possessed were the same sort of cotton bloomers, so comforting and familiar, that I had worn since earliest girlhood. They did not seem fitting for the occasion somehow. Perhaps I should have dispensed with underpants altogether. What does one wear to her deflowering? I wondered. Unfortunately, I was prevented from consulting my mother on this issue. My outer garments, carefully selected, consisted of a trench coat, a large brimmed hat slanted over one eye, and dark glasses, all of which I considered the appropriate costume for intrigue, but I was not at all sure. From the moment he called until I reached the hotel itself, Sonny was the furthest thought from my mind. Thus, I was sharply annoyed with him and, in fact, had trouble recognizing him as he approached the doorway from the opposite direction. He had forgotten to buy the prophylactics and was now returning from that errand. He said, "Nothing but the best for you, honey. Lubricated, Martha, lubricated!" I observed under my breath that I was quite capable of providing my own moisture. We rode the elevator up together, separated by a stocky middle-aged man and two old ladies, who were muttering about the unpredictable dribble of hot water and threatening to bring suit against the owner. When we reached the sixth floor I said, "Well, that was easy," and the door sealed behind us.

Room 613 contained a yellow dresser with three glass ashtrays upon it, in each of which was a book of matches inscribed with the hotel's name and the motto "Old Dutch hospitality in the heart of Manhattan." I slipped one of these into my bag as my only tangible souvenir. There was a stained orange rug on the floor, and across the narrow bed (it was a single room to avoid arousing suspicion) an orange chenille bedspread with a great cigarette burn in it, like a bruise. After Sonny and I kissed for a while, this bedspread was the item that I dragged off to the bathroom with me. There was another ashtray with a matchbook on the shelf over the sink, two glasses in little paper bags, and a strip of paper sealing the lid of the toilet seat to the bowl. I undressed without looking down at myself and re-entered the bedroom with the spread draped over me. Sonny, stark naked except for the glistening, viscous wrapping on his tuned-up organ, immediately pulled me into his embrace, and we kissed with borrowed passion, pretending we hadn't noticed that the spread had slipped to the floor. Then Sonny stepped back and admired my naked body for an excruciatingly long time. I didn't know what expression to put on my face. Sonny fell to his knees and commenced to worship me in that artificial way, kissing my feet in adoration. I knew, with certainty, that he thought I was hideous.

Every door opening and shutting, every toilet flushing, every phone ringing, every hallway step and whisper seemed thunderous to me as I lay under Sonny, who was trying to insert his penis I knew not where. At last he began to rock up and down, and I with him, in a fashion I assumed was correct from his account of how the prostitutes had performed. I was thinking, Well, so this is it. Well, it's nothing really. The footsteps outside our door were deafening. When I could bear it no longer, I began to moan and writhe, as I had seen some actress do in a movie. I wondered fleetingly whom she had been imitating. Sonny emerged triumphant. "You came! You came! And on your first try! Fantastic!" he roared. I began to cry. "It's all right," he said, "lots of girls cry when they have an orgasm." When I continued to cry he slapped my face smartly. I stopped instantly. "See," said Sonny, "that was the right thing to do. You needed that smack." I said, "Yes, I suppose I did." I rolled down Sonny's bag, which hung laden at the tip, put it to my lips, and blew it up like a balloon.

When the knock came at the door, I staggered, naked and exposed, to the bathroom. My heart was jumping wildly, striking me like a fist. I recalled the man in the elevator. Could he be a spy, hired by my father? Was he the house detective? Sonny called out, "Just a minute, please." He slipped into his pants and, bare-chested and barefooted, opened the door slightly, keeping the chain hooked. It was the elevator man. He poked his head through the chink and attempted to survey the room. I peeked out of the bathroom and observed his bristly, pockmarked face, with a look of severity in the shape of the eyes. He said, "I know you got a girl in there." Sonny replied, "Yes." Sonny went to great lengths to avoid being "phony," as he called it, with the result that there was a definite dishonesty to his trusting and open demeanor. It was one of the qualities in him I disdained the most. The intruder went on, "Well, your girlie dropped this belt to her raincoat in front of the elevator door. Here it is." He inserted a short arm with the belt dangling from the hairy fingers. "Thanks a lot," said Sonny, and he attempted to close the door, but the stranger's stubborn head was still blocking it. "I bet you thought I was a detective or something. Heh, heh! Must have given you quite a scare, buster. Listen, I know how you feel, pal. I once brung a lady up to a hotel room. Very classy. Met her on the Fifth Avenue bus. We gets right to work, you know what I mean? She gurgles. Foam comes dribbling from her mouth. I says to myself, 'Frankie, you sure gave her a good one today!' But she was dead. Heart attack. Right there under me. Boy, oh boy!" Sonny listened politely because he had this stupid romantic reverence for misfits, anticipating, I suppose, that he would become one himself someday. At last he closed the door. I came out of the bathroom fully dressed. I yanked the belt out of Sonny's hand and inserted it through the loops of my coat. "Let's get out of here," I said.

Over the next year my disgust for Sonny accumulated, but I continued to ride all sorts of elevators with all sorts of smells up to the hotel rooms he hired, because it was to Sonny I had given it. After each encounter I forced him to renew his pledge of secrecy. Then it happened that I fell in love with Hugh. "Goodbye," I said to Sonny. "Don't forget your promise." His last words to me were, "You know, Martha, I never did get to see you in a bathing suit." To Hugh I said, "I'm no longer a virgin." Hugh responded, "I'm filled with regret."

One night we lay on a beautiful but threadbare old Persian rug which my father had brought home from one of his hotels and spread out on the bathroom floor. Hugh let the water run, but despite it, I could hear my father pacing as he always did whenever a man lingered with me. Hugh rammed into me, and rammed again. "Why can't I get through?" Hugh wondered. Then a scream leaped from my throat. Blood gushed down my legs, disappearing into the scene of horses and maidens in the carpet. "You were a virgin after all," said Hugh.

I was filled with happiness.

It was mid-May when Mara completed the story. Each night after shopping she reread it, inserting small changes here and there in anticipation of presenting it to Luke Alfasi. Then she would tuck it under her pillow, whence her father slipped it out one afternoon while she was away prowling about the stores. Leon read the first two pages standing up beside his daughter's bed. Then he sat down and, breathing deeply, finished it. He closed the notebook and returned it to its spot under the pillow, upon which he took pains to resettle the eyeless head of Mara's old rag doll.

That night Leon was again sitting on the edge of his daughter's bed. He said to Mara, "I read your diary. You're some writer."

Mara was terrified. "You shouldn't have done that," she murmured. "It was private."

"If it was so private, why did you store it in a public place?" Leon asked.

"It was under my pillow, Daddy."

"Your pillow is mine. The pencil you wrote with belongs to me. I own the paper you wrote it on. Everything you have is mine."

Mara could barely speak. "It's not a diary," she managed. "It's a story. It's fiction."

"Do you know what would happen if Mommy read what you wrote about me? She would divorce me. Just like that. It would be over. Kaput!"

"But you could tell her it's only a story, Daddy."

"I could?"

"Besides, Mommy would never divorce you."

"You should show some respect for your mother," said Leon sadly.

Mara's head dropped onto her pillow. Her hand slid under and touched the stiff cardboard of the notebook's cover. She withdrew it suddenly, as if it had been contaminated.

"What's the difference?" Leon said at last. He spread the fingers of his daughter's cold hand in both of his own and inspected them closely. "I remember when this was such a tiny hand, Mara'le," he said. "A long time ago, before you had teeth to bite those nails. I would stick my finger into this little hand and it would lock into a tight fist. That was happiness! Now when I hold it, it's tense, waiting for me to let it go." He let her arm thud to her side. *"Nu,* so how is what's-his-name?" he inquired.

"He just got permission to leave Israel. He'll be arriving soon. I'm marrying him, you know."

"Certainly I know. Who do you think has been paying all these bills?" He indicated the heaps of merchandise. "Well, I suppose that now that we're sure your glamor boy can make it, we should send out the invitations. We'll call a caterer and fix the date. When are you clean?"

Mara felt the blood rushing to her face. She recalled how her parents had summoned her into the living room one Friday night when she was ten years old and informed her that in the near future she could expect blood to flow once a month from an unfamiliar hole between her legs. She had stood there in her pajamas and bathrobe, skinny, restless, blushing deeply, because her mother had been so indiscreet as to raise this subject in the presence of her father.

Now Leon dug into the pocket of his black jacket and pulled

out a narrow white box. "I brought you a present," he said. "Here, open it."

Mara snapped off the rubber band and lifted the cover. A slender cigarette holder was resting on a bed of white fluff. She raised it between her fingers and was surprised at its heaviness. Her father noticed. "Solid gold," he commented, and grinned. "Try it out." Mara pulled open the top drawer of her nightstand. She rummaged through her things until she found the old white sock in which she kept her pack of Gitanes. She took out a cigarette and inserted it into the gleaming holder. Leon extracted a book of matches from his pocket. The cover contained an idealized picture of one of his nursing homes, the Minnie Sweet Pavilion, and the slogan, "Where you're treated like one of the family." Leon struck a match and brought the flame up to Mara's cigarette, which she held between her thumb and forefinger, palm up, in what she deemed the more elegant European fashion. She breathed in deeply, setting the tip aglow. Then she let out, through the O of her lips, a great bush of smoke. As she brought the cigarette in its holder away from her face, she executed a saucy arc in mid-air.

Leon sighed. He pinched out the light slowly, almost as if he wished to burn himself. "For Shmerel also I bought something," he said. "It's a set of *Shass*. The complete Talmud. The works. If he wants to sit and learn all day, he can live on *kest*—I'll support him. If not, he'll have to go out and find a job. Maybe he can do something in one of my homes. Start from the bottom, work his way up—the American way. Or maybe I can open up a store for him. I hear he's an artist. *Nu*, so I'll rent a shop and he can stand behind the counter and sell his art."

This proposal was actually set before Sudah not many hours after he stepped off the plane in New York. Mara had been driven to the airport by Reb Anschel Frankel, who placed himself firmly at her side with his arms crossed over his chest as she greeted her betrothed. Standing next to Sudah was his mother, Jacqueline Mizrahi, who had accompanied her son for his wedding. Thus, the reunion of the lovers was, perforce, subdued, and this atmosphere was heightened by their mutual sense of having endured and been changed by suffering in each other's absence. Sudah grasped Mara's wrists. "Mara, hallo," he said. "You look to my eyes beautiful and strange."

In the back seat of the car they held hands with great intensity. The insides of their bodies seemed to them to be transformed into warm liquid which carried currents that sprang from their groins and surged to every corner of their beings and, through their entwined hands, to each other. Mara thought her form must surely be outlined in light. She looked at Sudah. He was staring ahead, his nostrils flared. They said not a word to each other. This union was broken abruptly when their car halted in front of the house. Sudah said to Mara, "That dress. Where did you buy her?" "Oh, I got it a long time ago," Mara said. "Don't you like it?" She was wearing the white knit that had hung, unused, in her closet since before her trip to Israel. Sudah inspected her critically, "It is bad. It is not from our life," he concluded.

He went ahead to assist his mother with their suitcases. Mara followed, walking slowly beside Anschel, who had a large trunk hoisted on his back. Without turning to her, Anschel said, "When you were eight years old I used to carry you on my back just like this trunk. You promised to marry me when you grew up." "I'm sorry, Red Anschie," said Mara, calling him by that dusty childhood name. But by now white hairs had mingled into his once flaming beard, and the shoulders of his powerful body were stooped. Anschel pushed the door open with his foot and stood aside as Mara passed through.

Thick steaks were served at dinner that night, and the juiciest slabs were placed before Sudah and his mother to demonstrate one of the matchless gifts of the United States. "You don't get steaks like that in Israel, now, do you?" Rose beamed. "Never mind, it's a young country" was Leon's comment, and he continued to chew and carve deliberately, glancing under his brow at his guests. Rose was eating too rapidly, as usual, pushing oversized pieces into her mouth. Sudah turned to her and spoke courteously: "You are right, Mrs. Lieb. In meat, who can compare? Also in other things America is best."

"In what, for instance?" demanded Leon.

Sudah waved the paper napkin that had been spread across his thighs. "In this. Also, toilet paper."

Leon leaned over his plate and clenched a rabbinical fist. "You can live without meat for your mouth or paper for your *myeh*, but you can't live without food for your spirit."

"Also in spirit food," Sudah observed, calmly forking up a piece of meat and inserting it into his mouth. "Israel acts to people like pigs."

"What people, may I ask?"

"Arab people." Sudah smiled, exhibiting his large, milk-white teeth, like a camel's.

"Now I understand everything," said Leon. "I forgot you were a holy man. So, tell me something, Moshe Rabbenu, how come the Arabs proclaim every day that they will throw us into the sea? How come there are always orders in the pockets of prisoners we capture to rape every female in Tel Aviv, grandmothers and babies included?"

Mara said, "Daddy, surely you see some justice in the Arabs' claims."

"Justice? Who's stopping them from returning to their homes? Mara, listen to me, you should recognize them for what they are. Plain, old-fashioned Jew haters, just like the Germans." Turning to Sudah, Leon put in sarcastically, "You remember, I presume, what the Nazis did to our people?"

"My people, no," said Sudah. "My people are coming from Yemen and Egypt."

"That's funny, and I was under the impression they came from France."

"Daddy!" Mara was half standing, a familiar position she took many a Friday night in readiness for her angry flight from the table.

"Sit down, Mara, relax." Leon sighed. "Well, I learned something tonight," he said. "I learned the meaning of a pacifist. A pacifist is someone who commits pacifism. And what is the meaning of pacifism, you may ask? I can give you the answer to that in a word: self-destruction."

Later, as they were sipping tea with lemon and sugar, and breaking off bits of apple strudel, Leon addressed Jacqueline: "We Ashkenazim have our customs, Mrs. Mizrahi, our traditions. When it comes time to marry off a child, the two fathers sit down at a table and negotiate. You pay for this, I pay for that. And so forth. But I see your respected husband has decided to stay home. I, personally, am a gentleman. I do not like to do business with a lady, especially a charming lady like yourself. But what does it matter, anyhow? I don't want anything from you. Usually the groom's family buys an engagement ring for the bride. A diamond, usually. Something valuable, a good investment for the future. So I'll buy it for my daughter this time. Big deal, it's not important. The groom usually pays for the music, the liquor, the flowers, the photography. But what do I care? I'll pay, it's all right. I ask only one thing from the children—that they be good Jews. That they observe the Sabbath, that they keep a kosher home, that your son lay *tefilin* every morning, that my daughter go to the *mikvah* once a month, after her period of uncleanness. Is that too much to ask? Tell me."

Jacqueline nodded thoughtfully. Her languages were

French, Arabic, and Hebrew, and she understood almost no English at all.

Then Leon outlined his proposals for Sudah and Mara's support after the marriage. Sudah listened gravely and agreed to consider all possibilities. "But I am an artist, not a peddler," Sudah reminded his bride's father. "Maybe I will ask you for to be my patron." Leon said, "I told Mara, if you would sit and learn all day, you would not have to worry for a thing. Steak every night. Think it over. It's up to you." He proceeded to lift out of the cartons his gift to the bridegroom, one enormous volume of the Talmud after another, and to pile them high on the table among the china teacups and saucers, enameled with red and yellow roses. Sudah opened each one, delighting in the crackling protest of uncut books. He inspected the stitching on the spine. He rubbed the paper between his thumb and index finger, relishing the supple texture. He slipped off the dust jackets to examine the covers and pointed out that the maroon of Volume Ten, *Masechet Gittin*, was noticeably redder in color than that of the other volumes. He wondered if it could be returned to the bookseller and exchanged. Leon watched this enterprise with doubt and curiosity.

Rose and Leon stood opposite each other, conferring in the kitchen. They assessed the situation. Rose commented, "Well, he's got a beautiful mother, hasn't he?" "She's not my type," said Leon. In the end it was decided that Sudah and Jacqueline would be accommodated in the Lieb apartment. Mara would go to Rashi's. The young couple would be permitted to meet during the day to attend to the remaining preparations, but for a few days before the wedding itself they would abstain totally from seeing each other, as was customary. Reb Anschel waited at the door as Mara and Sudah murmured their farewells. Sudah said softly in Hebrew, "Don't think I have forgotten, Mara. I shall pick the right time to explain. Before our wedding, not after. Trust me. You will be satisfied that I never meant to deceive you."

That explanation, unspoken, squatted over them as they fluttered in and out of the shops, trying to put together a spectacular wedding costume for Sudah. It was present in their rare moments of privacy, when they would shyly and hesitantly kiss. By the time the period of enforced separation commenced, Sudah had still not explained. Mara passed the long days at Rashi's reading to little Naomi, perfecting the latest episode in her "virginity" series, and talking over the phone to Sudah. The telephone was the least congenial of instruments for communicating an explanation of such importance, and so it remained buried.

One dawn in the Lieb apartment Jacqueline Mizrahi came upon Rose Lieb in the bathroom, nightgowned, leaning over the sink in front of the medicine cabinet, gulping down, without benefit of water, five days' quota of her prescribed medication. Leon quickly appeared in his red-striped boxer underpants and led his dazed wife away. Before he left for his office that day he shoved her bottles of pills into the pocket of his black jacket and began to dole them out according to a regimen established by Victor Asher. Rose took to her bed, moaning, tossing, weeping over the telephone to Rashi: "But I'm not getting an effect. I need the effect. I must have the lift. Tell Victor to let me have them, at least until after the wedding. Doesn't he have a heart? I'll cut down next week, I promise you." When she felt more tranquil she would call Rashi and implore her not to leave Mara alone. Not for a second. The evil eye will pounce instantly upon the unguarded bride. Mara protested, "Look, Rashi, I've got to have some time to myself. This is crazy." Rashi agreed, but whenever Mara went down for her walk, Rashi trailed her at a distance, with Naomi in a sack on her back, tugging at her mother's hair. On the eve of the wedding it was Rashi who accompanied her sister to the ritual baths, for Rose was distraught because Leon had just confiscated a half-emptied bottle of pills she had only that morning convinced a diet doctor to prescribe for her.

At first Mara blankly refused to "dunk in that filthy cesspool." "It's primitive," she declared. "Anyway, you might as well face it, Rashi, I'm no longer a virgin. Let's not and say we did. Okay?" But in the end she agreed to go, as a gift to her mother and simply for a change in scene. It was a slow night at the *mikvah,* and besides Rashi and Mara, the only ones there were the matron, who was the mother of one of Mara's school chums, Pearl Mintz, and an aged cleaning woman in a babushka, creakily pushing a dry mop. Rashi sat in the waiting room leafing through a bride's magazine, occasionally lifting her legs to accommodate the charwoman. Meanwhile, Mara took the requisite bath. Then she rang a bell to summon Rebbetzin Mintz, who came bustling in crying, *"Mazel tov, kallah, mazel tov!"* As she inspected the length and cleanliness of Mara's nails, as she examined Mara's hair for knots and her body for scratches and sores, Rebbetzin Mintz chattered on and on about her Pearl. "Thank God, my Pearl is keeping busy on the kibbutz. Picking apples, washing the laundry. *Nu,* it's what she wants. A real pioneer, God bless her. She hasn't found a young man yet, but we have faith in God. After all, my Pearlie is a pretty girl—no?—with a lot of common sense, right?" And on she went. When the inspection was completed she swiftly appraised Mara with a rival's eye. "You'll be a beauty when you fill out, darling. Marriage will do you good," she observed. Then she led Mara to the *mikvah* itself. Standing at the edge of the pool, pulling her kerchief over her brow, she gave the bride instruction in the immersion procedures and pronounced the blessings distinctly for the bride to repeat. When it was over she guided Mara back to the dressing room and said, "Now, was that so bad, darling? Tell me the truth. Every bride dreads it, believe me. You're not unique. I hope to see you now every month after your period. Remember what I say to you. You will have a successful marriage if you keep the laws of family purity. That is the woman's task. *Mazel tov, mazel tov!* I'll write to Pearlie and send your regards."

After the rebbetzin finally waddled out in her fuzzy pink slippers with the pompons, Mara sank into a chair, her elbows on her spread knees, her chin in her palms, her fingers veiling her eyes. She tried to amass the energy to begin the process of drying her hair and dressing herself, but a dull lethargy gripped her. She knew Rashi was out there waiting—patient accepter that she was—but she could not bestir herself. Then she heard the click of the door lock. Startled, she covered her breasts. It was the cleaning woman. The old lady must have been working in the adjacent bathroom the whole time. Her appearance was a shock. The crone hobbled on padded feet to the door and locked it from the inside. Mara instantly reached for the towel to protect herself. Sudah approached, slipping off his babushka. Grinning widely, he pushed the towel to the floor and drew her damp body to his pillowed breast. He whispered in Mara's ear, "Now you are so pure. Let's fuck." On the cold tile floor Sudah lifted his long flowered housedress and entered the naked Mara.

When it was over Mara was full of questions. "How did you get in here? How did you do it? Sudah, this is the funniest thing I've ever heard. Tell me everything." But Sudah merely drew a chair up to her and, placing his brown hands upon her knees, spoke softly in Hebrew about the lies he had told her. Had he been testing her loyalty? There were times, indeed, when he wondered. But no, that wasn't it. "To grow up a child must kill his father," Sudah said. "That is the only way to separate. It is something you, too, must do, Mara, if you want to become a person. You also must separate. I was teaching you the way." Mara wanted to ask him if it was necessary to separate so violently and ultimately. But Sudah said, "Think about it. You will understand in time. You must give up your old life for me. Totally. You must never allow people to talk to you about what has happened. You must never reveal to them the explanation. That is between us." Then he wrapped his babushka low over his head and halfway up his face to conceal his beard. "I'll see you tomorrow night," he said. He unlocked the door and followed the mop out of the room.

The next night Sudah was escorted into Mara's presence three hours after their wedding ceremony had been scheduled to begin, when it became obvious that the victims of the train crash would not be resourceful enough to hustle up some other conveyance, and when all hope that the storm would cease had vanished. They would be unable to raise the wedding canopy under the stars. Mara was seated on a red plush throne bedecked with lilies and carnations, set in the middle of the smorgasbord room, where she smiled in response to the congratulations of friends and kin until her cheeks ached. As the evening wore on, greasy plates loaded with chicken bones, olive pits, pickle stems, white fish skeletons, bread crusts, and balled napkins began to mount. When only a few brown specks remained of the chopped liver that had been molded into the form of a hen with three chicks, the band struck up a lively tune and a circle of clapping men danced into the room with Sudah in their midst. "Like a caged beast," Sudah described it later. The circle opened and Sudah was released to approach his bride. He bent over her wreath of wilted daisies, grasped the tips of her tea-stained tablecloth in each of his hands, and as he drew this veil over her head, he inclined his lips to her ear and whispered, "Feh, feh, feh!" Mara covered her mouth and lowered her head, her shoulders rocking with laughter, which the guests approved as the traditional bridal weeping at this most personal of moments. Sudah was led out. Leon placed both of his hands upon his daughter's head and blessed her with the virtues of the four mothers, Sarah, Rebecca, Rachel, and Leah. His arms dropped to his side and he stared down at the small lump of whiteness in the chair.

After the ceremony itself, as Rose sank in a cold sweat into one of the pews in the emptying chapel, a band of dancing men conducted the bride and groom into a secluded room and shut the door. Sudah removed his black silk top hat. He checked the tightness of his hair bun and stared into the mirror at the deep red welt the hat had dug into his brow. Mara walked around the room, inspecting it avidly. On a table against the wall was a round silver tray upon which were set two small glasses of sweet red wine and a dish of honey cake. With this they were supposed to break the fast of their wedding day, a day as holy as Yom Kippur, upon which all the sins of their past would be wiped away in one fierce stroke and no trace of their former selves would remain at all. Mara said, "All the girls used to wonder what goes on in this room. It was a great big juicy secret, you know. Now here I am at last, and I still don't know what I'm supposed to do." She drew aside a gold brocade curtain that was draped across the back wall and exposed a narrow cot across which a bare stained mattress was stretched. "Could this be it, do you think?" She sat down on the bed with her hands clutching her bouquet of daisies. Sudah was astride the pink velvet cushion of a gilded stool, his elbows on the marbleized counter, his face in his hands. He was watching the red stripe on his forehead fade in the mirror, and beyond his dark eyes he could see Mara and her flowers on the cot. This was the picture the photographers did not shoot as they burst just then into the room with their cameras and lights. Their brisk efficiency completely overwhelmed the couple, who permitted themselves to be set limply against the background of the gold drapes and maneuvered into a series of poses: bride's hand resting on top of groom's and both gazing pensively down at her shiny new ring; bride and groom's hands joined at waist level upon her bouquet, their eyes, in half smile, staring ahead, as into the future; bride and groom holding hands and facing each other, their noses in profile almost touching, with a hint of the approved lust that would soon be satisfied. Mara said to the photographers, "I suppose you've done lots of these weddings before," and the one with the camera, whose appearance was distinguished by sideburns that almost connected with his mustache and a massive belly in a white ruffled shirt, responded, "Honey, this is just another job to me. Now be a good girl and do like I say, or you won't have any memories. It's not my affair, right?" He then steered the pair into what would be the comic relief of their album: groom on one knee at bride's feet, bride's face disdainfully upturned to avoid the pathetic sight of groom's clasped hands, raised in amorous supplication. It was just as this pose had been frozen to the photographer's satisfaction that Herzl Lieb began pounding on the door, shouting, "C'mon, it's late already. We need the *chossen* and *kallah*. Everyone is waiting. What's going on in there, anyway?" The photographer yelled back, "Hold your horses, Tonto!" To Mara and Sudah he said, "Okay, terrific. Now hold it." In a flash the bride gathered up her skirt and bared her leg to the top of her thigh. "Hubba, hubba," said the photographer. This was the last formal picture to be taken on their wedding night. Immediately after, Herzl Lieb pushed them from behind into the reception room, where the male dancers dragged Sudah off into their wild ring and the women led Mara away into their circle of beaded and rustling dresses.

The women held hands and lifted their satin-shod feet steadily, round and round, while in the center of their circle Mara danced first with her mother, then with Rashi, with Jacqueline, with Sadie Stern, with Cookie Kalb, and afterward with various aunts and the substantial wives of her father's powerful friends. She stretched her arm around her partner's waist and arced the other arm in the air. Each dance ended with an embrace against a corseted bosom and a great rush into Mara's nostrils of perfume, talcum powder, sweat, and the pickled or spiced appetizer her partner had lately consumed. Suddenly, a band of singing and stomping men, wielding an empty chair, tore into their circle. The women began to clap their hands excitedly and sang along with the music in thin, high voices. They followed in the wake of the abductors. Now both Sudah and Mara were in their chairs, swaying on the shoulders of the dancers. With one hand the bride and groom clutched their seats, and with the other they held on to the white handkerchief that formed a bridge between them. Mara let go of her end of the cloth and stretched her fingers toward Sudah. Sudah reached out for her hand, almost toppling her from her seat. The dancers drew them apart and set them down in their seats on the floor.

The musicians had already torn off their ties. They mopped their necks with dinner napkins. Their faces were wet and swollen and crimson. The sounds coming from their instruments were growing more and more shrill and intense. The dance before the bride was rising to higher and higher pitches of frenzy. Sudah and Mara watched, laughing and commenting in each other's ear as another and still another dancer rose before them to fulfill the commandment of gladdening the groom and bride. How does one dance before the bride? Reb Anschel Frankel danced a lashing kazatzke around a glass filled with wine, threatening the wobbling red liquid with each fierce thrust of his leg, but never, never causing even a drop to spill over. Afterward he threw his head back, and with one hand pinning his black velvet yarmulka to his fading red hair, he drank the wine down in a gulp. Herzl Lieb leaped before the couple. He had disguised himself as an Arab, a white tablecloth wrapped like a kaffiyeh around his head, a long red candle flashing like a saber from under his robe. The women covered their faces in mock terror as Herzl glowered and charged, and some of the ladies were soon giggling as if they were being tickled. Rashi, who was standing behind Sudah's chair, bent her head to his ear and whispered, "That one is dedicated to you, you know." Rav Habakuk now presented himself, his guitar suspended from an embroidered ribbon around his neck. He spread his legs, taking the stance of the popular profane singers, and began a song in praise of the city of Jerusalem. Very soon his body was moving with heat and the guests were swaying with him. When they reached the words of the refrain —"Ye-*roo*-sha-la-yim, Ye-*roo*-sha-la-yim"—he and the crowd were shaking in an ecstasy of longing and love. "Friends, friends," cried Habakuk, "above all our joys we must remember the destruction of our beloved Yerushalayim. Why else did the *chossen* crush that glass? Sing it out again with me: 'Ye-*roo*-sha-la-yim, Ye-*roo*-sha-la-yim.' " Mara extracted a dying daisy from her bouquet and rose from her seat. She inserted this into Habakuk's dripping beard and the minstrel embraced her with a passion that still rebounded from his song. The ladies gasped. The bride is lovely, pleasant, and pious.

The circle now opened to admit the white-bearded stranger known as Berel from Delancey Street, who made his living dancing at weddings. He set a glass filled to the brim with wine on his forehead and performed many spectacular and intricate leaps. Someone passed him six small challa rolls which he juggled in the air, the full glass still on his head. He drank the wine and began to circulate among the wedding party, his palm outstretched. Leon drew him aside. "Look here, Delancey Berel," said Leon, "don't bother my guests." He slipped Berel a twenty-dollar bill. Berel glanced at the money and made a motion to resume his schnorring. Leon stuffed another twenty into his palm. Only after three more bills were scrutinized and pocketed by Berel was he content. "Now I have a night's wages," he said, as he danced toward the exit. *"Mazel tov,* Reb Leon. We shall meet on happy occasions only. I never dance at funerals."

While these negotiations were taking place, Manny Fish, bright silk scarves tied around his head and body, his pants rolled up to expose his hairy legs, crude red lipstick smeared over his face, was clowning with Mark Bavli before the bride and groom. Mark, with Sudah's hat perched awry on his head and a thick cigar between his lips, took the role of the stern male impervious to the grim flirtations of the female. At last he succumbs to her seductions. They embrace and cling to each other in exaggerated poses. Then comes their wedding. The pantomime ends with the female beating vigorously upon the male's back. He cowers and huddles on the floor. She crouches over him, pounding, pounding.

Mara bent down and mussed Manny's hair. He tore off his kerchiefs and briskly lit a cigarette, which he handed to her. She inserted it between her dry lips despite the perfumed lipstick stains on the tip.

Rose almost shouted into her daughter's ear. "Mara darling, you're embarrassing us. Put that thing out, darling. A bride can't be seen smoking a cigarette at her own wedding. It's a scandal!"

"It's not a cigarette, Mommy," said Mara. In fact, it was a marijuana joint. She puffed on it a bit longer and passed it to Sudah, who inhaled once, slowly and deeply, and stomped it out.

"Oh, thank you, Sudah! God bless you," said Rose. "At least you know what's proper."

More revelers took their turn before the bride and groom, including the strange partnership of Luke Alfasi and Victor Asher, who danced in a rather dignified and self-conscious fashion, boring the crowd immensely. However, one lady was heard remarking to her companion, "That's the son-in-law, the doctor. The other one looks to me like some sort of *meshug-geneh.*" And the wife of a state senator observed, "I believe the one with the mustache is the good son-in-law." But few among the witnesses recognized the significance of this event: that on a night when such hopeless contradictions as man and woman, East and West, were joined, so too were joined, if only for a brief moment, those traditional antagonists science and art, doctor and patient.

The last dance of this sequence began between Mara and her father, each grasping the opposite end of a handkerchief and prancing high in a circle. Mara moved closer to Leon. When it seemed as if she was actually about to brush against his body, her hand flew to her mouth, her face became contorted in feigned alarm, and she swiftly leaped back. The guests were amused by this harmless satire of extreme orthodoxy. Leon dropped his end of the handkerchief and drew his daughter into his embrace. "God take care of you, Mara'le," he whispered hoarsely. It was then that Sudah danced up, waving a handkerchief of his own. Mara bid her father farewell and went to her husband. Sudah and Mara danced around the handkerchief, now a crumpled white heap on the floor, never touching each other, as if the cloth itself were not necessary to separate them. They brought their bodies closer and then drew them apart, casting a dull shadow of their feverish nights dancing in the cellars of Tel Aviv. They were still dancing as the musicians blew the last blasts and the guests sat down to a choice of consommé with matzoh balls, vegetable soup, or cold borscht with a potato.

Between each course the guests rose from their tables, removing their napkins from their laps and wiping their lips, for another bout of dancing. However, the set between the soup and the entrée, while it lasted as long as any other, was uniquely lacking in exuberance and purpose, and this was because the bride and groom were not there. As hundreds of soup spoons were being elevated to hundreds of mouths, Rashi had gone up to the dais and performed a mute dance before Sudah and Mara, throughout which she had dangled over their heads the key to the bridal suite. Sometimes she would bring it closer to the couple, as if to present it to them, then she would teasingly withdraw it. Mara laughed good-naturedly, while Sudah pretended not to notice. But once, when Rashi let the key hover perilously close, Sudah's brown hand darted up and grabbed it. He grinned and slipped it into his pocket. With their arms encircling each other's waist, Sudah and Mara promptly left the dining room.

Rashi went back to her seat. She turned to the woman eating soup at her right. This happened to be Olga Kranz, a stylish gynecologist, trained in Moscow, whom Rose had once accused of flirting with Leon. "What do you think of this marriage, Olga?" Rashi asked; "terrible, isn't it?" Olga put down her spoon. She said, "I thought the two of us had something in common. I see now we do not." Rashi had expected polite, mumbled complicity, not this, certainly. "Don't count on me to be on your side," Olga warned; "I shall never agree with you —or them." Her gesture of disdain struck down all the unguarded diners. "All my life I have loved passion and risk. Well, Rashi, I once had hope for you. You showed some fire when you were a girl. What a pity it's gone!" A shameful sense of having been caught in the act of betraying her sister crept over Rashi. She moved out of Olga's range and never sat down beside her again for another course.

Above the dining hall, in room 218, Sudah sprawled across the bed, his arm folded under his head. With his right hand he was stroking Mara's flank. She was curled up beside him, her head tucked beneath his chin in the hollow of his shoulder, her bridal skirt bunched up to her waist to reveal no other article of clothing but her red ballet slippers tied with red ribbons. The curtains had been parted to expose a pitch-black window against which the storm continued to pound. Suddenly they felt calm and snug in this quiet, impersonal room, with the rain beating outside and the celebration below.

They were having a discussion in the Holy Tongue. The topic was, should they fuck or should they not fuck? Mara pointed out that "*they* probably think we're screwing up here." "That's a good reason not to do it," countered Sudah, who hated to be predictable. "But they would never know whether we did or we didn't. So we might as well do it." That was Mara's suggestion. Sudah wondered whether it would be better to fuck and say we didn't, or not to fuck and say we did. Mara thought it would be best to fuck and say nothing at all, but should someone happen to inquire, we could, of course, always say we did. "But we would lose our power if we held nothing back," said Sudah. Mara then raised for their joint consideration the special pleasure that could be derived from fucking while *they* were dancing their heads off downstairs. On the one hand, it would be like saying to them, "Fuck you!"; on the other hand, the revelers were, in a sense, observers, and might not their "presence" serve as a "turn on"? Sudah weighed these ideas. "Maybe so," he conceded, "but in that case it would be necessary for them to know we fucked. What if they don't even suspect it? What if they're too straight to even imagine it?" Then, of course, the problem arose of how to communicate the news. It had to be done discreetly. They could not very well re-enter the dining room screaming, "Just took a fucking break!" They could not even offhandedly reply to the inevitable questions of where they had been by casually saying, "Oh, upstairs, fucking." Perhaps Mara could forget to button her blouse. Perhaps she could change her costume entirely. Perhaps Sudah could leave his fly halfway open. Perhaps Mara could smear some blood on the front of her skirt.

They were growing tired of this conversation. Besides, Sudah disdained all intellectual discussion. As a matter of fact, it had been he who had persuaded Mara to abandon her university in Israel on the grounds that all that was taught there was lies, with no attachment to life. In any event, throughout their discussion they had been caressing one another's body to a delicate pitch, and so when the subject lost all flavor, Sudah set his mouth on Mara's genitals and she upon his, and in this way they resolved their dilemma to their mutual satisfaction and, they hoped, to the satisfaction of all those who were watching.

It was well after midnight when the last wilted guest left the wedding. Mara and Sudah re-entered their suite for the final time that night, their faces puckered with fatigue. This time they certainly had no intention of fucking. That is surely what would have been expected of them. Perhaps some traveler driving homeward through the storm would be leering to himself as he conjured up a cozy vision of what the newly married couple must be doing right this minute as he was pressing down on the gas. No, they would not fuck now, certainly not. Besides, they had business to complete. The couple sat down at opposite ends of a small table. Sudah extracted from all his pockets folded and crumpled envelopes containing gifts of cash, checks, and bonds. He tore each one open and broadcast the sum. Mara recorded the numbers, though not the names, and added them up, every so often announcing, with a fanfare, the newest total. The first envelope contained a check of one hundred dollars from Uncle Srulka, with the message "Stop counting and go to bed." This had been the advice he had given to Herzl and Rashi as well. The children continued to calculate as their benefactors struggled home in the storm.

The casualties of this wedding included the following: Irv Messer, who, in a huddle with Leon Lieb, was informed that he would not, after all his capitulations and compromises, be granted the franchise to the new downtown nursing home, the Parklawn; that it would go to Sidney Schneider instead.

Sid Schneider, who ignored his wife's warnings and celebrated by indulging in too many sour pickles and tomatoes, with the result that his ulcer began to bleed violently and he was rushed, drenched and nearly dead, to the hospital emergency room.

Peter Lustig, who in the course of one of the more frolicsome dances, was tossed up into the air and promptly forgotten until he hit the polished floor with a loud, bottom-crushing thud.

Dr. Lucille Sneed, the Negro general practitioner on call at Leon's homes, who was asked by a guest to hurry and bring over a knish and a wiener in a roll.

Aunt Lilly, upon whose white dress—which she had purchased only that morning and which she wore with the tags still attached—a plate of syrupy orange *tsimmes* had been spilled, rendering it impossible for her to return this article to the store the next day, as was her custom.

State Senator Teddy Schumacher, who laughed from deep within his belly, thumped Leon on the back, and boomed, sure he could arrange it, no sweat, what's a favor between friends?

Herzl Lieb, whose accelerator simply fell off during his journey home, causing his wife, Judy, to run out of the car, crying in the rain.

Rose Lieb, upon whose stiffened, strawberry-blond coiffure an absurd white wreath was set: who had been forced, in spite of her protests, to sit through the *mezinke* dance honoring her and Leon for having married off their youngest, for having thereby acquitted themselves of their parental obligation, when she knew very well that this wasn't a real wedding at all, not real at all, that it would end soon with a thunderclap and this queer boy would fade out of their sight like a cloud.

Mara rose from her seat. She stretched. "Five thousand seven hundred and eighteen dollars," she announced.

"Not bad," said Sudah. "Let's go to sleep."

He carefully folded his wedding clothes over a chair and lay down upon the bed. There he slept a child's sleep until the next afternoon, and Mara, her white body, beside him.

2 A hot night in September. Herzl Lieb, standing in the darkened kitchen of his parents' apartment, was cooled and lighted by the open refrigerator. This was by far his favorite mode of dining—alone and on his feet, fanned by the crisp breeze and comforted by the steady hum from that glowing cave with its heartwarming array of foods. The bottles of ketchup and horseradish, the jars of mustard and pickles, the milk, the juice, the soda, some leftover chicken and gefilte fish wrapped, like gifts, in silver foil, green peppers, carrots and plums in the drawer, round egg hillocks rising along the horizon of the wide open door. Herzl was feasting rapidly on one slice after another of packaged white bread, upon which he spread neither butter nor jam nor cheese nor chicken fat with *grieben,* but which he folded, stuffed into his mouth, and chewed briefly before dispatching it, in a damp, nicely painful lump, down his throat. The telephone receiver was pinned between his raised shoulder and his ear, and as he loaded and swallowed, he was listening to Sudah with disgust.

At last he lost patience with his brother-in-law's slow and irrelevant excuses. He opened his mouth and a rosette of spittle and bread crumbs, like a fireworks display, burst into the refrigerator's gut. "Look here, Sudah," Herzl was yelling, "I'm sick and tired of your crap! You get your people down there, you hear? I mean business! And you'd better not forget their equip-

ment! Wheelchairs, crutches, walkers, canes! The whole bit!"
He smashed the receiver down. Shaking his head in disbelief,
he grabbed a last slice of bread, which he squashed to a ball
in his fist, and trudged out of the kitchen in search of his father.

Even Leon had never permitted himself such an outburst
against Sudah. There were the testings and pickings, the
suggestions, the criticisms by word, by look, by silence, that
made each day loathsome, but certainly no ultimatum, no
showdown. What good would it have served? Leon was too
accomplished a businessman to force a break and thereby relin-
quish whatever control he still exercised, however shabby and
peripheral it was. On the other hand, the ten thousand dollars
that had long ago been designated as Mara's marriage gift was
still inaccessible in one of Leon's steel vaults. "Not until I have
proof you'd use it like a normal person" was his reply to Mara's
shrill claim. They wanted that money desperately, those two sly
children, and for it they would cede vast territories of themselves. But Leon himself so fiercely wanted something from
them, too, that he dreaded pushing his advantage to the limit
lest he lose his grip entirely. The more base and manipulated
he felt himself to be, the more unyielding he became with his
associates in business. Thus, after Herzl gulped down the bread
ball that swelled his cheek when he first appeared in his father's
study, and while he narrated the story of the fresh affront, Leon
tugged at his goatee and experienced a new surge of hope. It
was possible, he saw, to let his good children be the spokesper-
sons for his disapproval. It would be to the benefit of their
shared desires if Leon himself remained clean.

Herzl was convinced that Sudah was a Jewish anti-Semite.
"The worst kind," he declared, "just the worst!" He pronounced worst, "rurst," like world ("rurld"), and these, plus
some other minor residues of childhood, including a by-now
almost imperceptible lisp, were defects he took pains to guard
against in his role as rabbi and orator. Each Sabbath he offi-

ciated in a small East Side synagogue known locally as the
"Yekkie Shul" because its congregants were a certain unmis-
takable brand of proper and bourgeois, snobbish and fastidious
German Jew. However, the major portion of his earnings was
derived from his father's homes for the aged, where he was a
member of the board of directors with the official title of
"religious counselor and coordinator." "What's that?" demanded Sanford Gross, after reviewing the subpoenaed records
of the Lieb holdings. "And is this what your average rabbi is
pulling in these days?" he further inquired. Herzl was to call
Gross a "Jewish anti-Semite," too, but all this occurred much
later, though the first rumblings could already be felt in Lieb's
chambers.

The present friction between Herzl and Sudah grew out of
Herzl's plans for a protest to be carried out on one of the Ten
Days of Awe, between Rosh Hashana and Yom Kippur. By
some chance the world had inflicted no specific precipitating
injury upon the Jews at that time, but Herzl and his loose clique
of young activists concluded that the days around the New
Year holiday would nevertheless serve as an appropriate occasion to recall certain long-standing grievances. Herzl was a
generalist, and then, of course, the Russians could always be
relied upon to deliver one outrage or another. A member of
Herzl's group commented, "Jews need to be reminded they are
suffering. Otherwise, they forget they're Jewish." The speaker
was Bernie Schultz, who thought all day long in the privacy of
the front seat of his taxicab. He had just dropped off a fare and
was still wearing the plaid woolen cap with the little metal
buckle in back which served as his public head covering wherever a yarmulka would render him too vulnerable. You can see
this cap in a good many cabdrivers' identification pictures,
since the rule was that every licensee must be photographed in
a hat; Schultz was the only person who had one that day, and
so his was passed from head to head until it found its way back

to its owner, its lining darkened and blotched with sweat. In Herzl's living room, some seven or eight men were chewing cookies and emptying the small fluted paper cups of schnapps that Judy had spread out on the coffee table before retiring upstairs to watch television. What they were searching for was an idea, some device to turn their demonstration into an event that would evoke hot public interest. Herzl telephoned Rashi, who suggested they stage a sit-in of pregnant women. That was because Rashi suspected she might be pregnant. Herzl re-entered the living room to impart this flippant idea—he had many misgivings about it—but for courtesy's sake was obliged to wait as someone uttered the punch line to a joke involving a rabbi, three little yeshiva boys named Herschel, Velvel, and Berel, onanism, and pederasty. Soon after it occurred to some-one—it could have been Bernie Schultz—that they might do well to exploit the resources available to them through Herzl. Why not stage a march of the "aged and infirm"? Let them come pouring out of all the Lieb nursing homes—the Minnie Sweet Pavilion, the Parklawn, the Roseleon, the Aishel, La Mahr (*M*ara, *H*erzl, *R*ashi), the Ben Ezra, Mount Morning, and so on and so on. Let them roll out in their wheelchairs and hobble out on their crutches and canes. If they sat down on the ground, their bones creaking like an earthquake, and blocked the entranceway to some public building, who would dare undertake the responsibility of physically removing them? Moreover, it would be salutary for the old folks themselves—wouldn't it?—an outing, an excursion, something to plan and look forward to, a chance to make a contribution, to participate once again, if only for the last time. Everyone was thrilled. Herzl set to work at once. He said to Judy in bed that night, "Honey, this one is going to be a killer!"

He was bursting with enthusiasm. The administrators at the various establishments rightly perceived how important this project was to Herzl. They diligently went about preparing the old people. Each institution designated a small delegation of geriatrics. The desired qualities of those selected included an appearance of progressive deterioration and frailty, coupled with some sort of medical assurance of their ability to tolerate the probable stress and excitement. Those not lucky enough to be chosen were nevertheless generous with their possessions and labor, freely offering the loan of dresses, coats, ties, and hats, polishing canes, oiling wheelchairs, arranging coiffures. The arts-and-crafts workshops were bustling with people painting signs and posters, outdoing each other and even themselves: "Will We Be the Last of the Jews?"; "Senior Citizens for a Strong State"; "Who Shall Live and Who Shall Die?"; "We May Be Old but We're Not Dead"; "No More Hitlers"; "Save Our Children." There were others, too; some in Yiddish. Only at the Parklawn was the enthusiasm mixed, and this was the fault of Sudah, with Mara as his accomplice.

After their wedding Sudah and Mara had taken up residence at the Parklawn, where Leon provided them with room and board in exchange for their services—Sudah as arts-and-crafts director and Mara as social coordinator. They were assigned a small room that ran the width of the tip of the U on the third-floor corridor. The room had two exposures: the east window faced a narrow alleyway and a faded Coca-Cola sign, and the west window looked over the small courtyard and into Fanny Gottlieb's room, which was at the opposite tip of the U. As soon as they moved in, Sudah and Mara dismantled the white iron bedstead and leaned it, with its wire springs, against the hallway wall outside their door, where it may still be standing to this day. They peeled the flowered paper off the back wall, and then the plaster and wood beneath it, to expose the brick of the building, which they whitewashed. The remaining three walls they painted a deep chocolate color. They affixed a layer of cork to the floor, and the sharp smell of the glue stung the nostrils of all who visited. They wrapped the Venetian blinds in the gray, tattered nylon curtains and carried this bundle into the alleyway, where they deposited it between the pile of old mattresses and the row of trash cans outside the cellar door that led to the boiler room and into the quarters of Russell Boomer, the janitor. Their two windows were now bare of all covering, but they were still able to maintain the privacy of most of their intimate activities, which usually took place on and around the mattress pushed against the brick wall on the floor. The only other items in the room were the tall dresser they had found there and painted a vivid yellow, and the sink. One night, when it was known that the young couple was away, a contingent of residents, led by Fanny Gottlieb, stole into the room, flicked on the light, gaped in wonder, opened the drawers, rummaged through their contents, leafed through the notebooks and sketch pads, fingered every object. They were in agreement: dark, cold, smelly; and that bed? you could crack your bones getting up and down. With his index finger, Julius Fleischer made spirals near his temple. Cuckoo, that's what it was, cuckoo!

They all adjourned back to Fanny's room. She placed a kettle of water on her hot plate. The weak tea, sweet and lemony, was served in old *yahrzeit* glasses. Fanny unwrapped a grease-stained napkin and offered her guests bits of crumbling sponge cake saved from a Sabbath dinner. As they munched and sipped, she entertained them with stories of the sights she could see through her window. They walked around naked all the time, she informed her listeners. From the waist up you couldn't tell which one was the boy and which one was the girl, except for the beard—on the boy, of course. No bust, that girl has no bust. And I hear she's a rabbi's a daughter! After considerable coaxing, Fanny agreed to describe what she had witnessed two nights ago, but only if they swore not to look at her as she spoke. They swore. That girl, Mrs. Mizrahi, the social director, was standing in the sink, and that boy, Mr. Mizrahi, the arts-and-crafts director, was washing her all over, and I mean all over, first soap, then rinse with the water, then pat, pat, pat with the towel. Then the young lady sits herself down on the rim of the sink, like on a toilet bowl, you should excuse me, with one leg hanging over each side, and he goes right in there between them, and all you could see is his shoulders going up and down, and his behind going in and out, and her legs around his waist like a belt. "Your eyes are pretty good for an old lady," said Julius Fleischer. Dora Popper observed, "Well, at least she was getting a bath. She could sure use a bath, darling." Dora had been a socialist and a cynic in her prime, and those of her lovers who were not yet dead were dying. Fanny, on the other hand, was a romantic, and as she told her story, she removed the tortoise-shell combs and pins, one by one, from her heavy white hair, which fell down her back almost to her waist. She ran her fingers through it like a rake.

That same night, as was their custom, Mara and Sudah were smoking hashish on the roof of the Parklawn, directly over Fanny's room. Mark Bavli was with them, and the white clay pipe with the red tip was passed from mouth to mouth. They were feeling cozy, a bit silly. Loosened by the drug, they allowed themselves to amuse Mark with stories of the old people. Sudah told about Henry Friedman, who had marched purposefully into the workshop one morning bearing a glass of water in which his pink and white dentures floated. He took a lump of clay out of the barrel and set to work molding an ashtray from the impression of his false teeth. "For my grandchildren," he explained, "so they won't forget me." And what about Stanley Boxer? Boxer had grabbed the enormous breast of one of the Negro aides and cackled, "Titty, titty, give me titty!" He was dragged away to his room screaming, "Put me in a straitjacket, I don't care! I copped a feel, boys! I got it! It may be my last one, but it's mine, boys, all mine!" That reminded Mara of Sylvia Upright, who always placed her long fingers with the wrinkled skin, like an oversized, spotted glove, directly on Mara's bosom and declared, "No brassiere, darling? Well, you can get away with it!" Almost two-dimensional in her thinness, Sylvia dressed herself painstakingly each morning in false eyelashes and stiletto heels. At breakfast time Mara glided from table to table to greet the diners. Julius Fleischer never failed to rub her hand warmly between both of his own and beckon her to bend down so he could whisper in her ear. "Sweetheart, could you do me a favor? Could you get me a glass of prune juice with some hot water and a lemon? The old machine ain't what she used to be, ha, ha!" One day, according to Mara, a young intern was ushered up to the second-floor hallway to look at an aged man who had been lying there until a room could be emptied for him. For nearly an hour the intern struggled to draw blood from the patient as Dora Popper watched coolly. At last he threw down his instruments and exclaimed, "Damn it! I can't get a drop from this man!" "Of course not, Doctor'l," said Dora, "he's been dead for seven hours." The smell of excrement was strong around them. A few days later this same intern, a short, round fellow with inflamed pimples, was brought back to examine another patient. He placed the cold metal piece of his gleaming new stethoscope on her chest and screwed up his face to listen. Shaking his head ominously, he set the piece down on another spot. At last he declared, "Damn it! I don't hear a thing! This lady is dead." Dora Popper then said, "Maybe it would help if you put the earpieces into your ears instead of around your neck. A stethoscope is not a necklace, honey." Dora had once been a nurse. Over the years she had cultivated a hard disrespect for doctors, which she sought to translate into action by adding her presence, whenever possible, to the medical consultations at the

Parklawn. Her folded arms, her raised eyebrow, her pursed-lipped, expectant silence seldom failed to bring about an episode of sputtering humiliation.

It was Dora who had revealed to Mara some of the secrets from Fanny's past. Under Fanny's bed was an old shoebox filled with packets of crumbling, brown-edged letters bound in velvet ribbons, blue, red, and black. Blue for Vladimir Jabotinsky, red for Arthur Schnitzler, black for Herbert G. Wells. The old men had laid eyes on Fanny in the spas of Eastern Europe—Carlsbad, Marienbad, Franzensbad—and had been instantly devastated by her matchless red hair, her pale skin, and the pure white ascot that topped her blue tailored suit, over which three seamstresses had squinted long hours in a Kraków cellar. Each morning of a certain bright summer a messenger would knock at the door of Fanny's villa and present her with a bouquet of white roses from Doktor Schnitzler. Promptly at eight o'clock every evening the white-bearded writer would escort her back to her veranda and say, "A young girl needs a good night's sleep." As soon as he was gone, she would skip out the back way into the dark woods to sing and dance the night through with her wild young friends. There was a moonlit night long ago when the venerable Schnitzler had placed his chin upon his clasped hands, which rested on the knob of his cane, and declared, "You, Fanya, have surpassed them all!" "Those letters are worth a fortune," Dora said. "God forbid the administration should ever find out about them." Mara was flattered by Dora's trust, but most of all by Dora's implied distinction of her from the rest of the staff.

Fanny, however, never mentioned these romances, not that Mara withheld the opportunities. Mara spent hours in the lobby behind Fanny's chair, combing the long hair. Fanny loved the tremor that the comb's teeth along her scalp sent through her body. "But why do you bother with an old lady like me?" she sometimes asked the girl. Mara arranged the hair

in a variety of lavish, old-fashioned styles. One day she gave
Fanny a present of a silver barrette engraved with a bird on a
berry branch. The beautiful old woman listened as Mara described the events that led to her own recent marriage: making
love on the bed of her parents' hotel room, making love in Tel
Aviv as her sister slept beside her, making love on the cold tiles
of the *mikvah* floor. These were the details she selected and
offered up, because she hoped to elicit like stories from Fanny's
memory. Fanny rarely contributed to the conversation, however, and then only to say such things as, "Thank God you
didn't catch pneumonia!" or "You should really try to put on
a little weight, sweetie." Nevertheless, Mara felt a kinship with
Fanny. In Fanny she sensed she had an ally. Watching from
the roof as Fanny and the gang invaded her room and possessions, Mara knew she had been betrayed.

"Maybe I'll squeal to Sid about those letters," said Mara.
She laughed when she said this, as if to indicate that her words
did not betoken serious intention, but both Mark and Sudah
recognized how damaged she felt herself to be. Mara pressed
the heels of her palms against her eyes. "Oh, cheer up, Mara,"
Mark said. He stuck a finger in each corner of his mouth and
stretched his lips into a grotesque elastic smile. This was his
strategy whenever Mara would sink into one of her glooms: he
would transform himself into the buffoon. "Did they hurt any
of your precious things?" he went on. "Did they steal something? Did they leave a piss puddle on the floor? An old turd?
What are you so upset about? So now they got their thrills, the
poor, miserable jerks." "Shut up, Mark," said Mara.

But Mark would not retreat. He leaned over the low brick
parapet of the roof and with a broom handle began to beat on
the curtained window of Fanny's room. There was no reaction.
"They're deaf, the old farts," commented Mark. He let his
body dangle over the wall and reached tentatively with his toes
for a perch on Fanny's windowsill. Once he was securely estab-

lished, he began pounding with his fists on the pane, yelling, "Help! Help! Save me! Someone save me!" At last the curtains parted. What Mark saw were three old people huddled together with dropped jaws. What the old people saw was a man spread across their window, arms extended with palms upturned, ankles crossed, head drooped on shoulder. Dora resolutely approached and drew the curtains shut.

Sudah went down the flight of stairs and knocked on Fanny's door. They let him in. Fanny exclaimed, "Oh, Mr. Mizrahi! Thank God it's you!" "What's all this noisiness, kids?" said Sudah. They all began jabbering at once. "A minute, please. Now you, Julius, you who are the man. Talk." Julius succeeded finally in getting the story out. He indicated the window. Sudah walked calmly up to it and parted the curtains. A moonlit night and stars, nothing more. "You now see?" inquired Sudah. "Maybe I am mistaking to let the three of you scoundrels play after the curfew. You drink the tea with the lemon and sugar, you tell the stories about the ghost, and what then do you see? On your window, Jesus Christ himself. Maybe the rules are not so stupid, eh?" Sudah led Fanny to her bed, where she wriggled modestly into her nightgown under the covers. He splayed her hair across the pillow, pulled the blanket stamped three times with PROPERTY OF THE PARKLAWN to her chin, and flicked out the light. Then he escorted Julius and Dora to their rooms. They marched down the hallway, Sudah between them with his left arm over Julius Fleischer's shoulder and his right arm stretched diagonally up the back of Dora Popper, who was nearly three inches taller than he.

What Sudah noticed at once when he returned to his own room was that it struck him as starker than ever. The mattress and goose-down quilts were gone. The dresser drawers were all partially open, jutting out like irregular teeth, and you could sense instantly that they were empty. Mara was sitting cross-legged in the middle of the floor, calmly turning the pages of her "virginity" notebook. Next to her were Sudah's sketching pads. Without looking up Mara said, "You can go through them to see what you want to throw out."

"Where everything?" Sudah wanted to know. "I dumped it all," said Mara. She pointed to the window opposite Fanny's. He walked over and stared down into the courtyard. There, in a sad heap, was all their bedding and clothing, and rising from its center, like the devil from his hole, was the janitor, Russell Boomer, the cheeks of his black face gleaming in the moonlight, his sharp little goatee jutting out. He was shaking a fist and shouting, "You git dat crazy pussy down here, you heah? You heah?" Sudah turned to Mara. "Where Mark?" he asked. "Where is Mark?" she corrected.

Sudah said in Hebrew, "Are you protecting Mark from my bad English?"

"Mark was tired. He went home."

"Of course, tired. It is hard work to defend the lady against all violators." There was a long silence. Mara was now even more intensely engaged in her notebooks. "What you doing?" Sudah asked in English. "I am disinfecting the art," she replied. Sudah sat down on the floor beside her. He gathered his sketchbooks into his lap and began to leaf through them. On the first page of each pad, and sometimes on the second as well, Sudah had made a small, whimsical line drawing, usually of a figure in some state of motion. These were intended to be the inspirations and illustrations for a series of short, delightful children's tales that Mara had yet to compose. Other than these few rough pictures, however, the books were crackling new. A day or two after their wedding Mara had insisted they go out and buy the finest equipment. "Sketching materials," she had specified, "to make the sketches for that big canvas you told me about." Sudah loved to shop and did so in grand style.

He glanced at his sketches, murmuring every now and then,

"Nice, very nice." It was like a cat purring. Then he heard the sound of paper tearing. "What you doing, Mara?" he demanded. Mara said, "It's crap anyway, and now it's been crapped on." She was ripping out page after page covered with her small round writing, and since it was one of those notebooks sewn together with a large stitch seam, blank pages from the back were tumbling out as well. "Give me, you crazy girl!" Sudah grabbed the paper in handfuls and stuffed them into his pants.

Sudah found a pencil. He admired the velvety look of the slate-colored point, which he passed over the plate of his tongue. This tongue, cherry-red and narrow, was now pinned between his long white teeth, its tip protruding slightly from between the full lips. Sudah was deeply absorbed in sketching. After some minutes he nudged Mara to show her. What she looked upon then was a painstaking drawing of an enormous toilet bowl, and floating in the bowl you could see all sorts of words, such as "love," "pain," "art," "fart." Mara laughed, but she was angry, and grew even angrier now that Sudah had dealt with her as with a child, making her laugh when she preferred to be sad. "Well, I guess that's the most ambitious piece of work you've done in your entire career," she said.

"The lady says foo-yah!" Sudah announced. He ripped out the page and crumpled it into a ball, which he tossed out the window into the courtyard. In the bottom right-hand corner of a clean page he now drew a young girl with her forehead resting on the caps of her drawn-up knees, her arms braceleted around her ankles. At first Mara would not even look at it. Sudah refused to give up, however. "This you will okay," he promised. At last she lifted her head and stretched out her legs. She gazed at it a long time. "It's good," Mara said, "it's very good."

"Do you know what we call it?" Mara waited. Sudah pointed

to the small inscription underneath: "How I found my virginity."

"It's better untitled," said Mara. "You're a brilliant son-of-a-bitch, Sudah Mizrahi."

"No, no. It quite stinks, Mara. It's rubbish. It's dung!" He tore it from the pad, squeezed it savagely in his fist, and hurled it through the window to its just reward. Mara looked out in time to see it land. "I'm going to get it," she said. "I want it. It's mine."

Sudah followed her down. Russell Boomer was waiting for them in the courtyard. All he was wearing was a pair of pants, which were unfastened, and you could see the black hairs trailing downward in the direction of his groin. "How come you throwin' dem dirty pictures down on me? You wanna insult me?" Russell's voice was raw and menacing. He spat out a glob of chewing tobacco, which missed them narrowly. Sudah apologized. He tried to explain that neither the objects nor their descent into the courtyard had anything at all to do with Russell Boomer as a person. Russell said, "You talkin' English, man? I don' unnerstan' a word yo' saying!" Then Russell agreed to transport their belongings back upstairs for an advance payment of fifteen dollars. Mara and Sudah walked chastised behind the mattress on the black man's back.

Some nights later they could once again be found smoking on the roof, this time in the company of Manny Fish. Manny produced from deep within his sock a fairly large chunk of hashish, which he passed to Sudah. Sudah had established himself as the connoisseur in their group by virtue of his long and notorious experience, both in the United States and abroad. Sudah sniffed at the lump for a long time, his eyelids drooping. Then he examined it carefully by the light of a burning match. "It look good," he said at last. A sigh of relief was audible. "But the last test is the smoke," he added. He was cutting off slivers of the hashish with his silver penknife and inserting them into the bowl of the pipe, and as he performed this operation he explained that while sniffing he had been obliged to distinguish the essential fragrance of the hashish itself from the rather cheesy odor of Manny's feet. He advised that in the future a sweeter-smelling environment for conveying the stuff be found. Manny said that he had been racing down the four flights of stairs from Luke's apartment and was making haste to meet them here on the roof of the Parklawn when he had encountered Spin waiting calmly on the tenement stoop. *"Salaam Aleikem,"* Spin had said. "Are you eating your vegetables?" Spin was a young Negro with a dramatically scarred face and hair arranged in many upright little braids, as if charged with electricity. Even Sudah considered Spin crazy. Spin had said, "I have for your pleasure myrrh and frankincense from my spice garden." Manny had understood. "How much?" he had inquired. And so the transaction was completed and Manny certainly had no time to ponder the ideal mode of transportation.

The bitterness was lifted by the kef. Sudah inhaled and declared it good. Manny began to speak of his visit with Luke. He had brought Luke a poem about a pine tree stuck in the cleft of a mountainside. The line that Manny had created and that thrilled him the most was this one: "Frozen in coitus." As he pronounced it, *coi* rhymed with *oy*. Luke had said, yes, yes, you may have something there, but it is only a first draft; it is a question of art, after all, and you must travail over it. "From anyone else it would bother me," said Manny, "but from Luke, well, you know how long he's been revising his own poem." Manny told them that there was great tension at Luke's. Since his mother had been discharged from the hospital, Luke could get no rest. All day long she heard voices telling her joke after joke. She could not stop laughing. She laughed and laughed, and the side of her body, her jaw, and her throat were aching miserably. Her eyes were red and burning from the tears that streamed down with the laughter. At night in Luke's neighborhood there was no peace to be found, either. She sat by the window watching the events in the street—children squealing, squatting men making business, women in housedresses slandering each other, prostitutes strutting on their heels, pushers negotiating. Sometimes her head would nod on her chest, but that was all the sleep she ever got. Luke was of the opinion that what she needed was more tranquil surroundings. He had no money, so he could not send her for a holiday to the country. He wondered if perhaps Sudah or Mara could find a room for his mother at the Parklawn. Naturally, it could not be done officially, and this for two reasons: neither Luke nor his mother would ever accept the shame of her descent to the status of an inmate at a nursing home; and second, Luke could not afford to pay a penny. Mara and Sudah looked at each other. Simultaneously they thought of August Vesci, the old piano tuner who was dying two doors away from them. Mara said, "Okay. When Vesci goes, I'll tell Sid we need the room for a studio."

Mara was feeling detached, powerful. She said to Manny, "To tell you the truth, I think your beard is dreadful." What she was referring to were the clumps of wiry hairs that sprouted wildly from Manny's face. Manny spent long stretches of time gazing at this growth in the mirror, wondering at the contrast between its burnt-orange color and the brown of his hair, fretting over the rosy patch of baby skin from which nothing could be coaxed. Mara elaborated: "When I look at it, I know all about your pubic region." She disappeared into the building and returned with a mirror, a bowl of soapy water, and a razor. She handed these items to Manny. "Here," she said, "take it off." Manny held the rusty razor up to the light. It was caked with the old hairs that Mara had stripped off her legs as she had readied herself for Sudah's arrival from Israel months earlier. Two days after that event Sudah had informed her that the hairs on a woman's legs had always served to trigger his lust. Now, on the Parklawn's roof, you could see the matting of brown hair over her legs, and the little tufts sticking out over the chubby folds near her armpits.

Manny said, "I've never used a razor before, Mara." He was referring to his new mode of dealing with religion—selectively —forsaking certain precepts but clinging to others. For instance, he had reached the level where he would consume fried potatoes in a restaurant, knowing full well they were anointed in lard, but still he shunned the forbidden razor. To this objection, however, Mara responded, "Oh, don't be such a jackass, Manny." Manny coated his cheeks with the soapsuds and applied the weapon. He worked his way down from the left sideburn into the fullness and plumpness of his cheek. Every once in a while he opened the dispenser and blew a spray of coiled hairs into the night air. When half his face was embarrassingly naked, and the other half furred and foamy, steps could be heard ascending to the roof. The tread was heavy and brisk, heavier and brisker than the familiar movements of the female aides and the old people. Instantly, Sudah cast the pipe out of his hand, as if he had suddenly been scorched by it. It landed at the feet of the first of the two police officers to appear, the stem shattering into crumbs of pottery, the bowl miraculously preserved. Mara later asserted that she had noticed the curtain of Fanny's room parting ever so slightly as they were led away. They filed into the patrol car one by one. Sudah was to claim that Russell Boomer could be seen watching from a perch atop a trash can, his arms folded across his naked chest, the slice of his smile gleaming in the dark.

It was after midnight at the precinct building. The light inside glared with a cutting whiteness. Two officers in shirtsleeves were seated behind the counter. The first was filling out a long form and shaping the words with his lips as he labored. The second was pecking with a tentative finger at a typewriter.

Sudah, Mara, and Manny, with his semi-barbered face, were directed to a hard wooden bench opposite a green tile wall, a cigarette-dispensing machine, and these two indifferent workers. Sudah sat perfectly rigid, his cheeks drained of all color, his unblinking eyes seeming to protrude slightly. Manny was continuously rubbing the raw side of his face and contemplating halfheartedly how to divest himself of the evidence that now bulged in his pocket, waiting to incriminate him. Mara was giddy. A stream of sarcastic comments flowed from her, most of them having to do with her perception of the average policeman's mental capacity. She could not control herself. Sudah glanced at her in horror.

The sergeant who questioned them after a wait of nearly two hours was a solemn young man with a poorly developed chin. The badge on his lapel announced that his name was Barry Sherman. Mara insisted on referring to him by his initials. Sherman meticulously recorded the information as Mara gave it. Occasionally she would offer up some detail that had not been specifically requested, such as her father's name and estimated fortune, and the family's religion. Sudah's powers of speech seemed to have deserted him altogether. Mara explained that he could hardly understand the language anyhow, much less speak it. That, too, was a bit of unsolicited information, which prompted Sherman to observe, "An alien, eh? That's serious." At one point, however, when Sherman inquired about the source of the cannabis, Sudah quickly pointed a finger at Mara. It seemed to Mara, at that moment, that the heart in her chest had leaped up and socked her in the throat. But she said, "The source? Why, a plant, of course. From a Mexican garden." At the end of the interview Sherman gave this assessment: "Eighteen years old. First offenders. Minuscule amount in pipe. Still, it's trouble. A foreigner. It's bad news."

Dawn came, and with it an insistent exhaustion fastened

itself to Mara. She tried to rest her head on Sudah's shoulder. It was stiff and unwelcoming. She was fidgeting, seeking out a comfortable nook for her head, when Leon strode into the room, chatting amiably with the captain. *"Nu,"* said Leon, "get a load of my hot-stuff criminals." He stared at the half-shaven Manny in amazement. "This one looks to me definitely abnormal," he volunteered. The captain made a sign to Sherman, who proceeded to run his hands up and down the boy, frisking him attentively. Manny's pockets were turned out, and in addition to the hashish the following items tumbled to the floor: a pad containing his "frozen in coitus" poem, three combs, an envelope of prophylactics, two dollars and some change, a cluster of keys, a half-eaten cream-cheese-and-olive sandwich that his mother had plied on him, and a folded yarmulka. As Manny was led away to an inner chamber, Sudah and Mara left with Leon. Directly in front of the station house Reb Anschel Frankel was waiting. The engine of Lieb's big black limousine was running comfortingly, and Anschel was standing beside it, looking toward the east, immersed in the Eighteen Benedictions of the morning prayers, so that it was impossible to disturb him. On his forehead and arm were the black phylactery boxes. Around his waist a rope belt was tied, to separate the spiritual portion of his person from the earthly. They climbed into the back seat. Mara, who sat between Leon and Sudah, let her head sink into her father's lap and fell asleep instantly. Leon passed his hand through her unkempt hair, feeling the familiar bumps of the scalp underneath. Anschel took his three steps backward, bowed to either side, and stepped forward thrice. Leon saw that the devotions of his loyal sexton were now coming to an end. He leaned toward Sudah across his humped-over daughter and whispered, "I bet you were pretty worried in there, no? You probably thought you were seeing your visa fly right out the window, eh? You must have been *pishing* in your pants!" He chuckled warmly, fondling Sudah's biceps. Toward evening of that day, after Sudah and Mara awoke from a deep sleep in the Liebs' apartment, Leon accompanied them to an exclusive shop where he purchased for each of them a magnificent embroidered cape lined with the fur of a fox.

Later, in recounting this adventure to Rashi, Mara observed that she had never seen Sudah look the way he had looked that night at the police station. Utterly terrified and numb. She explained to Rashi that afterward Sudah had told her that he had been smothered by a heavy despair. He had thought to himself as they were being led away, Again I am in the hands of these savages. They are the same in every corner of the earth. The wound of his incarceration in the military dungeons of Israel was still raw. He had been tortured there. In his bread they had buried stones. His resistance they had sought to label madness, subjecting him to night-long interrogations by committees of psychiatrists sitting there judging him behind tightly crossed legs and tightly pursed lips. They had read her love letters aloud to each other in his presence. Ha, ha! What a laugh! They had mocked him.

Sudah had never before described this period of their separation to Mara. On the occasions that she had inquired, he had indicated that the injury still burned when probed. Nor did he hasten to bring up the subject after they were sprung from their brief police captivity. The air between them thickened with doubt. A tentativeness crept in, causing them to feel unsafe in each other's zone. It was only after Sudah had been removed from the crafts workshop as a consequence of his refusal to cooperate in the preparations for Herzl's demonstration that things began to mend between them. He had been excommunicated. Naturally Mara rushed to his defense. They were then brought even closer together as a consequence of Sudah's telephone conversation with Herzl, when it seemed for a time as if the ditch between them and Mara's family had widened perilously. Naked, they would lie between the furs of Leon's two foxes and Sudah would repeat the objections he had voiced to Mara's brother. His opinions, like all his possessions, were zealously personalized and shaped into aspects of his style. Again and again he presented to Mara the case as he had set it before Herzl. It was an unfair exploitation of these helpless, dependent oldies, Sudah had insisted to Herzl. No different from abusing children or cripples or idiots. Herzl, with his accursed demonstration, was taking advantage of his power, forcing his views down the throats of those who could not afford to vomit them back, endangering the very persons he had contracted to protect. Mara embraced Sudah and cradled his head on her breast. It had been on one of these tender nights that Sudah revealed the cause of his strange behavior at the police station.

Heeding the dictates of caution, Herzl had come to the conclusion that the Parklawn should contribute fewer representatives to the demonstration than the other homes. Why ask for trouble? A perfectly acceptable-looking geriatric could, in fact, be Sudah's stooge and sabotage the whole enterprise. Thus, Dora Popper was turned down, and not only because of the robust appearance that belied a dangerous heart condition, but above all because she was a famous troublemaker. Henry Friedman was similarly rejected; he was celebrated as an atheist and a pseudo-intellectual. Julius Fleischer, on the other hand, was among those selected; he possessed a carved cane of unsurpassed elegance, a plaid shawl that he knew how to drape over his bent shoulders for the supreme effect, and an awesome mane of white hair. Another lucky one was Fanny Gottlieb, with her face finely webbed, and her frail, brittle body. Moreover, it had not been too long ago that Fanny had knocked on the door to Sid Schneider's office to complain about that Mr. Mizrahi from arts and crafts. Mr. Mizrahi, she had said, gives them no instruction whatsoever. He tells them to do whatever they please. Be free spirits, he tells them. Now what kind of nonsense is that? "Soon enough I'll be a spirit," Fanny said. "Meanwhile, I'm still flesh and blood, thanks the Lord!"

The demonstration was scheduled for the Fast of Gedalya, the day after Rosh Hashana. By the time the holidays came around, all preparations had been completed. Fanny draped her pink silk dress with the lace inserts at the sleeves over her chair. Under it was her most reliable corset. Ready on her bureau was the silver barrette Mara had given her. At night she liked to lie in bed and look at her cherished costume by the flickering light of the *yahrzeit* candles.

A section of the Parklawn's dining room had been converted into a small chapel for the High Holy Days. The old people took their seats. They wept and prayed. God was deciding destinies on this day, they knew. Theirs were especially precarious. When the cantor sang of God the shepherd stretching forth His staff, causing His flock to pass under it, counting them, numbering them, sealing their fates, the crying became loud and husky. He was a sweet-voiced boy, this cantor, only eighteen years old, or so they had heard. What did he know about life? He had been recruited by Herzl from the yeshiva to serve in the dual role of rabbi and cantor. The sermon he delivered was painfully appropriate and moving. It was about a parent's love for a child. He told a story about a son who had brutally slain his mother to gain early access to the inheritance. The boy had cut the heart right out of his mother's poor body and buried it in the earth. While engaged in this sinful activity he stumbled, this bad boy, and the heart spoke. "Did you hurt yourself, my son?" said the heart. The story was called "A Mother's Heart." It provoked profound tears. During the recesses in the services this cantor-rabbi made ardent love in the workers' quarters to a Norwegian kitchen girl named Solveig. Solveig appeared in the synagogue during one of the rabbi's speeches. She had covered her white-blond hair with a black lace mantilla. The rabbi wordlessly expressed his appreciation to God for the podium behind which the lower portion of his body could be concealed. Solveig admired his shofar-blowing skills. Later that afternoon she insisted that he bring along this amazing instrument. She placed it over his member, like a sheath over a knife, and blew feebly into it. When they climaxed, however, she trumpeted a hearty blast. She really knew how all along, mused the rabbi. What a tricky wench. Sudah and Mara spent the holy days closeted in their room. They smoked, they stroked each other, they performed many acts that would have terrified Leon and put him in fear for his daughter's future. Sudah said, "All rabbis are bullshit," and Mara did not choose to argue. But they were young, after all. Most of the old people would never have dared to take such risks. Even some of the gentiles attended services, reflecting that it couldn't hurt and might even help a little, who knows? Only Dora Popper and Henry Friedman refused to collaborate. They could be found in the boiler room playing poker with Russell Boomer.

The night between the two days of Rosh Hashana was dark and cordial. The old people, armed with their hours at prayer, slid into it with confidence. They would certainly awake in the morning; they had no doubts. The rabbi lay beside Solveig, troubled and guilt-ridden. The melody of the *Hineni* prayer he had chanted that afternoon hummed incessantly in his head and would not unfasten itself from him. In it he had presented his humble credentials before God, as the ambassador of his congregation. What could those poor old people hope for, with so tainted a spokesman making the case in their behalf? Solveig slept with her mouth seductively open beside him. He stared at the big gentile teeth and did nothing. Upstairs Mara slept with her mouth clamped shut, some drool trickling from a corner. She was deep into an ancient, recurrent dream—that she was still at school, that it was examination time, and suddenly there was a course she had forgotten about, had never attended, had now to face its test. When Sudah shook her awake, her body twanged like a plucked string, but she was relieved to be liberated from the humid corridors of her old school. He had just returned from a walk, Sudah explained, and had been undressing by the window overlooking the courtyard. Would she rise and stand at the window with him?

Her naked body unfolded on its mattress and stumbled to his side. "What do you see?" Sudah asked. Sleep still moistened and filmed her eyes. Down in the courtyard there was darkness, almost total, except for flashes of scarlet light at one end. She was drawn to this light, jolted suddenly into alertness by it. "Fire, Sudah!" she cried, "it's on fire!" He embraced her. "Yes, *fasfusah!* Our eyes are eating together the same sight, like one piece of food! It is so sexy!" "We've got to get everyone out of here!" she said, struggling from him. "It's the mattresses," Sudah commented, "dry mattresses. I already warn that dumb Boomer!" Sudah volunteered to run down and call the appropriate officials. Only two public telephones were available in the building, and these were located in the bustling lobby outside the Director's door, so that a watch could be kept on which residents used them, how frequently, and even what they said and to whom, which could be accomplished by softly lifting the extension in the inner room. "But they might not understand you!" Mara shouted after him. He was already gone. She pulled on her shorts and halter. Grabbing Sudah's sketch pads, she began running up and down the hallways, pushing open the lockless doors and rousing the sleepers. "Get up! Get out!" she screamed. "Fire! Fire!" So many doors stretched out before her. Panic inflated in her chest like a balloon. Sudah stationed himself at the main entrance, meanwhile, and from this position he ushered the old people out onto the sidewalk. Fanny Gottlieb was clutching her shoebox. They stood there in the night, wretched, bewildered. Solveig ran out, wrapped in a sheet. The rabbi declared he would remain inside and burn to death, but as he was making his way back to his own room, where he wished to be discovered, he thought better of it and hurried off to rescue an aged woman on his floor, whom he carried out into the street cradled like a baby, her wasted legs dangling exposed over his arm. Terror engulfed most of the night aides, and they escaped without a thought for the welfare of their charges. Mara was the last one to leave the building, with old Vesci draped like a rag over her shoulder. He had refused to go at first. He was scheduled to die soon, anyway, he said with a cackle. Would she crawl into bed beside him and keep him warm? It mattered little to him that she wasn't a virgin. He himself was no King David, after all. As she pulled him out of his bed he inserted his ancient claw up her shorts and grabbed a fistful of her young behind.

Monsters, huge, arbitrary, encased in glistening rubber, leaped from the red trucks, uncoiling a thick black snake. The old people huddled together. "Only the righteous die on Rosh Hashana," Julius Fleischer muttered to Dora Popper, recalling the teachings of a dead rabbi. "Your brain is melting from the heat," remarked Dora. Dragging their hose, the firemen sliced brutally into the crowd, weaving toward the row of trash cans at the gate of the courtyard. Boomer took a position behind the cans, as behind a barricade, his hastily drawn up pants split in a V to his crotch. "What you want?" he demanded. His hands planted on his hips, he would not let them pass. "Where's the fire, buddy?" their leader spoke. "What fire, man?" said Boomer. Leaning out from the doorway to the boiler room, a slender Negro man in a tight shocking-pink shirt was pushing back the giggles with a dazzling manicured hand. "You nothin' but a bunch of shitasses," Boomer commented. He made way and they trooped by. They toppled over the pile of mattresses, invading the cellar with their axes, hacking, as the spirit moved them, at suspicious partitions. Boomer chased them, cursing over the rubble. They spread through the building like a plague until they reached the roof. Then they dropped down like a cloud of dirt and were gone. They left behind them their smell of metal and rubber. Slowly the old people filed back inside and sought out their cold beds.

On the second day of Rosh Hashana they prayed dutifully, but without much hope. Solveig cried for hours in her room over the rabbi's desertion. She sipped, sniffling, from the bottle of wine he had refused to share, for it had been contaminated by contact with a gentile. Sudah carried his sketchbook up to the roof. Leaning over the parapet, he drew the chaos in the courtyard. That afternoon Mara was able to capture an episode in her "virginity" series that had long eluded her.

### How I Lost My Virginity: Marsha

My mother tried, tried diligently, to be helpful to me in my preparations. In the morning she scrubbed my hair over the sink, as she had done so often when I was a child—sudsing it, combing out the tangles, standing behind my chair at the breakfast table and braiding it as I poked morosely at my cereal. This time, however, she rolled hanks of my wet hair around large mesh cylinders and fashioned a tiara of metal pincurls on my head. Then she wrapped an old red towel into a turban around her construction and encouraged me to take a sybaritic hot bath in a nest of soap bubbles, like the girls in the movies and the magazines. She knew a big night awaited me. I had told her Buddy and I were going to the opera—*Ariadne auf Naxos*. Actually, that was something we had done the week before, as part of my campaign to introduce an element of culture into our relationship. Buddy had reluctantly acceded to my petition. He purchased two tickets to the performance. Unfortunately, the seats he selected were located directly behind a pillar of imposing opacity and circumference. After a mere five minutes of suffering he rose and roared, "Ariadne Obnoxious! That's what this damn thing is! Ariadne Obnoxious!" All the binoculars in the second balcony swiveled toward us like pointed guns. We rushed out and saw a pornographic movie instead. Buddy was a barbarian.

The program for this evening, then, was not quite as my mother had been informed. "Let's get rid of it on Saturday night," Buddy had proposed, and I had no recourse but to agree. He had total charge of the schedule of my deflowering: petal by petal he plucked, and I did not resist, for I had read somewhere that the way to be was passionate and earthbound. He was the teacher and I the student, albeit neither of us had completed two decades. "You don't kiss correctly," he informed me one night, "and your breath smells like you're constipated." From then on I faithfully gargled a spicy red mouthwash to be fresh for each ordeal. As the days passed he proceeded to insult the length of my legs, the breadth of my hips, the sag of my breasts, the quality of my hair. I was not his dream girl. He would say, "Tonight we will take out your breasts," and in due course, out they would pop on my parents' sofa, pale and blinded. Over coffee he would announce, "Tonight I will jerk off for you," and I would wait patiently to learn what this "jerk off" could mean, knowing full well it could not betoken anything to my advantage. I discovered, however, at the designated hour, that it was not such a bad show after all, though a bit pompous and absurd. "Tonight when we get home I will stick my finger in your cunt," he had declared. That is how I discovered my cunt. We sat side by side like strangers on a train, connected merely by a finger. When the hour arrived for the train to stop at the next station on its route, I, certainly, could not be expected to be the one to plant myself on the tracks and halt its mighty rush with my upraised pink palms.

Buddy and my mother had become excellent friends. They would face each other for hours across a late-Sunday-morning breakfast table littered with newspapers and egg-stained dishes and carry on intimate conversations, in the course of which they would exchange unhappinesses and optimistic declarations. Each considered the other to be afflicted with a similar malaise, yet each felt secretly superior to the other, in a better position to extend consolations, in greater command of events. But despite her secret cynicism about Buddy, my mother was quite happy to hand me over to him. The reason for his presence at the breakfast table, I should explain, was the custom he and I had established of having him sleep in our cellar after each Saturday night's grueling episode, instead of venturing on the treacherous journey home by subway at dawn. I shall admit it: it was my fault entirely. When he escorted me home after our first night out together, I slipped my hand under his shirt and murmured huskily, "I want to keep you here always, like a captive." It was a romantic lie, plagiarized from plagiarizers. Buddy believed it whole. As for myself, the time had come for me to scrounge up a man. I figured he was my fate.

My father, on the other hand, shared my opinion of Buddy. Very little was exchanged between them, except, of course, for me. Each regarded the other with suspicion. My father and I had some conspiratorial fun one afternoon in the car, as Buddy sat hunched between us and my father controlled the steering wheel with his left hand and shaved his stubble with the electric razor in his right. I said to Buddy, "Why don't you take off your Vandyke?" My father wordlessly passed him the machine. In less than five minutes Buddy's cheeks were obscenely bare-assed. He could be very docile, Buddy could, but oh, how I feared his rage.

As I marinated in the tub, my mother called out from my room, "What will you be wearing tonight, Marsha?" "The black wool," I replied. She was deep in my closet, inhaling the musk of my clothing. Each school night of my childhood she had selected my dress for the coming morning and hung it on the door knob of the closet. There it would await me. As the years passed, the skirts I saw when I first opened my eyes grew longer and longer, until soon they were curtseying their good mornings to me from the floor. One day she announced, "I think you're old enough now to pick out your own clothing." And so for a week I had worn the same dress, a gray polished cotton with black velvet polka dots pasted all over it, like braille. By week's end I had picked off each and every dot, and all that remained was an ugly stippling of rough glue spots. My mother dutifully resumed her role as mistress of my wardrobe.

The black wool was not the one I eventually stripped off for Buddy's entertainment that night. It lay rejected on the pink carpet of my bedroom, at the bottom of a heap of crumpled dresses, shirts, skirts, and pants, which, with mounting panic, I had tried and discarded. In the end I clothed myself in my stained green velvet smock, with black tights my only undergarment. As I sat down at the kitchen table to allow my mother to comb out my hair, I warned her: "Don't say anything, Ma. This is what I'm wearing." My mother sighed occasionally as she worked with brush and comb, patting, fluffing, wetting, constructing. At last she handed me the mirror. I stared at my tense, sullen face framed in that coiffure—the dips, the curls, the folds. "Oh, Mother, it's awful," I cried, "just awful!" I rushed to the sink and put my head under the running water. My mother's arms hung limply at her side, a comb in one hand and a brush in the other. She was crying. "Drop dead, Marsha!" she said.

By the time I walked out the door she was contrite. My damp hair was bound up in a tight scarf, and on top of this I wore a wide-brimmed hat, slouched low over one eye. I slipped on my dark glasses. All that could be seen of my face was the tip of my nose and my mouth, with a fresh colony of pimples on my chin. My mother said, "They will all wonder about the mystery lady at the opera." She was sorry. She knew it was a big night for me. She did not want to spoil it. People always try to be nice to soldiers setting out for battle. Mothers weep, but still they lead their children to the train.

Someone was trailing me down the long hotel corridor to the room Buddy had engaged. I began walking very quickly, my legs shooting straight out in front of me like a toy soldier's, but I dared not run lest he think I was afraid. I found, to my dismay, that I had taken the wrong turn. The number I needed was at the end of the opposite hallway. I pivoted swiftly. My pursuer somehow resumed his position behind me, though I never noticed him passing me by. His presence weighed upon my back. Each step forward was a struggle against his intense backward pull. I reached the wanted door at last and threw myself upon it. Buddy opened it a chink. He was wearing nothing but a gleaming rubber.

Inserting his hand under my coat and down my dress, he started immediately to squeeze my breasts. He called them tits. Nevertheless, though he was in the neighborhood, he did not seem to notice how violently my heart was pounding. It was a cold March night and goose bumps had risen all over my flesh. The room in which we lay was ugly, too.

A cheap blue velvet tapestry decorated the wall, showing dogs costumed as people playing cards around a table. Big cigars stuck out of their mouths. I gazed at it from under Buddy. He had released me long enough to allow me to remove my coat and tights. My dress was rolled up like a tire above my tits and under my arms. When it was all over I would rise, let it drop like a curtain, and walk away to sit down alone in a chair. I insisted that my hat and scarf remain on my head throughout, because of the state of my hair. Buddy, however, was pleased with this novel touch. He complimented me on my erotic imagination.

As he toiled away I thought of many things—of work I needed to complete for school, of the new boots I would buy, of what I wanted to eat. I wanted to eat a slice of bread and butter, spread all over with a thick layer of salted raw onions. Occasionally Buddy would instruct me to move my hips in rhythm with his, but this is the kind of task a person can perform while still thinking energetically of other things. However, even I considered it an unfitting occasion to let my mind drift freely in other rooms. I forced myself to return to our bleak chamber. This is it, I announced to myself without conviction. It's finally happening, I said without enthusiasm. Can you really believe it? I demanded of my spirit. My spirit certainly could not. I was feeling very little indeed. I could have eaten a whole bunch of hard white radishes, crunching them between my teeth. It was a very harmless business, this fucking, or "fertilization," as my mother called it. I decided that Buddy was really a woman. That was a most comforting thought.

Farina, warm and soothing on its trip down to your belly, the way my mother would fix it when I was sick, with a square of butter that melted into a golden pool in the center of that undulating smoothness and whiteness—that was the food I wanted to eat now, I decided, good, gentle cereal. This realization came to me just as Buddy began to stiffen on top of me, just as those small helpless yelps began to escape from him. I joined my cries to his. Farina can move me to ecstasy, I discovered. Our sweat sealed Buddy's collapsed body to mine. At last his panting ceased. He spoke. I dreaded the words that were about to come out. "Fantastic!" he declared. "We came together! And on our first time! Incredible!" What a fool! And I had just begun to regret my petty deception, lying there thinking I had overdone it surely, for at most I should have produced my grunts before or after his, so why did I shoot so grandiosely for that holy "coming together" he prized so dearly? But he believed me, thank God, for I could not have borne the shame of exposure. He did not consider for a moment how womanly and passionate I was. He swelled only at the thought of how excellent a man was he.

There was not a drop of blood to be found—not on the sheet, not on my thighs, not on his bag. Buddy said I must have broken it as a child, while mounting a bicycle. Buddy took great pride in his wisdom. He loved to explain. I walked across the room and sat down on the cold plastic chair. I crossed my legs.

It was my good fortune that the knock came at that moment. Good fortune, I say, because we had finished our business, and furthermore, it guaranteed there would be no fumbling encore. On the other hand, it shattered my just-born dignity, sending me flying in disarray to the bathroom. Buddy, in his simplicity, opened the door at once. He was vulnerable in his white underwear. The voice I could hear was low and punishing, the presence I could feel was that of the being who had pursued me up and down the hallways of this hotel. "I know you've got a girl in there," the voice spoke. Some sort of accent distinguished it. Buddy did not require further torture to confess. "Get dressed, both of you," commanded the voice. "I'll wait for you out here."

Meekly we emerged. The voice was clad in a checked coat with a capelet. The hat it wore had two visors, like beaks, one in front and the other in back. A curled pipe preceded it. "You a detective?" I asked. I was too bold. Buddy's elbow jabbed into my ribs. My breath was coming in giggles. It was all so hilarious. "How old are you?" demanded the voice. I said eighteen, endowing myself with an extra year. The voice continued: "What would your father say if he knew?"

"I don't know."

"I know," said the voice.

By now we had completed our descent into the lobby. Indifferent bodies swam past us. "This is our first time, sir," Buddy said. His teeth were chattering.

"No, it is not," said the voice. "Be grateful I caught you before it was too late." The laughter jumped out of me, like a sob.

"I will let you go this time," the voice went on. "Don't let me catch you again."

"You won't, you won't," I cried. We held hands and skipped down the clattering sidewalks of the city. I was grateful, grateful to have been caught in time. Buddy seemed delirious, too.

Mara was sitting naked on the floor in front of her typewriter. With her two index fingers she was banging into existence this latest virginity loss. Sudah's sleeping body on the mattress seemed to be wrapped in a gray blanket of dawn light, which saddened her and filled her with pity. This typewriter was an object she loved. She had come upon it in the cellar under the Parklawn, among the bloated and rusted cans of food which she recognized instantly as the collection her father had organized for distribution to the poor many years ago. She herself, a scrawny child in pigtails, had knocked on row after row of doors until the duffel bag on her shoulder was bulging and the sharp angles of the metal making dents in her back. But there, among all this rotten food, was the typewriter, black and stately, with a weight and a presence that captivated her. She had lugged it up to her room and cleaned it with devotion. It was perfect in every way. Each key required the firm pressure of her fingers to force it down, but this only enhanced its value, for it gave her an opportunity to ponder the gravity and profundity of the individual letter. The noise she made as she pounded this dawn insulated her from her surroundings. No one seemed to complain. Sudah slept on. In contrast, the quiet when she finished teemed with all sorts of disturbances—floors creaking, toilets gurgling, the early-morning stirrings in the kitchen three floors below. She heard a terrible crash. No doubt it was nothing, like gunshots in the night that might also be the backfiring of a car. She would have ignored it had she not been inclined to exercise her limbs after her long bout with creativity. She wrapped herself in Sudah's red silk robe, painted with blue Chinese dragons. The thud seemed to have come from Vesci's room. She entered. The shoulder and head of the old piano tuner were on the floor, sticking out the door of the tiny bathroom, where the rest of him lay. It was one of the better rooms in the place, Mara noted, with its own bathroom. Vesci had fallen off the toilet bowl, where he had been set the night before by an aide and promptly forgotten. Mara leaned over him. Her robe parted to the tasseled sash around her waist.

She stared at the deep welts the toilet seat had carved into his gray behind. Vesci seemed to be leering at her. "Get up, you old goat," said Mara.

They carried him out in a black sack on a stretcher. The shorter attendant was in front and the corpse kept sliding toward him. They rested the stretcher on the floor in the center of the lobby and strapped the old man to it. A death, when it was not hidden in the night or concealed by departure through the cellar, was generally the high point of the day, and the old people would turn and whisper to one another as the body was borne past their chairs in the lobby. Someone would rise, and soon a silent procession would form behind the victim, moving slowly to the ambulance. Afterward the survivors would rush to their rooms, searching frantically for a bite to eat. But this time the ambulance was parked in front of the bus that was collecting the delegates from each of the nursing homes to transport them to the demonstration. The Parklawn's contingent, with Julius Fleischer on his cane at the head, marched down an aisle lined with friends. As they made their slow way to the bus, they shook hands with well-wishers on both sides and accepted their blessings. Dora Popper leaned over and kissed Julius with a wet smack. "Don't worry, Julius," she reassured him, "no hickey. They should think you're old and dignified."

There were not enough seats on the bus and it was necessary for a few of the more able-bodied travelers to stand in the aisle. Bernie Schultz, in his plaid cabbie's cap, had taken the day off to drive. He sat at the steering wheel singing popular Hebrew and Yiddish songs at the top of his lungs. "Join in, my friends," he cried to his passengers. "Let them hear us coming!" He intended to raise their spirits. The response was mostly shy and self-conscious, except for the more boisterous few, such as a plump lady with whitish-blue hair arranged carefully in tiers who pulled a parchment-skinned man right out of his seat and attempted to dance a high-kicking hora with him to the tune of "Hava Nagila." It was a hot and bumpy trip. The destination was the Soviet Mission. The old people eyed each other suspiciously, wondering what qualities they shared that made them fellow travelers this day, each seeking to gauge if his own exterior betrayed age so hopelessly. A passenger from the Aishel, seated directly in front of Fanny Gottlieb, began to call out and gesticulate vigorously to the driver, but Bernie was too caught up in the enthusiasm of his songs to notice. Suddenly this passenger stuck his head out the window and retched in violent gusts. The vomit flew directly back into the bus, right through Fanny's window, onto her right cheek, into her splendid hair, soiling part of her costume. "It's all right," she said to the stunned old man sitting beside her, "it's all right." She refused all help. She did not want to be noticed now; now, in her humiliation, she rejected all attention passionately. At the Mission her outfit was further ruined by Herzl Lieb, who stood by the door as they filed out of the bus and wrapped around each participant's arm a white band with a yellow star of David glued on it, in the center of which JUDE was stenciled in red ink. When they were delivered back to the Parklawn that night, Fanny buried her head on Dora's breast. "He *breched* all over me," she sobbed. "All day long I *schmecked* something awful." Dora stroked the vomit-stiffened hair, averting her face from the smell, as Fanny cried and cried.

The policeman at the gate was stunned by the hobbling parade of ancient bodies and dust-white faces. It was a funeral march of the dead, faces and bodies long stashed tactfully out of sight, in the grave or the grave's anteroom. He was terrified. He let them pass. Some of them bid him good morning in their native Russian. Julius Fleischer poked his cane amiably into the policeman's midriff and declared in accented Russian, "I was a socialist like you as a boy. Don't worry, you'll grow out of it." The cop clutched his belly as if he had been stabbed. He was an American black, twenty-two years old, and he did not understand a word. They struggled up the steps. Herzl and his friends carried wheelchairs with crippled bodies clutching the armrests up to the very door. There, blocking their way with his wrestler's torso, was the Mission's private guard, with a black mole on his cheek. Herzl requested that the group be allowed to enter. "We are legitimate protesters," he read from a crumpled napkin with a lipstick stain on it. "Permit us to present our petition to your authorities and we will leave peacefully." This, of course, was not the plan. The plan was to occupy one of the rooms, an inner chamber if possible, with direct access to a toilet to provide for the needs of the old bladders and kidneys. But the guard merely shook his steel head from side to side and stretched his muscular arms across the width of the door. He looked like a Cossack. "Hey, Ivan!" Bernie Schultz called out, "show some respect for these grandfathers!" The guard spread his legs until the tips of his leather boots touched the bottom corners of the door, and he scratched his scrotum.

Herzl Lieb and his friends drew aside and huddled, quarreling intensely. After a few moments Herzl himself stepped forward with some dollar bills dangling from his fingertips. He approached the guard. "Ivan," he whispered, "I have here a little something for you." Herzl attempted to stuff the cash into the giant's pocket. The guard pulled the money out and waved it in the air like a filthy rag. He began to laugh—deep, husky laughs, slapping his thigh as he roared. Suddenly, sharply, without winding down, he stopped. "My name is not Ivan," he spoke in a voice of thunder, "it is Adolf!" "Ivan, Adolf. What's the difference?" said Bernie Schultz. The guard ignored him. "And I can see that you, too, are not Russians," the guard went on, as if addressing worms, "you don't know how to pass a bribe. Ha, ha, ha!" This new explosion of laughter, even more terrifying than the first, caused the old people to bend backward, like wheat lashed in a gusty field. Herzl waited for it to end. "Tell me, Ivan," inquired Herzl, "maybe it's not enough?" Adolf spat on the bills and threw them down to the ground, stamping on them savagely. "You a rabbi?" he boomed. Herzl nodded. "A rabbi giving a bribe! Ha, ha, ha! I should stuff it down your throat, Rabbi!" Herzl's face was crimson, as if he were choking. Another conference was held, at the end of which Bernie Schultz observed, "What a *putz!* *Nu,* maybe it's better this way, after all. We'll be more visible." And the order was given to the old people to commence the demonstration in the very spot on which they were standing. The organizers helped them to sit down, packing them in rows along the steps so that anyone who ventured to ascend or descend would be obliged to lift a leg obscenely over a stooped shoulder and a venerable gray head.

A crowd, consisting chiefly of young persons and idlers, formed on the pavement behind the spiked wrought-iron fence. The old people stared at them with the blinking curiosity of creatures who had just emerged from a cave. Fanny leaned toward Julius Fleischer and whispered, "Don't they all look to you like Mr. and Mrs. Mizrahi?" Fanny's gold-framed spectacles were lying in the drawer of her nightstand at the Parklawn. She preferred to make her public appearance without them. Julius said, "You can't tell the little *pishers* apart these days, Fanny." Several patrol cars soon drew up to the curb and a contingent of officers mounted the steps with heart-warming authority. Their leader was Frank Tucci, who for years had been dropping in on the Liebs at Christmastime. He approached Herzl. Gesturing in the direction of the aged squatters, he announced that they were trespassing. Herzl said, "Certainly, Sergeant Tucci. So order your men to drag them into the wagons." Tucci surveyed the protesters doubtfully. He and Herzl stepped to the side, shielded from view by Bernie Schultz and a few others. They exchanged some words, after which Herzl jovially slapped Tucci on the back and shook his hand. Tucci plunged the shaken hand deep into his pocket and strode back to his waiting men. "There's nothing we can do, boys. They're just a bunch of old *kockers*. They're harmless. We'd break them in half if we tried to move them." He assigned a token detail to remain throughout the demonstration, to insure the peace. Then he drove off in the lead car, siren screeching.

Now two of Herzl's men unfurled a large banner, which they rested against the brick of the Mission wall. This was its legend: WE SHALL SOON BE DEAD, BUT ISRAEL WILL LIVE ON. Julius Fleischer clutched his heart when he read this message. "Never mind what it says," he replied to Fanny's demand. The slogan's creator, Bernie Schultz, had declared, "This will grab them," and he was right. Herzl took a position in front of the banner and raised a megaphone to his lips. "Your grandmothers and grandfathers are here today to remind you of your past," he cried. "Look at their broken bodies! They have known Hitler and survived. Soon they will die, but the Jewish people will never die! We shall live on! But as long as any one of our brothers is not free, we are not free! As long as any one of us is in chains, we are in chains!" And here, to everyone's amazement, he dangled in the air a sort of visual aid, a long, thick chain, the kind that is used to secure bicycles. First he wrapped it around his waist and then around a lamp post. Bernie Schultz locked it with great flair and walked away with the key.

Rav Habakuk strode up the steps, his guitar banging against his chest. He seemed much older than at Mara's wedding, the gray hairs outnumbering the black. He was in shirtsleeves, and great coins of perspiration could be seen at each armpit. "Friends!" he called out, "my friends! Let us lift our voices to pierce the very walls of heaven! Let the Lord Almighty hear our song!" He began to strum his instrument violently. Very few of the old people joined in. They were beginning to experience the discomfort of rumbling stomachs and filling bladders.

Julius had not had an opportunity this morning to spend his ritual half hour on the toilet seat with the Yiddish daily spread open across his knees. Habakuk paused and shook his head from side to side in exaggerated disapproval. "This is *schvach,* my dear friends, very very weak! Do you want everyone here to think you're old? Come on! Where are your souls? Let's try it again!" And he galloped into two more songs, this time with far greater success, thanks to Bernie Schultz and the other organizers, who joined in and danced in a stomping circle around Herzl's lamp post. Just as Habakuk was tuning up for a third number, the lady with the blue-white hair rose and shouted, "Play 'Rumania,' Rabbi! Rumania, Rumania, Rumaaan-ya," she wailed, and she began to dance a meaningful tango with an imaginary partner along the step. Someone hustled her back to her place. "The body may be decaying," Habakuk joked, "but the spirit is still young!"

Around lunchtime Herzl again raised the megaphone to his lips, partly to remind the onlookers of his presence, but chiefly to proclaim that the old people had nobly decided to forgo the midday meal. "Today is *Tsom Gedalya,* the Fast Day of Gedalya," he announced. "We shall fast to remember our past, to protest the present, to demand a better future!"

It was early afternoon. Inside the Mission a plan had been conceived to put an end to the nuisance at the front door. Final preparations were now being made to carry it out. The besieged Russians had been pondering how to rid themselves of the undesirables on their steps when someone remembered the old ebony coffin with the brass handles which was stashed in a closet for unpredictable emergencies but which had not had much use of late. Old folks, it was reasoned, would be particularly deferential to death. A heart attack would be announced, sudden and fatal, and four men would bear the coffin out to the top of the steps. An innocent ruse, really, quite harmless, which could not but succeed in forcing the pests to give way, for what is politics in the face of death? After that it would be an easy enough matter to disperse the rabble. Accordingly, four grim pallbearers, in dark glasses and double-breasted suits, appeared in the doorway of the Mission with the coffin atop their shoulders, just as Bernie Schultz and three of his people, with prayer shawls over their heads and chanting the *kaddish*, began to mount the steps with a plain pine coffin on their shoulders. The two coffins collided in mid-air. Only with great difficulty were the pallbearers able to prevent their respective burdens from crashing on the old heads underneath. The coffins were set down, and the overstuffed Russian box popped open immediately. Bitterly, the Russians pried the lid off the Jews'. It contained a cardboard mannequin clothed in a striped prisoner's suit from the concentration camps. On the featureless face the number 6,000,000 was painted in blood red. Inside the Russian coffin was the week's garbage, meat gristle and bones, potato peelings, empty vodka bottles, which the cleaning woman had prevailed upon them to take along since they were going out anyway. The old people sat on, the coffins forsaken among them.

Bernie Schultz went to Herzl's side. "How are you doing, my friend?" he inquired. By way of an answer, Herzl raised the megaphone to his lips and proclaimed, "My comrade here asks me if I am perishing of hunger, if I am expiring from the bondage of this chain. This is my answer. Let boulders drop from the sky on my head! Let the earth split open under my feet! No sacrifice is too great for our people!" There was some applause, and Julius said to Fanny, "That boy has some *pisk* on him!"

They sat on, the old men and women, dreaming wistfully of food and bathrooms. The streets were starting to bustle with the close of another working day. Sirens could be heard in the distance, the screams growing louder and more shrill. "Are they coming for us?" Fanny asked Julius. "Don't worry,

Fanny," he reassured her, "everything is hotsy-totsy." But then, as from nowhere, two great fire engines appeared to dazzle them with their redness, then an ambulance, a paddy wagon, and three patrol cars, with Tucci himself in charge. The sergeant's voice boomed to the crowd: "Ladies and gentlemen, I want you to stay very calm and follow instructions. We have a bomb threat here. Now, remember, I said to be calm. I want you to file down to your buses as quickly and as quietly as you can. Be calm, I said, we'll take care of you." The firemen spread over the steps like a net. All sorts of Russians could be seen scrambling out of the building, leaping over people and coffins. Bernie Schultz and his men loaded ancient, stately bodies with their wheelchairs and other equipment into the bus. There was a skirmish among the onlookers behind the gate. Police penetrated the crowd, herding the limp forms of bearded young men into the paddy wagon. As it set off, its siren blaring, a thin girl with glasses placed herself directly in its path. She stood there absolutely motionless, her arms at her sides. Passively she waited to be struck. It was Mara. Tucci himself jumped out of his car, ran over to her, and lifted her up like an unreasonable baby who had toddled off into the center of the road. "Do you want to get yourself killed, you crazy girl?" he cried. "I should spank your bottom!" He tossed her into the bus. The engine was already roaring. Bernie glanced for a final time at what could have been a triumphant scene. There he noticed Herzl, abandoned at his lamp post, the megaphone opening over his face like a howl. "The key, Bernie, the key!" Herzl was screaming. Bernie flung it out the window and drove off.

Mara walked up and down the aisle of the bus offering the food she had taken pains to prepare. Something nourishing, for a change, unadulterated: peanut-butter sandwiches, the first apples of the fall. Most of the old people refused it, pointing regretfully to their teeth. One man clicked his grotesquely, for her edification. She also exhibited a bedpan she had thoughtfully brought along. This, too, was rejected, for there was no privacy. The teeth-clicker hissed, "Get away from me with your *pish tepel!*" "Oh, come on, Fanny," Mara cajoled, "I'll stand in front of you." "I don't have to go, Mrs. Mizrahi, thanks very much!" Fanny turned away and pressed her forehead against the pane of the closed window. Mara desperately wanted to be of service today, the more menial the better. At the Parklawn that night she told Sudah how she had been spurned. "What you expect?" he demanded. He had heard about her outrageous stand in the path of the paddy wagon. "You want to die?" he asked. "I thought you were in it," she answered.

On the eve of Yom Kippur two new residents nestled into the Parklawn. The first was Luba Alfasi, Luke's mother, who was escorted by her son down the long corridor to Vesci's haunted room. Mara had spent several days readying the chamber as befits a poet's mother. She wanted to create a self-contained environment that would afford sufficient variety and stimulation, for it would be essential that Luba remain exclusively within those four walls. On the door she tacked a sign: ARTIST IN RESIDENCE. KEEP OUT! She covered one entire wall with a collage of pictures cut from magazines; there would be adventures enough there to fill up many a leaden afternoon. The remaining three walls were painted white. She encouraged Luba to decorate these herself with the colors and brushes provided on a shelf for that purpose. Mara had heard somewhere that such free, and even, in a sense, destructive expression was salutary for the troubled spirit. An old rocking chair was positioned by the window. There Luba could sit and peek through the slats of the Venetian blinds into the courtyard, where, admittedly, not much activity was taking place, but this, Mara concluded, was an advantage, since an atmosphere too heady with excitement was precisely what Luba was escaping.

Luke surveyed the room and shook his head dolefully. "I don't think it will all fit in, Mama," he said. His mother turned sharply, as if to leave without further delay. "All right, Mama, all right. We'll give it a try," said Luke.

Manny Fish and Mark Bavli were waiting downstairs, perched atop the fender and hood of the rented truck. For the rest of that morning, under Luke's nervous supervision, and assisted perfunctorily by Sudah, they carted furniture up to Luba's new quarters. An oval mahogany dining table and six chairs, with a matching sideboard and china closet of massive proportions. A lavish sofa upholstered in green velvet, two armchairs with exposed stuffing and springs, three lamps with fringed shades and bases enameled with pastoral gentlemen in powdered wigs and ladies with elevated white bosoms, and a heavy brown marble coffee table. An oak dresser and chest with clawed feet and beveled mirrors, and the headboard of a huge bed carved with fat cupids. A kitchen table covered with knife-scarred linoleum, and four yellow chairs. Cartons of crockery and cutlery, pots and pans, towels and sheets, and several wooden crates with Luba's best crystal and dishes. These were set at the foot of her bed. Furniture was piled on top of furniture. Only the narrowest of aisles remained, along which even thin persons would be obliged to inch sideways. Luba lay down upon the bed. She covered herself with piles of old dresses and coats, satins and laces, silks and wools, cottons and furs.

The only elevator in the Parklawn was claimed by the movers. The old people jammed the lobby and watched the spectacle with pleasure. As each object was carried down the runway, they muttered their opinions: "Junk!" "Old-fashioned dreck!" "Shmatehs!" Julius dubbed it "crep." Dora Popper called it "flotsam and jetsam." "It's pathetic," she said, "it's wrong to look." And she marched up the stairs to her room. Russell Boomer, who had refused point-blank when he had been approached to help with the hauling, folded his arms across his chest and for a while stationed himself stonily by the elevator. "Sons of bitches! Lousy sons of bitches!" he grunted as piece after piece was presented for viewing and piled aboard. Mara paced distractedly up and down the mucus-green tile of the lobby floor, wringing her hands, raking her hair. Each time the front door opened she would clutch her breast in anguish. Her father was expected momentarily, on the rarest of visits. Sometimes she would race up the three flights of stairs and dash panting into her room, where she would discover Sudah fascinated by some stage of his late-morning toilet—cleaning his fingernails or untangling his beard so slowly, so terribly slowly, she nearly burst. "Hurry up, goddamn you! We need your help!" she screeched. Her rage had the effect of slowing him down even further. In turn, his serenity in the eye of her anger swelled her fury anew. She began to hurl paintbrushes and empty canvases and fat tubes of oil pigment against the wall, wailing all the time, "Goddamn it, my father will be here any minute! He'll find out! I can't stand it! Goddamn you!" Then she ran down again in panic.

Leon made a point of seldom, or, if possible, of never visiting his properties. He wanted his association with them to remain exclusively financial, and even on paper the signs of his affiliation were cryptic. But on this occasion there was a personal reason for his coming. His wife, Rose, had dropped to such depths of depression in their apartment that it was no longer possible for her to remain there. All day long she would lie curled up on the sofa, moaning endlessly. When she arose it would be to bang her head brutally against the wall, or to search and re-search every cupboard, drawer, and closet for pills in any shape and form. "I need some relief, I need some relief," she would cry. Leon kept her medication in the pocket of his black jacket. Only a few hours after he doled out her quota, she would begin to claw at him and scream for more, more. Once he had flung the bottles at her and declared, "Here, you take care of it yourself, I'm getting out of here!" When he returned she accused him of no longer loving her, of wanting to leave her, of desiring her death. He then again assumed the responsibility of controlling her dosage and she charged him with treating her like a child. When she was calm she would look around her rooms and lament that she was useless, useless, her home was neglected, she had no energy, no will, had ceased to function, her children needed her no longer. It was decided that she required a new environment, one that made no demands, even unspoken, on her. Leon was struck by the idea that the Parklawn would serve as a perfect haven. Mara was there, after all, and certainly it would not be too much to ask of a daughter to take over the care of her own mother, whose heart she was responsible for breaking anyway. Besides, Mara likes *meshuggenehs*, Leon reasoned to himself. Once Rose was comfortably settled, he could go back to the uninterrupted pursuit of his business affairs, which were suffering lately from onslaughts from several sources.

And so, on the eve of Yom Kippur, Rose entered the Parklawn on the arm of her husband. As soon as Mara noticed their black car pulling up, she fled to her bathroom, where she was afflicted with violent cramps. The Liebs were trailed by Reb Anschel Frankel, pushing a dolly piled high with cartons of prepared foods—roasted chickens, chopped liver, knishes, kugels, *tsimmes;* in short, everything necessary for the long holiday of Succot ahead—for Rose had agreed to come only on the condition that she be allowed to remain undisturbed in her room. "I will not show my face in that dining room," she had warned Leon. Even the short walk through the lobby to the elevator was excruciating for her, and she agreed to make it only after Leon's repeated assurances that nobody there could possibly recognize them. "You'll step into the elevator and disappear. Everyone will forget all about you." This is how Leon had put it.

Unfortunately, the elevator was occupied and all of Reb Anschel's insistent pressing with the heel of his great palm was to no avail in bringing it to their service. It appeared to be stuck at the third floor. Leon took the opportunity to step into the manager's office to review some financial matters with Sid Schneider. Rose stood there wretchedly, her face white and strained with embarrassment, for she dreaded public exhibitions of any sort, and on those occasions when she was obliged to sit through a sermon by her husband, or in the kosher resorts they frequented where Leon and Herzl would pound with their fists on the table as they roared the Sabbath tunes, she would cringe into the sheltering depths of her body and pretend she was elsewhere. Now she seemed on the verge of fainting. Reb Anschel led her to the ladies' room in the corner of the lobby and posted himself like a sentinel outside its door. Two aides were in there, craning their necks toward the mirror and applying lipstick. They giggled as Rose staggered in. "She so fat she cain' stan' on her feet," one of them remarked. The other puckered her thick lips and kissed the mirror, leaving a cracked orange stain on the glass. "No man kin love dat tub," she said. When Rose returned to the elevator, leaning on Reb Anschel's arm, it was waiting there agape, ready to swallow them up, but the dolly was gone and the cartons of food were scattered about and flooding the lobby with a festive aroma. What had happened was this: during Anschel and Rose's brief absence, the movers had ridden down on the emptied elevator; Sudah had spotted the dolly and had instantly laid claim to it as just the thing to ease the labors ahead. Anschel carried the cartons into the elevator one by one. Then he knocked on the office door to signal Leon and boarded the elevator with Rose. The two of them waited there, as in a display case, another century at least, until Leon brought his conference to a close.

When Leon Lieb stepped off the elevator again into the lobby, after having set into motion the process of settling his wife, he came face to face with a barricade of furniture. Manny Fish and Mark Bavli nodded a brief greeting to him and began loading at once. Luke, who had no recollection of Leon, brushed by him impatiently. Leon turned to Sudah. "What's going on here?" he demanded. Sudah was balancing two chairs in front of his face. "Old stuff," he explained, and moved past Leon to deposit his load. Leon grabbed his arm. "I have two eyes, thank God. I can see the junk. What's it doing here, if I may ask?" Sudah loosened Leon's grip, finger by finger. "Maybe to you, junk," he said. "To them"—pointing in the direction of the old people in the lobby and of customers in general—"antiques. I am going into business, *Aba!*"

Before he left, Leon summoned Mara and Sudah into Rose's room. They were each given a fistful of silver dollars, which they twirled around their heads as an emblem of the rooster or carp that on Yom Kippur eve was designated for slaughter in expiation of its master's sins. "This is the money that will go to charity," chanted Rose and Mara, "and I will go to a long and good and peaceful life." Sudah refused to partake of this ceremony. "You shall not buy life for me," he told Leon. Leon chuckled. "Now you're such a wheeler-dealer, you'll buy it for yourself." He was pleased. He did not want to invest in Sudah anyhow. He placed both his hands atop his daughter's head and blessed her with the qualities of the foremothers, adding quietly his special petition to God that as long as she was bound to this impostor, He seal Mara's womb as He had for so long sealed the wombs of Sarah, Rebecca, and Rachel.

It was on the day of Yom Kippur itself that Rose's debauch began. It started this way. She lay in the narrow bed of her room in the Parklawn, craving her pills. Mara, to whom Leon had entrusted a full bottle before his departure with the words "You take over now, lots of luck," had set the day's quota in a glass dish on the dresser. It was Mara's hope that Rose would be sensible, would apportion the pills to last through the day. Mara thought, I'll give her some independence, some responsibility. That way, little by little, she'll learn self-control. Rose eyed the tablets for some time, enjoying the exercise of withholding from herself a pleasure that was well within reach, seductive but available, waiting to be claimed, soon to be her own. Slowly she got off the bed and drew near to her heart's desire. She was wearing a lovely white nightgown with lace at the collar and cuffs, which Mara had purchased for her own trousseau with Rose's charge plates, but finding it far too large had sold to her mother at a profit. Rose scooped up the pills. Just as she was about to stuff them all at once into her mouth and swallow them in a single gulp, as was her habit, it occurred to her that she was alone, not a soul could observe her, that she might comfortably extend the pleasure even further by setting the pills, one by one, on the back of her tongue and sending them off on a smooth journey through her mysterious tunnels with the help of a glass of water. Only after the final pill had been thus dispatched and the glass of water emptied to the last drop did Rose remember that today was the holy fast day of Yom Kippur, upon which even a sip of liquid was forbidden except in the most restricted of circumstances. She said to herself, Well, it looks as if I've broken my fast, I might as well go all the way. And that is when she began to eat her way into the cartons of food that Reb Anschel had stacked in the corner.

She did it in bed, propped up against the pillows. She ate very quickly, slurping cold chicken soup out of its plastic container and letting it spill down her chin. The noodles hung over her lips like worms. She made loud, smacking noises as she ate, chewing with her mouth wide open, occasionally raising a hand mirror to her face to enjoy the spectacle of the food being processed by her tongue and teeth. She tore whole chickens apart, biting off large chunks of crackling skin and meat, sucking the marrow from the bones and gnawing them to bits, tossing the crushed remains on the bedclothes around her. Her nose glistened with the grease. She stuck her hand deep into the bowels of the golden, crusty challa, extracting lumps of the soft white bread and packing them into her mouth as she had always longed to do but had never dared, even in the solitary kitchen of her home, lest someone suddenly discover her, for what is more foul than a fat creature gorging herself? As a matter of fact, she always ate minuscule portions in the presence of others. She rolled the chopped liver, slightly sour by now, into large brown balls and pushed them in, driving them down with the jellied sauce of the gefilte fish. She consumed whole potato kugels flecked with onions, and sweet, cinnamony noodle kugels. She held them up to her face like a harmonica, devouring the instrument as she played. Pickle juice squirted into her eyes. She wiped her face with the back of her hand, scratching her cheek with her wedding ring. She loaded the kasha knishes and potato knishes into her mouth. Matzoh balls went in whole. She licked her fingers to extract the last bit of the carrot stew's sweetness. She wielded the salami and *kishka* like giant drumsticks and gnawed at them until they disappeared. Peanut shells and egg shells, apple cores and beef gristle, oily cans of sardines and tuna fish, emptied soda bottles were strewn on the bed and the floor. When Mara knocked at the door to call her for the *Yizkor* services, Rose claimed she was not feeling well. She glanced defiantly at the poor flames flickering with disapproval in the wax of the two memorial glasses on her dresser, one for her dead mother, the other for her dead father. She did not allow Mara into the room for days and ordered her to slide the pill rations under the door each morning. Mara concluded that her mother was seeking to restore her own health by insisting on the privacy long denied her. "Mommy needs a room of her own," she explained to Sudah. Through the door Rose requested that Mara tell Leon, should he happen to call, to bring along her diaphragm when he visited. At last Mara telephoned her father. Stuttering noticeably, her face scarlet, she succeeded at last in relaying the message. Leon laughed. "So, has she found a boyfriend already?" he asked.

When not a single morsel remained of the food Rose had brought with her, she began her early-morning raids of the Parklawn kitchen. "It's my kitchen, after all," she reasoned, "and my food is in it." She would rouse herself after midnight, stricken by the familiar pangs of hunger that had often driven her from Leon's bed into his kitchen and had placed her before his open refrigerator, into which her hand would move mechanically, claiming anything that was displayed. There was a night in their apartment when Leon had found her crouching under the kitchen table, stuffing herself on one chocolate doughnut after another, an empty box on the floor beside her. She noticed his maroon carpet slippers and wept inconsolably. He was tender, as it happened, but she would not be comforted. At the Parklawn, however, she equipped herself with one of her cartons and descended the stairs with cold determination. The kitchen was open. She loaded her box with institution-size cans of fruit compote, strawberry jam, the thick syrup base for an apple drink, blueberry pie filling, packages of sweet breakfast cereals, five-pound bags of sugar. She did not forget to claim a can opener. Back in her room she devoured her plunder methodically, plunging her hand like a shovel deep into the can, squeezing her face into its tin-smell opening to lick out the last scrap, wounding her tongue on the jagged edges. Night after night, in the hours between twelve o'clock and dawn, she carried out her forays between the kitchen and her bedroom. She took everything in sight. All day long she ate in bed. Then one night she made her descent into the kitchen and found it locked and bolted. The next morning she permitted Mara to enter her room for the first time.

Mara was stunned. The smell overwhelmed her. Dizzy and nauseated, she slumped against the door. Every surface in the room was concealed by layers of garbage. "What's happening, Mommy?" she managed at last.

"I've been eating," said Rose.

Mara indicated that she had surmised as much.

"And now they've gone and locked up the kitchen," Rose went on.

Her daughter lifted a large can from the floor beside her. The label disclosed that it had once contained chocolate syrup. Peering inside it, Mara could see the paths her mother's tongue had taken.

"I disgust you, don't I?" Rose observed.

"No, of course not." Mara walked over to the bed and made a place for herself by pushing aside some gnawed bones and a blackened banana peel. She placed her cold hand on Rose's forehead and cleared away the sticky hair.

"You probably think I'm crazy," Rose said.

Mara shook her head.

"Well, think what you please, I don't care."

"Mommy, I don't think you're crazy, I promise you. I think you're just"— and here Mara paused to pinpoint the precise word—"*hungry!* That's what you are, you're hungry!"

"I'm starved!"

Mara nodded in sympathy. "Are you still?" she asked.

"Up here," said Rose, tapping her head, "not here." And she spread her hand over the part of her stained nightgown that shrouded her swollen belly. Mara stared at that hand, which she knew so well.

"I was having a binge," Rose explained. "I made a decision to have a binge and that's what I was doing. Nobody would interfere. Nobody would prevent me. I would eat until the eating came to an end, naturally. And now the stinker has gone and locked the kitchen. I'm still not finished."

"Are you feeling well?" Mara inquired.

"There, you see!" Rose pounced. "You do think I'm crazy!"

"No, I mean physically. From all the food."

"Mara, it makes no difference to me whatsoever if you consider me a slob. I've given up hiding my true self from you. I'm feeling all right, thank you very much for your concern. I can take in quite a bit, for your information. It's just that I'm constipated. I've been constipated for two years, ever since they shipped me off to that hospital the year before you left for Israel and the bathrooms had no locks at all. Anyone could walk straight in. I couldn't do a thing in those bathrooms. By the way, it's not just me. Your father is constipated, too, you know."

Mara knew. Her old bedroom shared a wall with the family's favorite bathroom, and the memory of her father's early-morning struggles still echoed. Her brother liked to sing secular songs on the bowl. Rashi used to run the water in the sink, and Rose would flush the toilet as soon as she sat down.

"It's the worst possible thing they could have done, to lock the kitchen," Rose went on. "And here I am more than two-thirds through my binge. I hope to God I can get some more food fast, because if I have to wait too long, I might be forced to start bingeing from the beginning again. All my work over the past two weeks will be wasted. Then when will I ever be able to return to civilization?"

Mara considered her mother's case. She had read somewhere of a type of therapy in which a person was encouraged to pursue even his most bizarre inclinations to their extreme limits. The result was healing. Rose knew, knew instinctively, where her cure would lie, Mara concluded. So she told her mother about the cans of food stashed in the Parklawn's cellar. She even volunteered to deliver a cartonful every morning to her mother's room. There were hundreds of cans down there that had somehow lost their way to the poor. Mara surveyed them purposefully each day. Carefully she examined each one, rejecting those that were bloated and those that had burst and those that showed any sign at all of being defective. She dreaded becoming the unwitting instrument of her poor mother's poisoning. But to Mara's great surprise, though the food was more than ten years old and many of the labels brown and peeling, much of it seemed to be quite usable. Thus Rose was able to carry on with her orgy, tearing the lids off cans of vegetables—string beans, corn, beets, peas, carrots—fruits and soups and fish, tipping them up against her lips and letting their contents spill, unchewed and untasted, down, down, down.

In describing her enterprise to Sudah, Mara called the food she procured for Rose "fodder." Sudah assumed she meant "father," and the whole undertaking struck him as amusingly metaphysical. "Soon your fodder shall be shit," he said. "I hope so," said Mara, "for Mommy's sake." Mara derived great pleasure from emptying the cellar shelves. Victor was right, she said to herself, it's all process. "Getting and spending, eating and eliminating, in and out, in and out" was how Victor had put it. He had made this observation during Mara's fanatic shopping spree. Mara hovered in and around Rose's room as much as she could, alarmed that her mother might at any moment be taking in the bolus that would kill her. It was a period of uncommon activity, of intense strain for Mara, and not only because of her concern about her mother. She also had to deal with Luba Alfasi, who was with each passing day becoming more and more difficult to contain.

One of the first signs of Luba's revolt against the restrictions that Mara had, of necessity, to impose upon her was her insistence on pulling up the Venetian blinds to acquire a better view of the courtyard. At first she merely sat in her chair by the window, rocking back and forth, chuckling quietly to herself. Soon, however, she began to demonstrate her need for contact by gesturing animatedly to any passer-by, waving, clapping, banging on the pane. Whenever a face peered at her from an opposite window, she would go to great lengths to win it over with a short, original entertainment, which generally consisted of thumbing her nose or stretching her features grotesquely, as if she were made of rubber. The captured bystander would vanish swiftly, like one who had been caught glimpsing a forbidden act, and Luba would slap her thigh with glee. Luba began to dress up for her window shows, in black silks with a lace mantilla over her hair, pulled flirtatiously across the lower portion of her face; in taffeta gowns bedecked with hundreds of buttons from old election campaigns. Fanny Gottlieb happened to notice Luba's window performance one afternoon and drew her curtains firmly together. But she could not resist lifting the side panel slightly and peeking out. Fanny's curiosity did not escape old Luba, who happily began to play a teasing game with her coy audience, hiding behind her own curtain and then, suddenly, popping out a leg, an arm, and sometimes even a triumphant face, stretched by a grin. Fanny was terrified but transfixed. She considered approaching Dora Popper to discuss these strange apparitions, but rejected the idea, anticipating her friend's cold rationality. "Your window giving you some trouble again?" Dora would crack, or maybe she would advise Fanny to stop hallucinating and take two aspirins. At last Fanny revealed her secret to Julius Fleischer. They kept watch at the window for several days. Nothing unusual happened. Julius began taking to patting Fanny on the back and murmuring, "It will be all right, Fanny, it will soon be all right, I promise you." Her senility evoked genuine sympathy from him, and he wordlessly thanked God that he had been spared. Then, with no warning at all, the Venetian blind in Luba's room shot up. There stood Luba, frozen like a corpse.

She was stark naked. Fanny and Julius dropped their curtain as if it had suddenly bitten them. They discussed for many hours what they had been privy to—the sagging breasts, the shriveled belly, the skinny limbs, wrinkled, crisscrossed with veins. They came to the conclusion that Mr. Mizrahi, the art director, was fashioning sculptures of old ladies in his studio, drawing his inspiration from the poor folks at the Parklawn. "That *momzer!*" said Julius, and he spat in the direction of the window. "He should pay us, that rotten pervert!"

The reason for Luba's absence from her window during the first few days of Fanny and Julius's patrol was an indiscretion she had committed which forced Mara to summon Luke to the Parklawn. Luke shuffled into his mother's room in his stocking feet, a towel wrapped around his neck. Mara hoisted herself up on a dresser and Luke sat down on a chair which was on top of a table, from where he glared down at his mother, who was huddled on her bed under a heap of clothing. "Mara tells me you threw a corset out the window," said Luke. It was an old, flesh-colored affair, stiffened with whalebone and dangling with laces. Luba neither confirmed nor denied this accusation. Luke went on: "Did you know that it landed on the head of the janitor of this building?" His mother gave no indication that she knew. "Did you know," Luke continued, "that as a result of your behavior it has become necessary to pay a certain amount of money regularly to this janitor to keep his mouth shut?" Still Luba made no answer. Luke motioned to Mara to leave the room. When she was gone, he climbed down from his chair and off the table. He walked up to his mother's body and put his mouth on her ear. "One more stunt like this and back you go to the nut house!" he roared. His scream flipped her over like a hot cake. Luba stared at her son with empty eyes.

Not too long after this event, Mara encountered Luba dancing down the hallway in a gold lace dress, on top of which she had strapped the guilty corset. As Luba twirled and twirled, her dress flew up like a saucer around her. Underneath she was wearing nothing at all. Luba sang as she danced, "I've got fireballs in my eucharist, ta ta tatata, fireballs in my eucharist, ta ta tatata, fireballs in my eucharist, ta ta tatata." She whirled straight into Mara's arms. Mara led her back to the room and locked the door on the outside. I wonder if I caught her on her first trip through the hall, she mused. She rather doubted it. To Sudah she said, "I hate to say this, but I think Luke's mother might really be crazy." "What you mean *might?*" said Sudah.

The climax came when Luba took to accosting the old people of the Parklawn as they made their way up and down the corridor. She would seize any occasion when Mara had neglected to bolt the door. She would scurry out into the hallway, her face twisted with the excitement of intrigue and adventure. Across her arms some ancient garment would be draped. She would coo to it like a cradled baby. Whenever she heard aged footsteps, she would dart out of her corner, her head moving to and fro to detect a pursuer. She would present the rags to the old man or woman who had the misfortune to cross her path. "Take it, take it," she would urge, "I have mine all picked out. This one is you, darling, believe me. To wear in your coffin." The complaints from residents and their relatives began to pour into Sid Schneider's office.

When Sid had telephoned him with the news that the kitchen was being routinely burglarized, Leon had snapped into the mouthpiece, "So what are you bothering me for? Put a lock on the door, shmuck!" But word of a maniac haunting the halls of the Parklawn brought Leon down at once. He stormed into Rose's room. "You've gone crazy!" he yelled. "You're *pishing* out the window! You're stinking up the hallways! You're scaring the living daylights out of these old *kockers!* You've gone over the edge, Rose, I'm telling you! Are you happy now? Have you got your revenge? Are you happy?"

"I am not happy," said Rose. Leon quieted. He made an effort to see her.

Rose looked back at him dully. She said, "To you it may seem that I've gone crazy. Let me assure you that I've had no such luck. Now, help me off this bed, Leon. I think I can finally go."

Rose's sadness hypnotized him. He went to her aid. She leaned heavily upon him as they made their way to the bathroom. Unfortunately, they did not quite reach it when her bowels gave out. She began to cry in bewilderment. He sat her down on the toilet and held her hand. He was sorry to see her lose her new dignity so fast. Afterward he cleaned her like a baby. He pulled her nightgown over her head and washed her poor stretched body with a cloth. He combed her hair. He sought out a spot where she might sit down and rest, and for the first time he seemed to notice the decaying remains, the mountains of rubbish, that stuffed the room. "I see you've been *noshing,*" said Leon.

He dragged the mattress off the bed and flung it into the hall. Underneath, trapped in the springs, was more garbage: chunks of meat, the skin and bones of herrings. He disappeared for a while, abandoning Rose in a fresh nightgown, standing there lost amid her leavings. He returned with a new mattress, fresh linen, and great plastic bags for the trash. He made the bed and led Rose to it. She fell asleep instantly. As she slept he cleaned the room, collecting the garbage, rubbing the sticky glaze off the floor with a damp towel, opening the windows and welcoming in the new air. Rose was the one who had always enjoyed throwing things out. He had a habit, in fact, of poring through her pails and salvaging what he could. But now he sensed the pleasure in it. God allots to each person in this life a finite amount of rubbish. Leon felt he was laboring toward an end. When he had finished he pulled a chair up to the bed and watched Rose sleep. She began to moan softly. Suddenly she sat up, screaming in terror. "You've been having a bad dream," he consoled. "Tell me what you dreamed." "A chicken!" Rose cried, "I'm a chicken!" She was clucking. She was scratching at Leon's chest. Soon she was deep into her black sleep again. Leon sat on by her side, thinking quietly.

He remembered how she had fought as a young girl. She had fought to get him. She was so American, it had enchanted him. She thought life could be controlled. Events could be explained, and she had explained them. Together they would rehearse the sermons he would deliver to the old people in the home where he was then the rabbi. She helped him improve his English. "Say *that*, not *dot!*" she would admonish him, sticking the tip of her pink tongue out between her small white teeth. Her mouth was rather small, actually. She considered it her finest feature and would paint it lovingly with moist red lipstick. Now she desired death by mouth. Leon wondered how he could ever have been so foolish as to attribute to Rose the exhibitionistic behavior of the Parklawn maniac. It obviously was not Rose. Obviously it was Sudah, having his fun wrecking Leon's investment as he had wrecked Herzl's parade, getting a big kick out of disguising himself as an old woman and terrorizing the inmates. After a while Leon left Rose's room, closing the door softly behind him. He entered the room of his daughter and her husband without knocking.

"Where is that *paskoodnyak?*" he demanded.

Mara was sprawled on her mattress, listening to jazz on the radio. "I don't know who you're talking about," she said.

"That little *shmendrik* you married. What's his name? You know who I mean."

"No. Who?"

"Don't play games with me, Mara. Where is he?" Mara decided she would persevere. She would force her father to utter the despised name for once. She began tapping her fingers to the music.

"Is he in his—what do you call it?—his studio? It's about time I had a look at what he's doing in there, anyhow." Mara was up in a flash. Leon was already out the door. She caught up with her father.

"You can't go in there," said Mara. "Don't you see the sign on the door?"

"Keep out," Leon read. "Can you order the landlord of the house himself to keep out? Ha, ha!"

"Daddy, try to understand. It's a very delicate business, this art. You simply can't interrupt a working artist just like that. The juices might dry up. It's touch and go, Daddy, touch and go. You'll block him, Daddy, you'll block him and I'll never forgive you!"

Leon had already kicked open the door. It crashed against the back of an old dresser. A fine silver netting burst open in the mirror on the other side. He squeezed himself into the room, Mara following hopelessly behind. He meandered among the mountains of furniture, muttering, "So this is what they call a studio. This, a studio?" At last he came to the bed. Luba, in pale-blue silk and an Indian's feathered headdress, was standing on it. She was holding a chair in front of herself like a shield, jerking it out menacingly as Leon drew nearer and nearer. "Is this how an artist looks when he's working?" Leon inquired of Mara.

"She's sick, Daddy. Leave her alone," said Mara.

Luba was waving the chair in front of her wildly. "Get the undertaker out of here!" she was screaming. "I'm not dead yet!"

3 That day Leon Lieb banished his daughter and her husband from the Parklawn. They stuffed their carpet-bags and moved into Mara's old room in her parents' apartment, where they were to remain for more than a year. Rose came home with them. Thus they were able to share the comfort of a taxicab. When Leon returned from his office late that night, he trudged past Mara's room on his way to the bathroom, his customary transition station. He noticed the door at once, shut ominously. Mara had tacked upon it the old ARTIST IN RESIDENCE sign, which had, until that morning, barred entry to Luba's cell. Leon had suffered an immensely difficult day, both at the Parklawn and at his desk. The sign was a dull memory. He stared at it with clogged understanding. "A guest?" he inquired. Rose told him the truth. Leon took several paces backward and prepared to hurl himself against the door. Rose placed herself directly in his path, her heavy arms crossed over her bosom. "Your child you may never throw out!" she declared. But Leon had already been launched and the momentum could not be halted. He crashed into the great softness that was his wife. They both toppled in a heap to the floor, giggling helplessly.

Inside the room, Sudah and Mara slept on. They lay on that girlhood bed, Mara curled into a question mark under her quilt, Sudah on his back, naked, uncovered, his nostrils flaring as he breathed, his beard tilted to the ceiling, his penis nesting in its black shrubbery. It was a dark room, paneled in oiled walnut with a greenish tint. The floor was stained a deep brown. The bamboo shades could have been rolled down over the windows, but Sudah and Mara were so exhausted they had pounced on the bed at once, the sun of the late afternoon casting stripes across their limbs. Mara turned away from her husband. He began to murmur into the bumps of her spine, swearing to shelter her, to care for her. She shook her head sorrowfully. "I hate this place," she moaned; "I never wanted to end up here." Sudah assured her she was not there, only her body was present. Do you suppose, he demanded of her inert back, that he would ever consent to such an environment for his own person? Mara was not convinced. Sudah dug his teeth into her buttock. She smothered her cry in the mattress for fear of alerting her mother. A big blot of drool spread where her mouth was pressed. Sudah bit harder. Mara swung over, her arms flailing in vain. Sudah pinned them over her head, causing her breasts to stand up fetchingly. He climbed on top of her. He entered and said, "It was wonderful funny, no? Luba sticking out chair. And your fodder, he was surprised, no?" Mara started to laugh. The tears that streamed down her face sparkled with the dying sun. "She kept on screaming, Luba just went on screaming," Mara said, choking on her laughter. " 'I'll kick him in the testaments,' she was yelling. 'I'll cut off his gentiles!' " Sudah collapsed on her. They fell asleep instantly.

Mara thought of this room as Sudah's, anyhow, as soaked with his essence, though they had never, until this day, slept in it together. She had completed her painstaking redecoration of it close to her departure for Israel, ridding herself of the flowered pink-and-white wallpaper, the fluffy pink rug, and the white dotted-Swiss curtains crisscrossed over the windows that she had chosen four years earlier and that her friends had admired so sincerely. Upon viewing her new room, her friends recognized at once that Mara Lieb was embarked on a deviant career. It was in this room that she had pined for Sudah after her return from Israel. Here she had lain, receiving visitors like the bereaved, when Sudah's stories were laid out like carcasses at the crossroads. The room would forever evoke Sudah for her, in the way that a tune revives, as nothing else does, the texture of a lost time to which it had been the background.

In their bedroom down the hall Rose and Leon were struggling to an arrangement. On one point, however, Rose would not budge: her home was the children's home for as long as they needed it. Leon railed against her mulishness, calling her a bad mother, declaring that the best thing for the little bloodsuckers would be to throw them out on their behinds. Rose folded her arm across her brow. Her two vertical wrinkles ascended from between her eyes. Leon could hear her teeth grinding. "Listen to me, Rose," Leon said, "that boy will rob your false teeth right out of your mouth." "If they go, I go, too," she replied. "Ha, ha! Where will you go? Do you think they'll let you have a corner of their sleeping bag?"

They reached a compromise. Leon would tolerate the invasion, but only on these terms: that Rose would not slip them a single penny, not a coin; let them drain their wedding hoard until they are forced to grasp Leon's knees in supplication. That Sudah lay *tefilin* each morning and pray with genuine devotion. That he cover his head with a yarmulka at all times. That he spend his days looking for work. That Mara spend her days looking for an apartment. That they all spend the Sabbath together, in the proper manner, Sudah walking beside Leon to synagogue and inflicting upon him no embarrassment whatsoever. "I'll lay it out to them in the morning," said Leon. "If they agree, fine. We'll write a contract. If not, I'll throw them to the wolves! Frankly, it would be the kindest thing I could do for them."

There was the silence of completion. Then Rose said,

"Leon, how come you didn't bring my diaphragm to the Park-lawn?"

"What for?"

"I thought, maybe, in case you visited."

Leon touched her cheek. "I've been working every minute, Rosie," he said. "There's this little politician in town, a new boy who still can't wipe his own *tuches*. A rising star, may he slip in the tub and squash his poppy. He's been trying to give me a hard time, Rosie. I can handle it, don't worry, but I've got to keep my eyes open every minute. It's not easy. Rosie, I want your friendship. Why don't you slip off your bloomers now?"

As she wiggled out of them under her quilt, Rose said, "Your sister Bluma told me that her Max jumps in, empties out—and finished! As if she were a toilet bowl."

"Max is a busy man," said Leon as he mounted.

"Well, maybe it's better for her that Max is still so speedy," Rose mused. "A man gets older, after all. He huffs and he puffs. It could take him a year and a Wednesday before he finishes up."

"Besides," Leon went on, "Bluma is nuts. Maybe not so nuts as Mara's old lady at the Parklawn today, but definitely crazy! I'm telling you, Rosie, Mara really picks them crazy!"

"Am I crazier than Bluma?"

"What's the matter with you, Rosie? Now, be quiet. This is no time for a conversation."

"All right, Leon, all right. But turn out your light. Hurry."

Weeks passed before Leon could find a suitable occasion on which to present his conditions to Sudah and Mara. And the occasion, in the end, did not arrive spontaneously but was snatched by Leon in desperation. There was a Saturday within this period upon which Leon ventured to open negotiations, but he was blocked by Sudah mid-sentence with the admonition that surely one does not discuss business matters on the holy Sabbath. What could Leon say? In any case, it would have been totally impossible to write up the contract on this day. But other than the Sabbath, when Mara and Sudah stayed home out of an instinct for stopping short at the limit, Leon simply never saw them. When he rose in the morning to prepare himself for the day's work, he would struggle to avoid the bald face of their closed door. Beyond it they were sleeping serenely. Leon averted his eyes lest he trigger the rage in his breast and blast himself to bits. In the evening, when he returned home, of late more and more dejected, they were gone. They did not come back until the early hours of dawn, between the dark and the light. In his troubled sleep Leon could hear the key twisting in the front door, the hum of their whispers, the sucking noise of the refrigerator door opening and shutting, the toilet flushing once, then once again, the footsteps to Mara's room, the door sealing with no reprieve. Leon could not summon the spirit to rise and confront them at that hour.

For Rose, the best part of the day was the time between the children's awakening, which occurred about three o'clock in the afternoon, and their departure from the house an hour later. She molded her day around that hour, dozing till noon, swallowing her second dose of pills for the day (the first consumed at dawn, when, disturbed by the noises of their return, she would stagger, eyes closed, to the bathroom), then sitting for three hours over the newspapers at the breakfast table, comfortable in her loose flowered housecoat, her glasses sliding down her nose. She was shopping. When an article of clothing pictured in an advertisement seemed suitable, she would rip out the page and order the goods. She hated to enter a store in person, hated trying things on. Her method resulted in closets overstuffed with garments of all sizes, some chosen in times of hope, others in times of resignation. The bright appearance of Sudah and Mara would send her flurrying in the direction of the stove, clattering frying pans and banging coffee pots. She would say, "I don't know what to serve you, breakfast, lunch, or maybe dinner." Mara would hug her and respond, "You're so cute, Mommy. Sit down, I'll do it." Mara would then cut off slabs of pumpernickel bread, smear them with mayonnaise, and set thick slices of cheese on top. Alongside the sandwiches she would place scallions and olives, and a sprig of parsley. She would explain to her mother, "What you eat is important. How it looks like, that is important, too. You must to eat beautiful food in elegance and with finesse." She was cultivating Sudah's syntax and accent as her own. Then she would clear the newspapers and scummy dishes off the table, toss a clean cloth over it, and place a vase of flowers in the center. In this way Rose acquired the habit of eating a second breakfast. While eating she would tell them of her worries that she slept too much, that her energy had eluded her, slipped away. "I just can't seem to function any more," she would lament. Sudah would say, "You are inside good. Why should you do?" Mara would say, "Mommy, put down your sandwich between bites." Rose would say, "It would sure be nice if the two of you would *do* a little. It would make Daddy happy." "You're a pure spirit, Mommy," Mara would say, "Sudah and I have decided."

They would leave, and Rose would tell the maid to clean up after them. Then she would take a long bath, preparing herself for a childless evening face to face with her husband. Rose was fastidious. Leon, on the other hand, bathed annually, on the eve of Yom Kippur, or so Rashi told it. This story had become part of the oral tradition of the family, and even Leon chuckled when it was repeated. He enjoyed hearing himself transformed into a legend. Rashi always finished off by asserting, "But still Daddy always smells so sweet, like a Negro." Leon boasted that he changed his underwear once a week, on Friday afternoon, in honor of the descent of Queen Sabbath. His shock at discovering that his then future son-in-law, Victor Asher, changed his underwear at least once a day was so profound and filled him with such consternation about the quality of Victor's masculinity that he did not even think of inquiring how Rashi came to know this intimate detail. In the end he concluded that Victor's aberration was a function of the excessive hygiene natural to a doctor. But Rose's bath was something her children knew about, for when they were small she would separate from them to enact this daily ritual, closing the bathroom door firmly, and they would hover anxiously outside, sensing the link between her splashes and their returning father.

The children also knew about Leon's chair at the head of the dining table, which no one but their father was permitted to occupy. When Leon was not there this chair stood empty, so that even in his absence he was present. Leon sat there these days, brooding into the plate of soft beef and string beans that Rose placed before him. His gloom was so thick it began to seep even into the circle of melancholy within which Rose made her way. "Trouble?" she asked. "It's getting hot, Rosie, it's getting very, very hot, but I can take it." At last he would shove away his drooping food. "Where is he, the little dope?" he would inquire with a scornful toss of his head in the direction of Mara's room. Rose would shrug. "Wasting their lives! Jumping into sewers and coming back to *shmeer* the *kocky* all over my walls!"

Leon rose in disgust from the table. At the kitchen sink he gulped down two pills to calm his traitorous stomach, which always attacked him in hours of stress. Then he walked into Mara's room and threw the door wide open defiantly. "Come over here, Rosie," he called. With a sigh she obeyed. "Look at this mess! Just look at this mess, Rose! I want you to give me your word that you won't lift a finger, not one finger, to clean this up."

Clothing, damp books, cigarette butts, fruit pits, soiled laundry, newspapers, balls of soggy tissues, and many nameless exotic objects were scattered everywhere. The bed sheet was stained with blood and dirty footprints. "This place stinks like a corpse!" Leon said.

"God forbid, Leon!"

"And where did they get that television set, may I ask? I hope to God you didn't finance it, Rose."

"What are you saying, Leon? I gave you my word."

"I don't want to speak out loud what I'm thinking now, but if that *momzer* is bringing stolen goods into my house, I'll turn him in personally. That's all I need at this time of my life."

"Leon, I am telling you right now, I will not listen to such talk about our daughter's husband."

"Okay, okay. But what I want to know is, where is his art? That's what I want to know!" He rummaged through a pile of papers and came upon one showing a heart pierced by an arrow and enclosing the statement "Sudah fuck Mara." Leon held on to it with his left hand and began smacking it with his right. "Is it for *shmuts* like this that we're giving him a grant?"

"Take it easy. Sit down."

"All right, I'll sit." He lowered himself onto the foul-smelling bed. "I'll tell you one thing, though," he said, "this does not look like the room of a religious person."

"You never can tell, Leon." With the tips of her fingers, Rose plucked out a flimsy black object from the pile beside them.

"What's that?" demanded Leon. Rose shook her head. "Is it Mara's?" he persisted. Rose simply did not recognize it. "Maybe it's his," said Leon. "Some fancy underpants, a new-fangled jockstrap, God help us!"

"Mara doesn't wear any underwear at all," Rose said. "You must to let the body free," she added softly, mimicking her daughter's new accent.

Leon clutched his forehead in his hands. "They run around

all night, like wild Indians, like gypsies. What are they doing, Rosie, can you tell me that? They're not kissing the mezuzah until five in the morning, believe me!"

At first they roamed the streets waiting for something to find them and change their lives. Arms looped around each other's waist, they stepped with a high spring, their hair flapping like a sheet as they walked. Passers-by were offended by their youth and their mutual absorption, so private and smug. They dressed alike, taking turns with their two pairs of loose corduroy pants, one forest green, the other brown, shortened to above the ankles, snug shirts that were actually the gray upper halves of old-fashioned long underwear, and on top of all this, Leon's fox cloaks. They spent their wedding money freely on whatever struck their fancy—embroidered shirts from India, Chinese slippers made of silk, old Persian boxes. Sometimes they would bring home a present for Rose, a carved ivory pipe, a brass samovar. One day they bought a very expensive German camera. Mara fidgeted for hours as Sudah slowly inspected it over the counter, as he painstakingly selected a supply of extra lenses and a fine brown leather carrying case. She worried a bit over the cost but did not wish to deprive Sudah of any of his heart's desires in the new American life she was providing for him. But she did venture to express her preference for the Japanese camera, equal in every respect, cost included. "To my past the Germans do nothing," said Sudah. The clerk would not accept their check, they looked so strange and irregular, and they were obliged to draw cash out of the bank. Sudah loved the look of the camera slung over his shoulder, he loved the feel of it bumping against his hip as they made their way up and down the streets.

Sometimes they would stop at Rashi's place, bearing gifts for little Naomi, a doll in a royal dress inset with broken mirror fragments, a red and gold string hammock from Mexico, for which they eagerly drilled holes into the two walls of an arch-way and inserted the steel hooks. As soon as the child was bundled in, down it came, baby and all, ripping out hunks of plaster. Mara brought a stiff pair of leather sandals two sizes too large for her sister, and another time she came with antique eyeglasses rimmed with silver, though she knew very well that Rashi did not need glasses at all and, furthermore, could not abide any useless object straddling her face. Rashi would place some rice and salad in front of them, and Sudah and Mara would eat out of the same plate, inserting tidbits into each other's mouth with the ivory chopsticks that Sudah always carried in a silk pouch at his waist. From beneath a lowered brow Rashi observed them, feeling herself an intruder at some intimate ceremony, but glad, nonetheless, for their presence, for all day long she was alone, and while Naomi slept she stood by the window staring out and wringing her hands. Now that Rashi had assured herself she was not pregnant, she would occasionally consent to smoke with them, marijuana or hash-ish. Mara would nod approvingly as her sister erupted in foolish giggles or delivered banal pronouncements as if they were weighty fresh insights. One day Rashi traded an extra television set she owned for a few ounces of their good cannabis. This deal was arranged by Sudah, who loved to watch television, especially cowboy shows, but found his pleasure vastly dimin-ished in the common living room of the Lieb household, where the family set had its honored spot, underneath a studio por-trait of the three Lieb children, Mara with four front teeth missing. Traveling back home by subway that dawn, Sudah lugging the television, they were stopped by a policeman who, putting together the object with its bearer, concluded that the former was stolen and the latter was the thief. All three re-turned to Rashi's apartment. Sudah was grudgingly released, thanks only to Victor's credentials. But he was deeply insulted.

But more and more now they were taking the subway down

to Luke's. Sudah would spend hours adjusting lights and constructing settings for photographs of Luke and Luba, who was back with all her goods. Luke's toothless face above the towel he habitually wrapped around his neck and below the village cap was charted with suffering. Sudah was never satisfied enough to shoot more than three pictures a visit, which he tore to shreds as soon as they were printed, for the reality of his work could never match what Luke no doubt imagined it to be. There were always others there, too, sipping tea out of saucers around the kitchen table and inclining their heads in the dark for a message from Luke. Mark Bavli would come, and so would Manny Fish, with his new friend, Gila, a husky divorced woman ten years his senior, an instructor in Holocaust literature at one of the universities. Strangers also would quietly draw a chair up to the table in a way that suggested they were initiates, for Luke was a secret that was confided only to the privileged. Bogdan Chmielnicki was often there. He was a Ukrainian who wrote poems in Yiddish, a language he had taught himself with much difficulty in atonemen for an ancestor's sin. Another guest was Jim Palmer, once a Baptist preacher and now a housepainter, a baker of nutty loaves of bread, and the father of half a dozen black and crippled orphans. Christopher Hill, the heir, would come lumbering up the steps, booming at the top of his voice one of the thousands of folk songs he knew in one of a hundred languages. He would let his guitar case drop with a crash on the table, click it open to expose the plush green interior, and present to each person there assembled a ring box, wrapped and bowed in sparkling silver, inside of which a nugget of hashish was set like a gem. Sometimes Hill would be accompanied by his friend Joe Gold, the psychiatrist, who was known to all who knew of him as "Joseph the Interpreter of Dreams."

Mara and Sudah would squeeze themselves into a single chair, his head resting on hers, hers nestled in his shoulder.

Sudah's bushy eyebrows would be drawn upward and joined in an expression of amused detachment. He never spoke. Everyone was beguiled by them. He was an artist, she a writer. They were a unit apart, meant to be on view. Like twins they were, curled up together in a transparent egg. Though they were known to be lovers, they were almost indistinguishable in sex, each neither boy nor girl. Joe Gold invited them up to his place. In time they began to go directly there late each afternoon and linger till the dawn.

Gold had just taken over a large apartment on the West Side, in an old building in which his mother had an apartment, too. For a long time Gold had sought his own place in that building, for while he preferred not to share the same quarters with his mother, he valued her nearness and, especially, her services as keeper of his house and keeper of the peace among his women. Then one day the inhabitants of the apartment Gold was eventually to acquire posted an advertisement in the lobby for a boarder. Gold knocked at the door at five that afternoon. The rooms were dark and hushed. In the distance he could see long, lit tapers and stooped figures clothed in black. The master of the house, an obliging Englishman, showed Gold the room, explaining, as he did so, that his daughter had just died that afternoon, quite suddenly. Her remains would be laid out in the living room for some days, he hoped Gold would not mind. Gold offered to return at a more suitable time. The Englishman immediately lowered the rent by ten dollars. They bargained discreetly for a while. At last the matter was settled. When one of his girlfriends demanded to know how he could be so callous as live in an apartment with a dead body, Gold replied enigmatically, "There is no house without its corpse." He was paraphrasing his favorite book.

Soon Joe Gold's complete household joined him in his rented quarters. This consisted not of objects or possessions but of a constant revolving entourage of beautiful women and idle men. They overflowed his room and engulfed the Englishman's entire apartment. Gold's mother bustled in each morning, elbowing everyone aside, to cook and clean and set things in order, which became absolutely necessary now that Gold had begun to conduct a few of his therapy sessions on the couch in the living room, beside a sealed coffin. The situation at last became so intolerable that the Englishman and the surviving members of his family had no choice but to move out. They did so one day, leaving behind all their furniture, some unused caskets, and, in addition, several months' unpaid rent, which Gold paid gladly. The gloomy furniture was piled on the curb. Within minutes every splinter was stolen. By the time Sudah and Mara had become faithful visitors at the apartment, it was totally bare, save for some plain coffins and Gold's large round bed, set like an island in the center of what must have been his bedroom.

An evening at Joe Gold's varied little. People wandered through the rooms, pouring wine from large jugs and sipping it out of plastic cups, which Mrs. Gold collected and rinsed out the next morning. Chris Hill would distribute his presents, arcing his finger to the stubble on his cheek for a kiss in payment. Then he would cautiously lower his bottom to the kitchen floor—he was quite stout and wheezy—and begin strumming his guitar. A circle would soon form around him. A canopy of smoke would hang suspended from the ceiling. Sometimes Joe would tap two or three women on the shoulder. They would rise without a murmur and follow him to the bedroom. Once he even invited Mara, who shook her head passionately and brought it to rest on Sudah's lap, to indicate where she belonged. "Well, then, let him come along, too," said Joe. Thus it happened that Sudah and Mara were granted a permanent corner of Joe Gold's bedroom from which to view the events. No one complained. They were as still as cats, like cats, ornaments. They were furniture. They huddled on the floor with their arms around each other, Sudah's face in a knowing half smile, Mara's reflecting no sign that what she was viewing was anything other than her standard fare. Joe favored several women laboring over him at once. He tried his best to satisfy all of them equally, but he charmingly acknowledged that there were limits to what one man could perform, even a psychiatrist. When he failed, he would encourage them to satisfy each other. These sessions would often be abruptly interrupted by Gold's mother, who would come waddling in without a knock and briskly shoo the girls away, crying, "Get dressed, *maidlach*, get dressed! What do you think? Dr. Gold has to earn a living, too. There's a patient waiting in the living room, Yossel, quick!" His mother was his agent and manager. She carried stacks of his cards in her pocketbook, bound with rubber bands. While walking through the wealthier parts of the city she would occasionally encounter some rapt fellow conversing animatedly with himself, or a rouged lady picking through a garbage pail. With a sympathetic tap on the shoulder and a look of calm understanding, she would press one of Joe's cards on the poor creature. Joseph Gold had been trained in Sweden and in Switzerland. Many people bore witness to his healing ways.

Gold did not like the girls to tarry in his bedchamber, even on those rare nights when he was not too busy to finish up with them. They, in turn, were eager to get back to the group, where there was gaiety, singing, and laughter. Swiftly they departed. Then Joe would rise from his bed and dress before a narrow mirror fastened to the wall, his back to Mara and Sudah. He and their reflections would proceed to carry on long discussions on such impersonal subjects as ethics and art, about which they all had opinions. He took care never to tread in their private domain, except for two fleeting occasions: once, when he extended to them an invitation to sleep in his bed should they have no other place, and another time, when he offered them the job of decorating his apartment. They refused both flatly. But one night, as he was drawing his belt through his pant loops, he paused ominously, and Mara knew that something irreparable was about to be uttered. She waited in a stew of her own excitement and fatalism. No matter how bad it would be, she wanted it. "Well, Mara," Gold said at last, "I see you have a pretty good-looking father."

Mara was stunned. Had her father been checking up on her? She had always drawn comfort from what she thought was her anonymity at Gold's, an anonymity that her marriage had first endowed in the form of a new name. The Mara Lieb of old had been wiped out. Now, unknown, a stranger among strangers, she could be whatever they imagined her to be. She considered herself invisible. She was a transient, without a fixed future in which she could be held accountable, without a past. She said softly, "I didn't know you knew my father."

"I don't." Gold tossed her a rolled-up newspaper. Her eye immediately hooked on to the picture of her father, the brim of his black felt hat pulled down at an angle, his lips set above his goatee. She spotted the dark mole in the foothills of his nose. She skimmed the article in a daze. Something about his nursing homes. Some politician wanted to view the records. Mara did not know the meaning of the word subpoena. There were complaints about money, conditions. Mara shook her head and passed the papers to Sudah.

"It's just that his pants are too baggy," Gold went on, "like all the rabbis I've ever known. You should tell him. He can afford a better tailor. It would improve his image."

Sudah handed the newspaper back to Mara without a glance. He disdained the written word. She was still clutching it when they reached home that morning, earlier than usual. Murray Levine, her father's accountant, was just leaving the building as they entered, accompanied by a smartly dressed young man Mara did not recognize. Levine did not acknowledge them, his eyes were groveling. In the apartment Herzl was curled up in sleep on the living-room sofa, snoring fitfully. His mouth was open as it had always been in sleep since boyhood. Leon was leaning over him, trying to remove his shoes without waking him. Max Brody, Leon's brother-in-law, had fallen asleep with his head on the dining-room table, his pillow a mound of closely printed documents, his cheeks ink-stained. Reb Anschel Frankel was staring out the window watching the dawn arrive, rocking back and forth on his heels, chanting Psalms to a private melody. Mara's eye was drawn to his strong, familiar hands, red-furred and freckled, clasped behind his back. In the kitchen Sadie Stern was brewing a fresh pot of coffee.

Mara walked up behind Sadie and kissed her tenderly on the back of the neck. Sadie started, for ever since her years in the concentration camps any sudden movement or sound stabbed her with terror. Mara took the coffee pot from her hand. "Go rest, Sadie," she said, "I'll finish up." She emptied the soaked grinds on Leon's newspaper face, dumped the whole package into the garbage, poured out two cupfuls, and carried them to the table. She remembered how her father had always served a cup of coffee and a piece of cake to her mother in bed each Sabbath morning before he left for the synagogue. When Mara became a teenager he began to bring her some as well, but never once had she taken a sip or a nibble from his offering, feeling somehow that to do so would be incestuous. For the same reason she had never served her father at table. This was the first time. "Sit down, Daddy. I've brought you some coffee," she said.

Leon shuffled over to the table. Needles of grayish-black hair prickled his cheeks. He was in his stocking feet. Like a mourner, Mara thought. Leon always forbade them to walk around the house in socks, for that was a high symbol of mourning, and whom does a child mourn over but a parent?

"To what do I owe this honor?" Leon asked. His face was grinning, like a skull.

"What honor?"

"The coffee. The service. The early return. After all, it's only four a.m."

"I hear you're in trouble," said Mara.

Leon raised his hands to the crystal chandelier on the ceiling. "Do you see, Creator of the Universe? I have to sink to the lowest depths so that my daughter can stoop to show me a little sympathy and affection." His hands thudded onto the table, spilling some more coffee into the puddle already in the saucer. "Maybe if I were crazy, like that husband you brought home, I would have had a lousy cup of coffee from you a long time ago."

"Daddy!" Sudah's fat red tongue shot out, like a ripe secret. However, by the time Leon noticed him standing there, solemnly leafing through the *Guide of the Perplexed* of Maimonides, it was tucked safely inside again. Leon shrugged. "I didn't know you read the newspapers," he commented.

"I don't," Mara replied. "A friend showed it to me. A psychiatrist."

"A psychiatrist?" Leon groaned. "A big shot? That's too bad. Now he'll know what kind of a loose daughter I have!" They both began to laugh, like people who know each other's weaknesses too well. Suddenly Leon's face lengthened and turned severe. "Sadie!" he called, "come right over here with a piece of paper!"

"You!" Leon commanded, pointing to Sudah, "sit down!" Sudah did not budge. "He has a name, you know," Mara whispered.

Impending sarcasm gleamed in Leon's eye. "I see we have a scholar in our midst who cannot bear to tear himself away from the holy books," he said. "May I be so bold as to disturb you, Rabbi ben Ezra? The fortunate father of such a distinguished son is called Ezra, is he not? So why then doesn't he help you out a little bit? Ha, ha! What's the matter? Am I the only living father around here?" Sudah remained locked in his corner.

"Reb Sudah'le, please," said Leon, "would you be so kind as to honor my modest table?" Sudah kissed the page he had been poring over and shut the volume with a smack. He climbed on top of the table and sat down.

Leon trembled with disgust. "Such a learned man as you are, Reb Sudah'le, surely you are aware that our sages compare a table to a sacred altar. 'This table stands before the Lord,' our scholars teach us. Why, then, have you *plotzed* upon my innocent table the lowest, the most impure, the most defiled portion of your body?" Leon was almost shrieking.

"He simply did not understand you," said Mara. "It's the language problem, Daddy, that's all."

"As you say, daughter of mine. Okay, we'll try once again. Now, Reb Sudah'le, take a seat please, take a seat. We must get started. If I don't get some sleep tonight I will collapse."

Sudah took a seat and stood there holding it. There was a puzzled look on his face, as if he were awaiting further instruction on where to take it.

"Sit down, you imbecile!" Leon's face was bright red. He paused to master himself. "Reb Sudah'le, I am pleading with you to sit down at once, damn it!"

Sudah obeyed. He offered Leon a friendly smile. At Joe Gold's that night Sudah had smoked more than his usual share of hashish. His mind was rocking pleasantly back and forth on glimmering sea waves.

Leon cleared his throat. "I have problems of my own, as you know." Mara nodded. Sudah nodded, too, in the way that daydreaming pupils learn to nod to flatter the teacher into thinking that someone, at least, is listening. But in this case, their nods served only to stoke Leon's fury. "Maybe, had you been home and up at a normal hour, you would not have had to learn of my troubles from the newspapers," he said bitterly.

"We're prepared to help you in any way we can," Mara announced.

"Help me? How can you help me? You're an uneducated little nothing, are you aware of that? Did you think because you write those dirty little stories you have some standing in this world? The last thing you were trained for was the toilet. As for Reb Sudah'le here, even to finish high school was beneath his dignity—an artist of such genius! Next to him you're a veritable professor!"

"My father is naturally upset," Mara explained to Sudah.

"Do me a favor, Mara, spare me your understanding. Don't play games with me like you play with your nuts."

"Maybe we should go to bed, Daddy. We'll finish this discussion some other time, when you're feeling calmer."

"When, for instance? For weeks now I've been waiting to get you to this table. If I can't run the business in my own family, how can I be expected to manage it outside? Sadie, take notes! We are going to write up a contract, here and now. There is no creature on this earth who gets a roof over his head and food in his belly for nothing. Why should you be exceptions? Are you something special? You are animals, just like the rest of us. You have to eat and you have to *pish.*" Mara cringed as she always did when her father sullied conversations with gross references to bodily functions. Anyone else could speak in this way and even delight her, anyone but her father. Other children, gentiles in particular, did not have to put up with their father's humid, fetid, suffocating environment.

Sudah spoke for the first time. His voice creaked. "I piss with proudness," he declared.

"Pride," Mara corrected. (Later, in bed, he called her to task for this. "How can we do fucking now?" he asked. "I can see you are not to me married yet.")

"I piss with proudness," Sudah continued, allying himself on this masculine issue with Leon. "I am not ashame. This night I myself piss on the walls of the great Metropolitan Museum of Art. I am happy to piss on the head of any enemy of my Mara's *aba*."

"Thank you very much, Reb Sudah'le. My worries are now over." Sudah acknowledged Leon's gratitude by slowly lowering his dark-fringed lids over his eyes, which now consisted almost entirely of pupil. Max Brody lifted his head, muttered something that sounded like "Gimme a piece of smiley pie," and let it plop down again on top of the pile of papers.

Mara said, "Uncle Max doesn't look too comfortable."

"Of course not," said Leon. "Your Uncle Max is a reasonable man. Why should he expect to be comfortable? He knows this is not his own house."

"But it is my house, Daddy." Mara said this, well aware that she was striding straight into her father's unsubtle trap. Her lust for disaster drove her on.

"No, Mara," Leon said, not triumphantly but wearily, "this is not your house, not any more. It is my house. Nowadays my enemies are attacking me from every side, just as, sooner or later, they always gang up on the stranger from a strange land. It's an old story. But my house is my own. If I open the door and let someone in, I expect him, while he is sheltered within my four walls, to live by my rules. If he leaves a pile of doody on the living-room rug, out he goes, no ifs, ands, or buts. But you are a special case."

Mara winced. "That's right. I'm your daughter."

"You are a special case," Leon went on, "because I never invited you in the first place. And now that you are here, your mother, in the cruel way that mothers always damage their children, your mother will not allow me to throw you out. That is the situation. 'These are not strangers,' your mother says, 'this is a special case.' 'If this is such a special case,' I said to

Rose, 'I will treat it in a special way, not like I deal with ordinary guests who are polite, who are grateful, who have a home of their own and go there sooner or later. With this special case I will write a contract.' "

Mara strained to hear the regular breathing, the soothing heartbeat of her mother sleeping alone beyond the bedroom door.

"A contract, a lease," said Leon. "I am the landlord, you are the tenants. On a piece of paper we shall write out the terms. If it has to be at a time when I am already suffering under more burdens than any mortal should bear, if it has to be at this miserable hour, so be it! I shall dictate the conditions. Sadie will write them down. We shall put our signatures on the bottom line, though God alone knows what yours are worth. You keep your end, I'll keep mine. You break your word and out you go with all your junk. I will evict you without mercy. Maybe it would be the most merciful thing I have ever done for you. Sadie, are you writing? First, I provide the room and board and nothing else—do you hear?—not a penny more. Don't try to squeeze any money out of Mommy. You won't get a cent. She is my partner and ally."

"Have I asked you for money, tell me that? Have I asked you for a rotten dime?" Mara's voice was bruised.

"Not yet, but you will."

"You owe me ten thousand dollars, Daddy, you haven't forgotten that, I hope."

"Owe you? Since when is a gift something a person owes? I might just as well use it for toilet paper as hand it over to you today. That's exactly what it would be worth." Leon pulled a wrinkled handkerchief out of his pocket, cleared his throat, and spat some phlegm into it. He gazed at his output with interest.

"New paragraph, Sadie," he continued. "Under the heading of 'Religion.' And these are points I should not even have to mention. It's only common decency to respect the custom of

the house. It's what is meant by being a *mensch*. If you stepped
into an Arab's hovel, you would take off your shoes and drink
the Turkish coffee he *shtupps* into your face even when you
don't know what the hell he puts in it! Why, Rashi told me
that Reb Sudah'le here would not even speak Hebrew in the
Arab quarter lest he offend them with the despised tongue of
the conqueror. Such sensitivity, why is there none left over for
me? *Nu*, so pretend like I'm an Arab. I won't be insulted. Now,
Reb Sudah'le, I ask you always to keep your head covered,
inside my house and out."

Sudah pointed proudly to the African skullcap on top of his
curls, gaily embroidered with fish-headed monsters dancing in
an idolatrous ring. In fact, lately he had been wearing it almost
constantly, it pleased him so immensely.

"*Nu*, what choice do I have?" Leon addressed the chandelier. "It does not look like a yarmulka. It does not fit like a
yarmulka. It is not a yarmulka, there's no doubt about that, but
the head is covered, so what is to be done?" He shrugged. "And
now, Reb Sudah'le, I'm asking you also to put on your *tefilin*
every morning. I noticed them under Mara's bed, in a fancy
silver bag smeared with dust. I want you to pray to God. The
Jewish God. It can't hurt."

Here Sudah broke into a lengthy Hebrew dissertation, in the
singsong style of the talmudic scholar, waving his thumb
grandly in the air, in which he raised the question and provided
conflicting opinions on the subject of whether or not he ought
to lay *tefilin* at all, since when he awoke, after all, it was no
longer morning, but, in fact, nearly dusk, the hour for the
afternoon prayer, and so on and so on. Thus he argued pro and
con with himself while Leon stared at him incredulously. At
last Leon cut him short. "Put them on at sunrise, before you
go to sleep," he said. "Enough with the *pilpul*. Was that your
bar mitzvah speech, by the way? As a matter of fact, were you
ever bar mitzvah? Never mind. Why should I ask questions

when I don't want to know the answers? Next, Sadie. About the Sabbath. While you are living in my house, you must observe the Sabbath like a member of my household."

"But we do, Daddy," Mara protested. "Doesn't Sudah go to *shul* with you every Shabbos morning?"

"It is pure agony to wake him up in the morning, let me tell you," said Leon. "Then, after he's finally up and dressed, his company is more of an embarrassment to me than a pleasure. My friends all sit there waiting for the show. What do you imagine they think when they see my son-in-law come in at my side, all fancied up in that velvet suit from the wedding, with the cape? When he takes off that top hat, they all expect a rabbit to hop out of it. There he sits in his jungle yarmulka, without once moving his lips in prayer. What do you suppose goes through their minds when they see such a spectacle, huh?"

"Maybe they think he's one of your employees," said Mara.

A stricken look passed across Leon's eyes. "Unfortunately, they know who he is," said Leon.

Mara said, "We like living in this house at least as much as you like having us here. We would be out in a minute if we could find the right place."

Leon banged the table with his fist, pitching Max's head off its pile of papers. "When I was a young man I would sleep in the gutter rather than live like a parasite! I had nothing, but I was a man! I took care of my wife! What do you mean, the right place? A room with a toilet, that's all you would need if you had some pride."

"You forget, Daddy, that Sudah is an artist. An artist is not an ordinary creature. He needs a certain environment. What will do for everyone else will not do for an artist. Right now Sudah is planning a massive canvas. We're looking for a loft, with high ceilings and plenty of space."

"Good! Then find it! Find it fast! That's one of my conditions; write it down, Sadie. And one thing more. Far be it from me to deprive the world of an artist of such promise even for one dark minute, but while he continues under my roof, he'd better go out and look for a job."

"Who's the 'he'?" demanded Mara, echoing her father, who would never permit his children to refer to a respected adult by a pronoun.

"He! He! Him! That lump of clay over there! Tell him to get to work! I don't care what he does, as long as it's honest!"

There was a long uneasy pause here, during which Sudah's smile expanded from a slit and wrapped itself slowly around his face. His cheeks puffed out, his face taking the shape of a queer amphora.

"What's the matter with him?" Leon asked at last. "Is he normal?"

Sudah said, "I smile because I am happy this day to make you happy. I will tell you now we already have job. To fix up apartment of our psychiatrist friend Joe Gold. He is the man what showed to us the picture of you. He say you a very very handsome man, by the way, but to tell you for your own good not always to wear black suits. It make you look like a funeral parlor."

Reb Anschel Frankel swiveled around, for the first time betraying that he had been privy to anything that was spoken. He gazed at the audacious boy, babbling away there so impudently. Sudah gave Anschel a cocky salute. "How, Chief!" he said. Then, with his springy walk, Sudah emptied the room of himself. Mara rose to follow. She hesitated for a moment and came up behind Leon. She bent over and kissed him on the top of his head, inhaling his warmth. "Will you be all right?" she whispered. Leon took her hand and stared at it blankly. "You're still biting your nails, what a pity," he said. She tried to draw her hand back into safety, but Leon held fast, lifting it briefly to his face and brushing his lips against it. He let it fall. "We have suffered in the past and we have survived. We shall endure through this one also," he said. "I have always fought like a lion to get the best for my family. But your mother is not taking it well."

Late the next afternoon, as she was preparing the first meal of the day for herself and Sudah, Mara turned gravely to Rose. "I'm worried about you, Mother," she said. A warm sadness spread through Rose. That formal word "mother," so portentously stressed, meant that her condition was now about to be discussed with seriousness and purpose. For a change it would not be necessary to personally steer the conversation into her own sphere, scorning herself the while for her obnoxious dependency, her self-riveted invalid state. "About me?" Rose replied. "But why, Mara? I'm fine, perfectly fine, as you can see." "There will be rough times ahead for you," said Mara. "You'll need some extra support."

Rose slid her glasses down her nose and peered at Mara over the frame. "If you mean a psychiatrist, sweetheart, forget it. I've had a bellyful of the species, thank you very much. They want to remodel me. Well, it's too late for me to change. They tell me to lose weight. So what else is new? I tell them I sleep too much. Do you know what they answer? 'Stop sleeping so much,' they say. For that they had to go to medical school? They want me to talk, to start with year one. I have nothing to say to them. When I ask for some lousy pills they make me go down on my knees. It's not enough I have to pay through the nose, I also have to pay with a confession, a dream, a lie from my past. They turn me into a child. If I make too much trouble, they have a plot to put me away. No thank you, Mara. I despise them."

Sudah nodded. "They are worms. They pop my brain like blackhead." He was recalling the ordeal of his imprisonment and interrogation as a pacifist.

Mara was vexed. "But Joe is not like the others, right, Sudah?" Chastised, he agreed. "Mother," said Mara, with her collected authority, "I want you to start seeing our friend Joe Gold. He's different. He doesn't think he's God. He could be a patient, too, and he knows it. He has a very original technique, which he developed himself. He cures through dreams."

"Dreams! Very original, ha!" Rose eyed Mara shrewdly. She went back to her shopping, licking her finger before turning over each page of the newspaper. "All right, sweetie," Rose said, almost inaudibly, "I'll go." She looked up sharply and grinned. "Surprised you, eh?" Mara's face was stretched in astonishment. As they were leaving home a short while later, Mara observed to Sudah, "I think that deep down she really loves going to a shrink almost as much as she loves being hospitalized, but not quite." To Leon, Rose commented that night, "I want to see for myself where they go, what kind of life they lead. When will I get another opportunity like this?" Leon was amazed at her energy. But he remembered how, in their early days together, she had always gained vitality as he weakened. It had been to her detriment that his power over the years had been so sustained.

Her very first step into Gold's apartment was a calamity. Her knees caved in, and with her fingers grasping in vain for Mara's sleeve, her rump hit the floor and her legs shot out into a V straight in front of her. The pink patch of underwear at her crotch was revealed. She had labored to put herself together and now she was in disarray. She blamed her collapse on the sudden darkness of Gold's rooms. It flattened her like a boulder. Candlelight flickered here and there; slim, alien shadows glided by; and the smell of incense smothered her like a hood. The bareness of the rooms was what really terrified her. She could see in an instant that there would be no chair for her to sit on, and furthermore, how could her child, her irresponsible Mara, ever succeed in the job of filling up this cavernous void?

Mara and Sudah slipped their hands into her armpits and lifted her off the floor. "It's all right, Mommy. You'll be all right. Don't be ashamed." They led her into the living room and left her standing there by the cold fireplace.

The need to sit down pressed upon her. She was alone; merry sounds were coming from somewhere. A few long, narrow, wooden boxes were pushed against the wall, but she could not gauge the strength of their lids. If she sat down on one of them and cracked the wood and fell in, she would be desperately ridiculous—she would want to die. She considered lowering herself to the floor—no one was watching—but later on, of course, she would be obliged to get back up on her feet in front of the psychiatrist. She began to wander through a bewildering arrangement of rooms, each alike in its emptiness. She passed the kitchen. This was where the music came from. Dancers were sealed together, moving slowly in place, making no progress at all. On the floor forms were interlocked, falling and rising like breathing. Strange moans could be heard. She hurried on. The old panic gripped her, of groups with members who belonged, and she the clumsy outcast, unable to conceal her bumpy body, betrayed by her real wishes and longings. At last she found a narrow door, slightly ajar. "This must be the bathroom," she concluded with relief, realizing, suddenly, that here, in fact, was the goal of her search. She entered tentatively. Luke Alfasi rose from the toilet, bowed slightly, and gallantly extended his arm to offer her his place. "It's the only seat in the house." He laughed. The lid was down. Rose accepted gratefully. Luke found a place for himself inside the tub. "I remember you from Mara's wedding," said Rose. "You're Luke, the poet."

"You honor me too much with the title of poet." Luke hung his head.

"Oh, no. Mara says you're the distilled essence of the poet. You are above writing poetry, she says. It's not a necessary thing for you to do. You and poet are synonyms. Sudah is the same, she says, only in art, of course. He is the artist, purified. I'll tell you the truth; when Mara told me all this I listened respectfully, naturally, as one should always listen to a daughter. But you know what I said? Forgive me, but I said to Mara, 'Well, if you have to pick a business, that's the business to pick!' I haven't insulted you, I hope." Luke laughed good-naturedly. "Tell me something, Luke the poet," Rose went on, "you look to be about my age. Can you tell me, please, what has happened to the children?"

Luke and Rose began to talk earnestly and quietly. He told her about his own family, his wife and three sons, Shadrach, Meshach, Abednego. Meshach committed suicide by drowning himself in a swimming pool. His wife gathered her surviving children to her side and went West, leaving him alone with his old mother, who, unfortunately, was insane. His wife took the children West, Luke said, to purge them of their father's Jewish madness and love of death. "But our children will come back to us someday," Luke reassured Rose. Luke and Rose had become friends. They sat without speaking in each other's presence, leafing through old issues of the *Archives of General Psychiatry*, which Gold kept in a bucket by the toilet.

There was a knock on the door. They looked up, saddened by the interruption. Without waiting for a reply, Joe Gold stuck his round face into the crack. His squat body followed. He strode past Luke, directly up to Rose, and extended his hand. "I've been looking all over for you. You must be Mrs. Lieb. I'm Joseph Gold." Rose got up. Out of habit she flushed the toilet. Gold led her back into the living room and directed her to a seat on one of the long boxes. It was sturdy enough after all. Rose tugged the hem of her skirt over her perpetually bruised knees. Joe dragged out another one of the boxes and sat down facing her, his legs spread apart.

He explained his method to her. It was very simple and

elegant, he said, like mathematics, like any correct solution to a puzzle. It consisted of charting, or "mapping," as it were, what he called the "dream landscape." Gold believed that each person lives two lives of equal reality, the waking life and the dream life. The dream life, he maintained, like the waking life, contains familiar persons and places, a home, a neighborhood, a regular flow of recognizable people coming and going, helping you and harming you. What happens in the dream world is as real as the events of the waking world. If someone hurts you in your dream, you are quite justified in avoiding him should you cross paths while you are awake. Indeed, Gold was at this time engaged in supporting his theory by mapping the dream landscapes of the people his patients dreamed about. He did not doubt that there would be a striking coincidence of events and environments, except from different points of view. That would be an astounding confirmation of the dream's reality, wouldn't it? As for the practical application of this theory to the individual sufferer, the cure would lie in thoroughly identifying the ingredients of the patient's dream life, thereby acquiring knowledge of the other world she inhabits and thus achieving wholeness. The patient must be prepared to work hard, Gold warned Rose. She must pay scrupulous attention to her dreams. Never, never allow a dream to evade you. Train yourself to jolt your body into wakefulness at the conclusion of a dream and write it down at once. Keep a little pad and pencil at your bedside. The material of these sessions would be dreams, nothing else, only dreams.

He finished and waited. There was a deepening hollow inside of Rose, filling up with silence. Her high-school yearbook had described her with this rhyme: "We can't accuse her of being dumb, / But she enjoys staying mum." She never enjoyed it certainly, she always knew that. But what she said when she spoke created an even more misleading impression than her silence. There was a clock ticking away somewhere. Her heartbeat was racing against it. Any second now she would be blown off the map, the waking map and the dream map. The slightest noises became deafening in her ears. Now Rose's silence was transforming itself into a panic. For the life of her she could not recall a single dream. She began to rub her knee, as if she wanted to grind herself down to a few forgettable specks of dust. Then she said huskily, "Well, lately I've been dreaming that I'm a chicken. You know, cluck, cluck, cluck!" She flapped her hands at her side. Then she blushed deeply. "Can you use that one?" she asked, looking at Gold hopefully, trying with her smile to elicit some approval from him.

Gold scribbled something on his clipboard. Rose's bottom was aching from the hard wooden surface it had been assigned. Her legs, drawn tightly together with the knees up, were cramped and falling asleep. She began rotating her thumbs around each other, a feat at which she was unmatched, both for speed and for her skill at keeping the thumbs extremely close but never quite touching. In despair she dropped her hands into her lap. "I dream about my mother a lot," she said. "My mother is dead but in my dreams she's alive. That's all I can remember, I'm afraid."

The next awful silence was broken by Gold himself. He suggested she lie down, stretch out. Perhaps a more relaxed posture would trigger her memory. Or she might even fall asleep and deliver a fresh dream for them right on the spot. He helped her stand up. Her legs were wobbly and she was overcome by a great rush of dizziness. She grabbed Gold's sleeve, stretching the knit fabric, and leaned heavily against him. "Are you all right now?" Gold asked after a while. Rose nodded. He lifted the lid off the box she had been using as a bench and helped her climb inside. It was quite narrow in there, making it rather difficult for her to stretch out on her back. Even on her side the walls of the box pushed against her, stuffing her in distressingly. Her left hip stuck out like a sea mammal's hump. Gold opened his own box and stepped in. However, he remained in a sitting position in order to keep an alert eye on the progress of his patient.

It was tight in that box, surely, but it held you after all. Rose soon seemed to be asleep. The balls of her eyes were rolling wildly under the lids. Gold took note of this. He was encouraged. It meant she had moved into the territory of dreams. He lit a pipe and puffed confidently. Soon he would awaken her. Even if he startled her and lost the dream as a result, the habit of nabbing a dream must at some time be implanted. It would be a worthwhile investment, yielding future profits. But before he could take a step toward carrying out his plan, Rose's head was bobbing up and down. She was screaming in terror, "Get me out of here! Help me, help me! Get me out of here!" She had somehow turned over and was now lying supine. Gold jumped out of his box and drew near. He patted her shoulder reassuringly. "It's all right, Mrs. Lieb, you've just been to a nightmare. Tell me about it." He rested his pad on his knee and aimed his pen.

"I feel like I'm dead, Doctor. I feel like I'm in my grave. These walls are pushing into me. Help me out of here, please!"

"Let's have the dream first. This will be a good lesson in trapping the dreams."

"I'm begging you, Doctor. I'm going to suffocate. My breath is being squeezed right out of my body!"

"Now, now, Mrs. Lieb, you see I am right here by your side. What have you got to be afraid of?"

Rose recognized a stubborn man. She understood how hopeless her circumstance was. She felt the terror expanding in her again. She racked her brain for a dream. "I dreamed I was being born," she said, panting heavily. "I was struggling to push myself out, but my mother kept stuffing me back in. Is that good?"

"Not bad. What else?"

"Nothing much. Well, she stuffed me back in and I kept getting smaller and smaller."

"Yes. Then what?"

"Then what? Then I wanted out, and I tried to get out, believe me, but I kept growing larger and larger. That's all I can remember."

"All right. It reminds me of other dreams I've heard before, but it will have to do for a start." Gold was writing rapidly, crackling page after page as he flipped them over. He finished and put his pad down. "I would say it's about average for a first shot. We'll do better next time. Still, it gives me some clues. The outline of the map is coming faintly, faintly into view on the screen. Now, Mrs. Lieb, why don't you climb out of there? The session is over."

"But, Dr. Gold, it's what I've been try'ng to tell you. I'm stuck! I can't get out of here myself."

Gold extended his hand. Rose seized it hungrily. He pulled, and was surprised to find himself dragging the box toward himself with Rose still inside. He examined the situation. Her shoulders were the cause of the problem. They were wedged in tightly. Carefully he succeeded in freeing one. But as soon as he let go to grab her hand and pull her upright, it swung right back into its groove and had to be extricated again. "Mrs. Lieb, you're not trying hard enough," Gold complained, "you're not cooperating. You can't expect to be pulled out without any effort on your part. You have to do something for yourself, too. Now wiggle those shoulders and try to get them loose."

"I can't any more, I just can't," Rose cried. "It's tearing the skin off my back. I'm just going to die."

"Wait here," said Gold.

He disappeared for an eternity. When he returned, Mara and Sudah were with him. Gold took her right hand, the children her left, and they pulled. They managed, in fact, to lift Rose to her feet. The only trouble was, she was still in her box, like a turtle in its shell. She stared at them pop-eyed, like a big mama doll that opens its eyes only because it's been set upright. They let her down slowly, but their laughter so enfeebled them they could not hold fast, and they dropped Rose in her box before the upper part had touched the floor. There was a muted thump. To Rose it seemed as if her organs had snapped loose and were tossing chaotically about inside her. The three of them sat down on Gold's box, waiting for the savage laughter to subside. Sudah was the first to regain his composure. "I have idea," he announced. He assigned to Gold the task of holding the box down. "Put on all your might," he ordered. Meanwhile, he and Mara each took hold of a hand and pulled. In a minute Rose was free. The powder on her cheeks was caked with tracks of perspiration. Mara hugged her mother and battled to murmur some comforting words, but her body was still pumping up the laughter and it was impossible.

It was one of the most humiliating experiences of Rose's career. She shuddered whenever she thought of it. A screech would emerge from the depths of her being, surprising the silence around her. It was as if she were trying to drown out even the inward retelling of that day. For weeks after, the sides of her body were black and blue and raw. She refused to discuss her adventure with Leon. And naturally, she never went back to Gold. She could not even abide hearing his name mentioned. But Rashi was insistent that she put herself in the care of a psychiatrist. "When things get heavy you're going to start tossing in those pills like popcorn. You'd better make arrangements now," said Rashi.

So Rose began to see Hermann Weisz, a psychiatrist of Hungarian descent, a former professor of Victor Asher's at medical school. But even Victor could not obtain an appointment for his mother-in-law, so busy a practitioner was Weisz. It required the intercession of Leon Lieb himself to convince

Weisz to set aside twenty minutes twice a week for Rose, from six-forty to seven o'clock in the morning. "Ve are doing you ze biggest favor, dah-ling," said Madame Yolanda Weisz, Dr. Weisz's wife and nurse. A heavy woman with artificial blond hair and an extra skin of cosmetics, Yolanda had been a pedicurist in Budapest. A bright-orange sign used to swing from her parlor window and advertise it to the boulevard below: PEDICURE YOLANDA. When, for one reason or another, Hermann could not keep an appointment, Yolanda would sit in for him. She would even write the prescriptions for medication. "Act noh-mal!" she would scream at the patient, "ztop vhi-ning!" The truth was, Yolanda Weisz considered all mental patients malingerers and all mental illness a fraud. For Rose's sessions with him, Dr. Weisz would appear in his pajamas, bathrobe, and slippers. He would sip out of a mug of coffee in the saucer of his palm. He wore a gold ring, set with a large diamond cut in the old European fashion, on his upturned pinky. He was a natural aristocrat. In the patients' bathroom he had placed over the toilet bowl an upholstered chair with scrolled mahogany arms and a large hole cut through the cushion of the seat. He was a talking psychiatrist, which relieved Rose immensely. He did not dispossess Rose of her pills, nor did he force her to degrade herself for a refill. "Ve vill maintain you, Rosa," said Dr. Weisz. Accordingly, once a week, at the end of the session, he would shuffle over to the desk and scribble a prescription in what was probably Hungarian for the coming week, which he would hand over to Rose with a gentlemanly bow of the head. They chatted amiably. Rose avoided the topic of Leon's entanglements. She talked almost exclusively about Sudah and Mara, and the frictions that resulted from their presence in her household. This subject inspired Dr. Weisz to talk about art, to which he was devoted. He was at that time engaged in tearing down the walls to an adjacent apartment and remodeling it to house his growing collection. As she left Weisz's apartment,

Rose often saw the first of the workers trudging up, hauling equipment, the imprint of the pillow still on his face. There was nothing Dr. Weisz loved more than discovering a promising young artist. He liked to think of himself as both patron and crafty investor. He demanded from Rose a guarantee that, at the appropriate time, he would be the first to view Sudah's work.

As for Mara and Sudah, quite unabashed they returned to Joe Gold's in the early evening of the day after Rose got herself jammed in the coffin there. The door was unlocked, as usual, and at the usual time Joe beckoned to them to join the procession into the bedroom. People drifted behind their drinks from room to room, and even Mara could not fault anyone for casting, or seeming to cast, a mocking glance into her space. So the story of her fat mother's embarrassment had not become common coinage, to be passed from hand to hand and rubbed over for a moment of cheap glory. Gold continued to take his post-coital conversations with them—it was a habit by now, like brandy after dinner—but no hint of that unwanted moment of shared familial intimacy stained their talk. And as the days passed and it became clear that Rose would never return, the subject became truly prohibited, for now it was not only a matter of the woman's ridiculousness but of Gold's professional failure as well. Once again Mara was a phenomenon, without a family to explain and predict her, only this mysterious, rootless man at her side.

More and more now, their bedroom discussions focused on the topic of Joe's apartment, how best to do it. Mara and Sudah flung out a dazzling stream of ideas. Joe, who did not care a fig for things but prized ambience above all, declared his faith in their taste. "You know me, you know my style," he said. They nodded seriously. "If you find something right, buy it," said Joe. The antique dealers quickly overcame their instinctive distrust of this disreputable-looking pair and pocketed their checks with glee. Rose informed Leon that the children were up and on their way at an earlier hour. "To make the stores," she said, "for their job." Dr. Weisz admitted that these developments appeared on the surface to be symptoms of progress, "but do not ever trust za artist," he warned. He had had a few maddening disappointments in his time but still found it difficult to restrain himself from indulging that charming unreliability which he considered so alluring and vital in the artistic personality.

They genuinely loved to shop. And now, with the financial burden resting safely on Gold's shoulders, it was pure pleasure. At first they bought haphazardly, single items that appealed to them, without any concern for the total decorative scheme, which had yet to be devised: a bamboo desk with a wonderful array of secret cubbyholes, and without one of its legs. An old wicker rocking chair, slashed at the seat. An enormous armoire painted with a thick coat of glossy aqua, which they intended to strip down to the soft yellow oak underneath. An antique rattan chaise longue with a wrought-iron frame that needed some hardware to correct its tendency to collapse whenever a person attempted to lounge on it. A daguerreotype of a family posing stiffly in front of a house that was unique in its many narrow horizontal windows, which resembled slitted, judging eyes. A century-old fainting couch, still with its original bouquet-of-roses upholstery, that, with any change in the pressure on it, gave out discomfiting noises of armies of little legs scurrying frantically about deep inside in search of safe new niches. Sudah took one look at this couch and commented, "For the sicks. Better than coffin, no?" As a perch for Gold himself they found an old piano stool that, screeching madly, could be spun up to great heights or flat down almost to the floor, as the situation warranted. When each of these things arrived at Gold's apartment, Mara would set it in a particular way in a particular spot in one of the rooms, take a few paces backward, and with her hands on her hips and her tongue sticking out between her teeth (a mannerism she had picked up from Sudah), she would stare at it a long time, shaking her head disapprovingly from side to side. Then she would drag it to another corner and try it out there. Many hours were consumed in this way. Seldom was she satisfied. Sudah would occasionally collaborate with her in this enterprise, especially when the object in question was a heavy one, such as the couch. And sometimes he would squat down next to one of their purchases, snap open his brown leather pouch with its gleaming miniature tools, and slowly begin the work of restoration.

It soon became apparent that an overall plan was needed, a motif, a theme, something to draw together the disparate objects that were accumulating in each of the rooms. The absence of such a plan was what made everything they bought seem so isolated, so jarring, so shabby. They decided to devote themselves first to Gold's bedroom. It already contained his large round bed and a narrow full-length mirror. The aqua armoire, which they had vaguely intended for this room, was moved elsewhere almost at once. It disrupted the impact utterly, there was no denying it. The round bed standing alone in the center of an empty room was striking, very effective indeed. What was needed was some device to reinforce this bold effect.

One idle night they developed a scheme for the bedroom and presented it to Gold. He approved heartily. His faith in their talent had begun to suffer when the furniture first appeared. There were many nasty comments from the regulars. Chris Hill remarked that he, for one, preferred the necrophiliac's leavings. But this new plan was brilliant. Gold was completely reassured. The idea was to build two tiers of banquettes around the room, against all four walls, with space for storage underneath so that no other furniture would be needed. These banquettes would resemble the stands in a stadium. The bed would represent the center of the arena, toward which all eyes would naturally turn. The banquettes, walls, and floors would be entirely covered with the same substance—some material still to be chosen—and a round mirror, corresponding in size and position exactly to the bed below it, would be affixed to the center of the ceiling. Without delay Gold hired a carpenter to build the banquettes. While this work was going on, Sudah and Mara prowled the art galleries and came back with a group of life-sized plaster and metal figures—a family consisting of a stern-looking father with a mustache and suspenders, his bony, tense wife, their freckled child dragging a runt of a pup, and two other statues, the first bearing a strong resemblance to the pamphleteer Karl Marx, and the other to the physician Sigmund Freud. They propped these sculptures on the banquettes, one here, another there, like spectators at an event.

Gold was so excited by this project and by the way it was shaping up that he took the time to choose the covering material himself. Sudah and Mara presented a series of possibilities for his consideration. He rejected cork, burlap, grass cloth, suede, leather, little mirror squares, human hair, aluminum foil, feathers, wood paneling, stone, shells, and a variety of fabrics and carpeting. What he selected in the end was a long-haired fur of a lesser animal, in a deep shade of brown. It stirred him enormously. He insisted on having it, despite the warning that it might attract maggots and flies, that it was susceptible to damage by moths, and that it already emitted a mild organic stink which was likely only to intensify. It was also extremely expensive, and for this reason, seeing how attached Gold had become to it, Sudah and Mara offered to save him the cost of hiring a professional to lay it. "We'll stick it on for you," said Mara. Gold did not know how to express his appreciation.

The fur arrived in heavy rolls, which two sweating truckmen dropped in the corner of the bedroom, groaning with relief to be liberated from the embrace of these dead monkeys. Sudah unrolled each one, inspecting the goods carefully before paying and dismissing the men. All the cutting and piecing was done by Sudah. Mara did not possess the confidence to undertake this delicate job, so overawed was she by the preciousness of the stuff. However, she shared fully in the work of gluing the fur, first along the corners of the ceiling, which would not contain the mirror, then over the walls, the banquettes, and last across the floor. She was also given the task of stitching together two large semicircular pieces to serve as a spread for the bed. They kept the windows wide open as they worked. One night Mrs. Gold rushed in screaming that everyone's nose was frozen stiff and would drop off any minute like an icicle. It was the end of a bitter winter. They closed the windows, but the smell of the fur mixed with the glue was suffocating. They began to burn little sticks of incense in brass holders.

The bedroom was completely given over to them during the period that they were doing this work. They entered and closed the door. No one disturbed them. Gold found this spell of celibacy thoroughly refreshing; it gave him another reason to be grateful to them. Sudah was a very slow, painstaking craftsman. Their method was to work for a while, then to lie down on the bed and gaze critically at what they had just accomplished. They would share a pipe of hashish. A feeling of extreme peace and competence would enclose them. They would embrace with passion. Pretty soon they would be making exquisite love, in which each would all at once become transfixed by some detail of the other's body, Sudah by the two dimples at the base of Mara's back, for example, just above where her buttocks swelled out, or Mara by the map of blue rivulets on his poor pulsing neck. Occasionally they would invite someone into bed with them, one of the silent spectators, the father, the kid, Karl, or whoever suited their mood that night. Then they would fall asleep, very contented.

She was dreaming that Reb Anschel Frankel walked her in her sleep to the bathroom and sat her down on the toilet. He was her babysitter that night while her parents were away at some political function. Although she was already a girl of five years, she still wet her bed; Reb Anschel was only carrying out her mother's orders to prevent such an accident. All at once, sitting there on the toilet, she opened her eyes, and instead of finding Reb Anschel waiting there alone for her to finish, she saw everyone she knew—her mother, her father, her brother and sister with their spouses and children, Sadie Stern, Sudah and his parents, Luke Alfasi, his mother Luba, Fanny Gottlieb, Dora Popper, Julius Fleischer, Manny Fish, Mark Bavli, Cookie Kalb, Joe Gold—everyone. They were laughing and chattering in a bright circle around her, having a gay party as she sat there, mortified, her urine tinkling above the din, drop by drop, into the bowl. Her heart began to pound brutally. She grabbed Dr. Freud, who happened to be at her side that night. He was totally drenched. My God, have I peed on him? she thought. She feared the worst. She sat straight up in bed. It was soaked through and through. Joe Gold was standing there yelling out orders. People were darting back and forth, dumping buckets of water everywhere. The smell of scorched fur, like singed chicken feathers, fouled the air. Chris Hill was ramming the windows open to let out the black smoke. The bed was utterly ruined. Mrs. Gold was running around, waving their hashish pipe in the air. She was screaming hysterically. "They were *shmucking!* They were *shmucking* in my bed, the idiots! I'm gonna kill them! I'm gonna wring their necks! I'm gonna grind them to bits!" One of Gold's women was obliged to slap the old lady four times, twice on each cheek, to calm her down. Sudah dragged Mara to a corner. He dried her and dressed her efficiently. He found her glasses and mounted them on her face. They were dusted with a gray powder. He pulled her by the hand. "Let's go," he said. Right by the door he noticed their pipe, which Mrs. Gold in her frenzy had let fall. He picked it up and wiped it lovingly, for it had been with him since he was twelve. He slid it into his chopstick pouch. Their departure went unnoticed in the confusion. They ran down the steps, laughing wildly. In the quiet and cold of the early-morning streets, they walked with their arms around each other's waist. They had been saved, redeemed, liberated. They had not felt so happy in a long time. Mara's teeth were clacking uncontrollably, she was shivering at her core. Sudah hugged her. "We could been killed!" he said to her. "They give damn only for spider fur and asshole bed!"

Rose now noticed that Sudah and Mara no longer were in such haste to dispose of the subject she raised for discussion at the table. They took their time with her now, offering detailed advice on what to eat and how to eat, and, in general, on how to conduct oneself for a life of health and peace-of-mind. They announced that they had become vegetarians. They fixed elaborate salads for her, scooping globs of yogurt on top, and, over that, a sprinkling of granola. "I've never tasted canary seed before," said Rose, as she crunched her food. "Are you sure it's kosher?" "Eat slower, Mommy," Mara said. "Take smaller spoonfuls. Don't talk with food in your mouth. Don't make sounds when you eat. Chew carefully." More and more often now they would return to their room after their meal instead of heading straight out to their unwholesome haunts. They closed their door, sometimes even receiving visitors behind it. But every corner of the house was invaded by the noises from their machines—their record player, their radio, their television—and by the smells of the alien things they burned. Leon felt as if he were being besieged. Rose had to restrain him. "It was better when they were gone all night," he cried.

One afternoon, after Sudah had completed a description of the kind of shoe Rose should wear to raise her self-esteem, even going so far as to sketch his meaning on a napkin (which Rose saved for a few days, figuring it might have some future worth, and then threw out with the trash, having forgotten why she kept it in the first place), Rose cleared her throat and said, "I've been noticing some cockroaches around the house lately." Her words did not seem to impress them. "We never used to have cockroaches," Rose went on, a bit more assertively. Mara and Sudah were conferring over a pot. Mara was stirring, Sudah was sampling. "It certainly takes you a long time to cook your food," Rose complained. "By the time it's ready you've probably already lost your appetite. What's that you're pouring in now? How many vitamins does a person need, anyhow? Who wants to be so healthy? Haven't you heard me at all? I said there were cockroaches in the house."

"You shouldn't talk about cockroaches while we're preparing food," said Mara.

Rose did not really want to talk about cockroaches, in fact. She wanted to talk about why they were no longer going to Gold's, but that subject stuck in her throat. "Where do you think they're coming from, huh?" she persisted. "The roaches, I mean."

Mara stared at her innocently. Rose jerked her shoulder ever so slightly in the direction of their room, but could not bring herself to pronounce the undisputed source of the filthy bug. She sighed. "Well," she said, resigned, "when you see one, do me a favor, please, and kill it."

Sudah turned to face her, a wooden spoon in his hand. He was shaking his head. He seemed disappointed in Rose. "I would not ever kill a cockaroach," he said. Mara gave Rose a swift look of warning. Rose held her tongue. Sudah went back to mincing his ninth garlic clove and sprinkling it into the zucchini soup. Garlic brought good health, abundant hair, and calm, he maintained. Now Rose gathered up her courage and quickly, as if it were necessary to get it all out at once, she inquired about their friend, the quack, what's his name? Her face turned scarlet with the memory. Why were they no longer working for him? "You mean Joe Gold?" said Mara. Rose could not answer. Sudah explained that it was because of an aesthetic conflict. They simply could not compromise their artistic standards to suit Gold. "He is caveman!" Sudah declared.

"Tell her the real reason," said Mara.

Sudah looked at Mara in surprise. He shrugged. "Okay," he said, "it's because we burn his bed."

"Burn his bed? What do you mean, burn his bed?"

"It's just an expression, Mommy, an idiom, you know, 'to burn one's bed.' It means we forced him to re-evaluate his basic philosophy. He was so goddamn pompous and smug! But the real reason we quit is because Sudah needs to begin working on his painting at once."

It sometimes happens this way with creative people, Mara told Rose. A thing grabs hold of them and won't let go. Sudah had long had this idea in mind. They were hoping it could wait until they found the loft. Well, it turns out it can't. It's like being pregnant. When the baby is ready to be born, it just pushes itself out. It's not going to wait until you're high on the delivery table, white sheets and sterile instruments all around you.

"Yes, that's how Herzl was born," Rose said, "in the elevator. It was a mess!"

Mara conceded that it probably would be a big mess. Nevertheless, the living room and the dining room, which ran into each other, made up the only area large enough to accommodate the project Sudah had in mind.

Rose had many personal misgivings about the scheme. The prospect of her apartment in upheaval truly frightened her. She liked to retire to a hotel or to one of Leon's homes when the painting of her walls and the polishing of her floors could be put off no longer. Moreover, she saw no way to win her husband over to this crazy idea. But in the end she said she would present their proposal to Leon. His decision would prevail.

Leon looked at her in a glazed way. *"Nu,* and maybe they would also like to shave off the hair from my balls and use it for a paintbrush?" Rose could sense that he felt thoroughly trod upon. She took this as her answer, flicked out her light, and turned on her side in search of sleep. "All right," said Leon, "it's worth it just to see what he can do, the little *vantz.*"

Once again they went shopping. Sudah actually had two projects in mind, one a painting and the other a sculpture. They decided to buy materials for both. The painting, as Sudah conceived it, would be huge. It would consist of six canvases nailed together, each five feet by three feet in size. The predominant color would be gray. A certain commercial paint named Battleship Gray struck Sudah as exactly right. Mara laughed, calling it a strange choice for a pacifist. (It was all right for her to call him a pacifist in jest, but for Rose to do so in response to his declaration about the cockroaches would have been an intolerable liberty.) They bought twenty-four gallons. The proportions of the sculpture were to be less monumental, though certainly not small. Sudah selected a magnificent block of brown marble, and just in case he spoiled it by some mischance, he bought some back-up chunks as well.

All the furniture in the living room and the dining room was pushed against the walls. The Persian rugs were rolled up. Sheets were hung across the gold satin drapes. It was a dreadful sight. Rose carefully sidestepped these rooms, and even avoided looking into them as she passed by in the hall. Sudah covered the oak parquet floors with old newspapers. When all the preparations were completed, he stationed himself with his hands on his hips in the center of the transformed rooms and waited for it all to begin. He walked over to the window. He was very high up. The apartment was on the sixth story.

Shrunken people were dashing about to and fro on the sidewalk, their legs jerking stiffly out in front of them. Where were
they running? What could they have to do that was so important? They were utterly without consequence. He looked at the
door. Beyond it was the elevator, which would bear him down
like an object and spit him out on the sidewalk. He sat down
on the layer of newspapers. Soon he was crawling about on his
hands and knees. With his felt pen he was drawing mustaches,
eyeglasses, genitalia, and thick prison bars on the smorgasbord
of news faces lying there, ready to be devoured. He spent a long
time over the face of his father-in-law, accenting the eyes,
rouging the cheeks and lips, devising an elaborate hair style,
carefully transforming Leon into a painted woman.

While Sudah worked, Mara spent most of her time in their
room, her head resting on the keys of the old typewriter she
had brought with her from the Parklawn. She rose and stared
at herself in the mirror. Her forehead was carved with circlets.
She could discern the letters engraved there: F G H. Combine
them in infinite ways and, behold, words. Then sentences.
They were cutting their way into her. She wanted to write
again but dreaded doing so in her father's house, where nothing
of her own belonged to her. The memory of her father exposing
her manuscript still made her soul cringe. Nothing rendered
you more pathetic than to witness your possessions in the cold
hands of a stranger. Nevertheless, she found herself beginning
again. She reasoned as the work proceeded that this time was
different. She was married now. Her father would not enter her
room this time, clotted as it was with the stuff of her sexual
existence; it would embarrass and hurt him to do so far more
than it would her.

### How I Lost My Virginity: My Bourgeois Influence

I took her along with me that night. I wanted her to see for herself
how I scorned her. I wanted to shove it straight in her puss. Her name

is Pearl. I call her my bourgeois influence. I no longer see her but she visits me still in my dreams. I believe she knows this, comes clackety-clacking intentionally into my dreams in her white high-heel pumps. Her hair is always greasy the day before she washes and sets it. In my dream she still sits primly at the table for unmarried girls in the reception hall of one of our friends' weddings. She purses her lips and unfolds the linen napkin, smoothing it over her lap. With a cool eye she takes in the centerpiece. I know what she is thinking. The accessories at her wedding will be in better taste.

She is a sensitive girl. She puts her head down on the desk and sobs when the teacher scolds her. She is always correct. I rely on her. We are eight years old and best friends. We ask each other to list in order the ones in our class we like best. I tell her that of course I love her best, then Vivian, then Ellen, then so-and-so. When her turn arrives she bests me. She waits patiently to savor her triumph. She announces that first of all she likes Kenneth, then me. I accept it. Certainly a boy must be first. All the girls have declared their adoration of Kenneth. Kenneth strode out of his mother's womb carrying an attaché case. I once offered him an answer to copy off my paper during a test. He rejected me outright. Actually, the boy I loved was Attila. Attila told me plainly that there was no God. It was deliciously terrifying. He once grabbed the bow at my waist and pushed me down on the ice. My dress was torn. My face was bloodied. Pearl took my hand and dragged me to the teacher. "We're going to fix those boys," she said. My wounds in the mirror dazzled me. I wore them ecstatically, like medals, like jewels.

We compared fathers. Hers was very refined. Two walls of his study were lined with the thin spines of records—classical music. Unfortunately, he had no phonograph. My father belched at the table. He mixed together all the food on his plate—the meat, the vegetables, the potatoes—into a muddy mush, booming, "It all comes out together in the end, anyway!" Her father was civilized. I always sensed that mine was an outlaw.

When the time came for us to concern ourselves with men, she grew very secretive. She was superstitious, I think. She picked carefully, moderately accomplished men, intelligent, not too flashy, good prospects, well-zipped, never committing herself to them wholly. I knew in the end she would make a disastrous mistake. I was right. She married a man with her father's name. Even the surname was the same. It was a coincidence. In the dark of their bed her voice murmured the name over and over.

As for myself, I took Lenny. I was not in the least bit attracted to him. Nor he to me. Why, then, did I choose him? Why did he choose me? A wise man answers the first question first, the last last. I am a woman. He chose me because I pursued him. The girls he admired were always tall, with pimples for breasts, hips as sharp as blades, and the greater portion of their body wasted in superfluous leg. Like boys, actually. I am of average height with full breasts and hips, and the plump legs that men who like women cannot resist. Nevertheless, I moved in on him and he succumbed. He was obviously weak enough for my purposes.

He had been a basketball player in high school. Those were his headiest days. He still wore the glossy green and black jacket with the big number 2 on the back, though he was already growing much too flabby for it. They called him the Lion. It was his period of highest personal achievement. Nothing that came before could match it, nothing after ever would. It was the only time in his life that he strained for excellence, and in fact, he succeeded somehow in surpassing his own talents, though he never became truly first-rate. He was not a natural athlete. He was flat-footed. The military rejected him for that reason. Too bad. He would have enjoyed his army days, especially if war had broken out. They might even have exceeded in splendor his brief hour on the basketball court. For a short while, then, he was a small-time hero. My brother admired him. That was important, but it was not the only reason I fixed on him.

To put it quite simply, I had to get myself off the market. Some girls can bear presenting themselves as the merchandise, on display for your inspection, sir, while secretly they are the ones who are doing the shopping all along. Pearl could do that neatly. I could not. Even if I wanted to—or especially because I might have wanted to—I could not. To reveal your wants so openly renders you immensely vulnerable. Better not to want. Besides, I was different. I was not a bourgeois, like Pearl. Still, it was necessary to find a facsimile of a man. So I took Lenny. We acted most improperly in public, like lovers, particularly when we were not. But I was set. I had already found what Pearl was still hunting, but you could never accuse me of being like Pearl. I knew she would disapprove of Lenny and I was glad. I could picture her slitting her eyes and giving him the swift once-over. She would be thinking how she would do better.

Lenny resembled my father in one way only. He was not a frequent bather. But unlike my father, Lenny gave off a bad smell. Sitting beside him one afternoon at a movie, I was sure the clients were tiptoeing out, one by one, because of the humid stench that seemed to rise like steam from his crotch. It nearly made me faint. Afterward I told him that while there was no doubt that his odor was natural and served to fuel my passion, it was not the sort of thing one shared with the world. He thanked me profusely. He appreciated my guidance. He was relying on me to improve him. He began to powder himself with a lilac-scented talc. It made my head swim.

In every other way Lenny and my father were opposites. My father was a strong businessman because of his ability to get what he wanted in an indirect, calculated fashion. He was a strategist. He did not lunge like a fool, blaring out his intentions and thereby alerting his prey. No. Rather, patiently and smoothly, step by step, in novel, devious, and complex ways, he would circle in on his victim. He never had to seize a thing in the end. It and more would invariably be offered to him. This approach is an asset in a lover, too. Lenny did not possess it. "Your father is a crook," Lenny said. "I'm not a phony and a hypocrite like your old man." I agreed wholeheartedly. Lenny was an all-American boy. He was very sincere. Wooing was phony and hypocritical. He would say, "Let's this, let's that, let's fuck." A pig grunting to its sow. But at least there was no doubt about what he was after. He was safe. Safe, that is, within boundaries. As with all weak people, in his breast a sacred niche was lodged wherein the essentially pure and good child he and his mother still considered him to be was worshipped. Dare to trespass on this holy ground and you were in danger. He could turn suddenly into a monster, a primitive, an unpredictable roaring beast. He was not charming, in short. My father, on the other hand, did not think of himself as a child. He knew he was a sinner and an adult. He was a scoundrel, a cynic. He said to me, "Why are you throwing yourself away on that one?" Nevertheless, he fumed at my manner of conducting my relationship with Lenny. "You are not behaving like a respectable girl!" He was referring to our public kissing and pawing, for example, our filthy talk. It was all right for him to be unconventional, borderline. He trusted himself. In me he had no faith whatsoever. Naturally I defied him.

Early on, Lenny had said to me, "We'll get married, of course." This proposal took place over the telephone. It was a black telephone, smudged with fingerprints, and it stood on the night table by my mother's bed. I answered, "Yes, of course." It was my fate. It was understood that my maidenhead was doomed. My language was hot, as if I couldn't wait another minute to be popped. Where to get rid of it was the question. We had no place. Lenny had no car. We were always being chased out of doorways. We would sit clasped together for hours on the stoop of a stranger's house. Before our departure we would stuff my soiled panties into the mail slot of our host. Thank you and goodbye. We were kissing wetly on the subway-station platform near Pearl's house one night, when, to my regret, Kenneth strode by, swinging a briefcase. He nodded briskly. In this way I discovered that I was not invisible, that my choices would constrict me, that I would pay for my flamboyance.

Lenny gave me a packet of condoms to hold on to so that we would be prepared in case the golden opportunity should suddenly present itself. With pleasure he described the comradely leer of the clerk at the store. I stuffed his purchase deep into a shoe and shoved it under my bed. My father came into my room one evening and sat down on the edge. He picked up this shoe and examined it idly. I watched aghast. "What are you doing with my shoe?" I finally asked. My heart was jumping. "Can't I hold my own daughter's shoe?" he said. "When you were a baby I would put your whole foot into my mouth." He set the shoe down on the mattress between us. There was something he wanted to say to me. "I happened to pick up the phone the other day while you were on it with that boyfriend of yours," he began. "You should have hung up immediately," I replied coldly. "Why? It was such an interesting conversation. You know what I heard?" I waited, losing hope. "Nothing!" said my father. "Nothing at all! For five minutes breathing, nothing but breathing!" He dropped the shoe back on the floor. There was a slight thump, then the snap of a foil envelope striking a hard surface. "You can still get out of it," said my father. "You're too young to give up. What are you afraid of? You're not married to him yet."

It became essential to formalize it as quickly as possible. The following clinical steps had already been taken, in rapid succession and in the proper order: hand holding, arm over the shoulder, kissing on the lips, kissing with tongues probing the interior of partner's mouth, hand dangling innocently down, then swooping suddenly to cup the clothed breast, hand slipping into the brassiere and fondling the naked breast, mouth on breast, a period of time in which an above-the-waist holding pattern was sustained, then the crucial descent, finger plunged in cunt. His only previous experiences were with prostitutes and so he was ignorant of the clitoris. I decided to keep that as my own private preserve. He also introduced me to his prick, which was as fierce as the Wizard of Oz. We had reached a dead end. I handed him fifteen dollars and told him to engage a hotel room.

As I have said, he prided himself on a kind of stupid honesty, and so the little assignment I had given him was not at all easy for him to carry out. Three hotels turned him down. The first because he did not carry a suitcase. The second because, in his desire to be a nice guy, he volunteered that he would be using the room only for an hour or so, after which, by all means, rent it to another customer. The third because when the clerk inquired if he would be alone he replied by covering his mouth with his hand and giggling. The fourth was a grimy, run-down place where the rouged attendant behind the desk took his sweaty bills and handed him the key without looking at him once. By the time he called me and whispered the hotel name and room number, I was thoroughly disgusted. Nevertheless, I went dutifully. I was not the kind who would give off lusty signals, like Pearl, then break down in the clutch. My father drove me to the subway because he did not approve of me walking the night streets alone. "What kind of boy is it who doesn't pick up his girl at her home?" he demanded. All fathers are pimps.

In front of me on the train sat a couple, the woman with a freshly waved hairdo and a coy velvet bow, exactly like Pearl's on a date. I stared deeply into the back of her head, wondering whether I should tap her on the fur-collared shoulder specked with dandruff—it would be such an ironic and literary touch. My eyes sought out the roots of each hair for the oily droplets she could never hide from one who was her intimate. What I found instead were small patches of skull-gripping, flesh-colored horsehair mesh. It was a wig.

The first thing Lenny did when I entered the hotel room was to proudly hand me my change. This I promptly returned to him, for I had realized during my heart-stopping ride up the elevator that I had forgotten to bring along the condoms. While he was gone I looked around the room. How bleak and mean it was, my mother would grieve. In the sink was a coiled black hair. The top drawer of the nightstand contained one used, limp prophylactic and a Bible. I opened it up and began reading from the beginning. This was no Garden of Eden. I took the opportunity to undress, hoping to spare myself the anguish of stripping, fig leaf by fig leaf, for his entertainment. One thing I would not do, and that was to satisfy his cruder fantasies.

I was sitting in a chair wrapped up in a yellowed sheet and reading about snakes when Lenny barged back in. Without further ado, he tore off all his clothing. His member stuck out like a towel horse. He asked me to roll on the bag and I did, for all the world like a sausage maker. I rose, ungluing myself from the plastic seat with a smack, contriving to keep at least those parts of myself which I deemed least attractive covered by the sheet. We moved toward the bed. In two minutes the preliminaries were over. A minute later it was all over.

We lay there side by side, each forsaken in the thoughts of the other. His breathing glided soon into a rhythmic pattern, regularly interspersed by low whistles from his nostrils. He was asleep. My head was propped up on the foul pillow. I was staring straight in front of me, directly at the bathroom door. A toilet flushed. It seemed to be ours, so near and familiar was the sound. This was a vile place, this rathole he found, the walls were thinner than skin. It flushed again. A phantom flusher, pipes caked with excrement. I watched the bathroom door open. A man entered our room. In the dark I could barely make out his face. He was wearing a robe of some sort, with a hood.

"Is this your first time?" His voice was low.

I shook my head. "No."

"Come with me." I followed him, forgetting my sheet. The robe was stretched across his buttocks. We walked through the bathroom into the adjacent room. It was lit by a single candle. The walls were covered with pictures of men and women madly loving. All sorts of paraphernalia were strewn everywhere. The air was moist with the smell of open bodies. On the bed a naked woman was reclining. She smiled and tenderly combed the hair of her groin.

He left me and went to her. They began slowly to kiss. I approached the bed. The woman raised her hips and spread her legs gladly. The man descended. He emerged. I watched. I bent over and put out my hand. The woman turned her head and caught my nipple between her white teeth. "She's still a virgin," I could hear him whisper. With his fingers he parted my hair and stroked in the furrow. A great mass was gathering between my legs, hanging pendulous. All of myself seemed to be contracted there. In a moment it would drop to the ground like an overripe fruit they had forgotten to pick. Before my eyes was a sheet of sharp white light and beyond it the edges of calm space. In a moment I would be carried off to there. I would be cut off, lost, unwilling to return. "No," I screamed, "no, no, no, no, no!" I ran out of the room. When Lenny woke up I was already dressed, sitting in the chair, reading about the daughters of man and the sons of God.

There was a smug look on his face. "You seem a bit lighter," he said. He snickered at his own joke. I crossed over to the bed and hung my arms around his neck. His breath was stale. "You should feel proud of yourself," I said.

He grinned like a child who had just avoided punishment because his mischief was so cute. "Every boy deserves at least one virgin," he said coyly.

"You got what you deserve, then." I paused, focusing on him solemnly. "Promise me something." He waited. He sensed it would be a request he would just as soon not hear. "Promise me you won't tell anyone about this," I said.

"You're worried about your reputation? I didn't expect that of you."

"That's ridiculous! I don't give a damn what anyone thinks, and you know it! It's just that this is an intimate matter, something private between you and me. It's holy. You would be defiling it by sharing it with others. You understand that, don't you? I want you to promise you won't tell a soul. Not Eddie, not Mike, and certainly no one from the team. It's not the sort of thing you should boast about. Promise me!"

"Not even my analyst?"

"Oh, well, he's taken a vow of silence, anyway."

Lenny agreed, the poor sucker. He seemed quite forlorn. Just then the toilet flushed. He looked up, alarmed. "We share a bathroom," I explained. "God knows who's in the next room. It could even be a murderer."

Lenny's hands reached down involuntarily to protect his wilted nakedness. "Let's get out of here," he said.

Oh, my Lord, what an awful story! Mara was truly disturbed by it. She stapled the pages together and slipped them under a pile of cast-off clothing by her bed. She would not even show it to Sudah. She fled the room, wanting to be out of its reach. Sudah was at work in the living room, merrily whistling. He was applying broad strokes of the Battleship Gray with a wide housepainter's brush. "How are you doing?" she asked, always anxious in his behalf. He smiled an imp's smile. Darts of paint had stiffened in his beard. "Good, good!" he exclaimed, "I'm slopping him on!" "You mean, 'slapping it on,'" said Mara. "Yah, slopping *it* on."

She left the apartment and began wandering through the streets in tight agitation, expecting something to befall her. She passed a cheap diner. The smell of fried chicken drifted out the door, making the hair in her nostrils stand up. She entered and ordered a portion. The grease spilled down her chin and glued her fingers together. There were still some feathers in the puffy skin. Blood spurted out of the drumstick. She bared her teeth and tore off big chunks, swallowing great unchewed lumps. She considered, as she devoured the rubbery flesh, how with each bite she was defying two men, her kosher father and her vegetarian husband. She bought another helping. She slurped the ketchup off the wax paper. She sucked the fat from her fingers. She was back in the street now. Sloppy tears began to plop down her cheeks. "What's the matter, girlie?" A man in his sixties, with wet stains on his baggy pants, was squeezing her arm. "Nothing, nothing, I'm just looking for someone." She twisted herself free and ran away. A cab drove by. Sudah was in the passenger seat, his white teeth gleaming in his beard. He waved to her. She walked on with rapid, stiff steps, as if she were being pursued. She found her way to Rashi's building. She ran up the stairs.

No, she was not hungry. She told Rashi about the fried

chicken she had just consumed. Rashi said nothing. Mara could sense her sister's disapproval. It was necessary to win her as an ally all over again. How dreary it was! She tried to amuse her with the story of Joe Gold, of how she and Sudah had burned down Gold's bed. It was hilarious. She laughed wretchedly. "Joe's a philistine," she said, "a charlatan. He deserves to fry." Rashi listened grimly. "How long will you go on deceiving everyone?" she demanded at last.

"What do you mean?" said Mara, half hoping for a good fight to distract her from her inward despair.

"You deceive Mommy and Daddy about everything you do. About your work, about religion, about everything!"

"You're the one who made us swear to play at being religious, or have you forgotten so soon, Rashi?"

"Can't you see what's happening?" Rashi cried. "Don't you understand what a mess Daddy's in? They're chipping away at him, bit by bit. Soon there'll be nothing left. They're out to break his bones. You live under the same roof, yet you have absolutely no feeling for him, no sympathy whatsoever."

Mara was standing up. "How can you accuse me of deception, Rashi? You—you and Victor—you're the deceivers, the frauds, putting up a false front for them that you are the model children they worked to raise when actually you're no more religious than Sudah and I. You're cowards, afraid to disappoint. Sudah and I are not deceiving anyone. They know the truth about us. They're deceiving themselves. They're self-deceivers, petty self-deceivers."

"It's just no use talking to you," said Rashi. "You simply don't consider Daddy's problems serious or real. If he's lucky enough to be sent to jail, maybe then you'll feel something for him."

The two women fell silent. The small space between them had soured. Each was girding herself for a deadly assault from the other, yet each knew she would never be the one to plunge into her sister's weaknesses, which now lay more pitiful and exposed than ever. Mara went home. When she awoke the next afternoon, Sudah was no longer in bed beside her. Her father was standing over her, a colossal presence. Too much sleep had left her groggy. She had a headache. She needed her glasses. He seemed to be swaying up there, looking as if he were about to keel over. "Get out of here, Daddy!" Mara whispered, "I'm not dressed." The gases of undigested fried chicken filled her mouth. She groped for her quilt, drawing it up to her chin.

"I'm not looking at you, Mara. I'm a busy man. I'm here to say something to you."

"Where's Sudah?"

"He was *potchking* with his paint in the living room, like you and Herzl used to *potchke* with your *kocky* when you were babies. Now he's gone out, God knows where."

"Get out, Daddy. This is the room I sleep in with my husband."

"Once, in the distant past, this was a room. Now it's a pigsty." He bent down and scooped up an armful of junk from the floor. Mara saw the pages of her manuscript squashed against his chest. Oh, God, not again! Her heart sank. Leon began to pile things on top of her, item by item, as if he would bury her under her debris. "Dirty *gatchkes!*" he said. Down came a pair of stained underpants. "Poison!" Cigarette butts rained on top of her. "A present for the cockroaches!" A hard bagel and a rust-colored apple core bounced on her belly. "A fancy shroud, phooey!" Leon held his nose as he gingerly let drop from between the tips of his two fingers Sudah's long embroidered vest, which had been his unchanging, unlaundered uniform for months. Now Leon was fanning himself with her manuscript. "What can this be? Wait! Don't tell me, please! Another big production from the brain of Mara Lieb, in which, for your passing entertainment, ladies and gentlemen, she once again betrays everyone who ever did her a kindness! Well, never mind, it can't hurt a fly." And he sent the pages fluttering like slaps across Mara's face. They came to rest on her bare shoulder. And so it went, one despised object after another, until nothing remained in his hand but a strange, bulky package tied up with string. "Do you recognize this?" Leon inquired. Mara did not. "Look again."

"Stop playing games with me, Daddy."

"Oh, I see, so now I'm the one who's playing games. You don't seem to realize that I'm fighting for my life now, and for the life of my family, of which, by the way, you were at one time a member in good standing. I need every ounce of my strength for this struggle. Yet I'm forced to waste my precious time with your nonsense. I made a bargain with you, Mara. I have lived up to my end one hundred percent. I have even done more than my share. I have allowed that faker you married to turn my living room into a dump!"

"I don't know anything about your business affairs, Daddy. All I know is, it's wrong for a father to write a contract with his daughter. All my life you've been making deals with me. They don't mean a thing."

"Listen to me, Mara, you have not kept your word!" Leon pounded the package he was still clutching. "Do you see this? Do you know what it is?"

"I don't know and I don't care." She shrugged, and the corner of one of her manuscript pages sliced painfully into her neck. Her finger found the trickle of blood and carried it to her mouth.

"Take a guess; go on, guess." Leon would not let go.

Mara sighed. "Okay, Daddy. It's a time bomb."

"Ha! 'A time bomb,' she says. Maybe that's what it is, in a way. And now it's about to go off. A religious wife would have no trouble recognizing this. It's your husband's *tefilin* bag."

"Really? Sudah's *tefilin* bag? Why is it all tied up?"

" 'Why is it all tied up?' she asks. I'll tell you why. It's tied up, my dear, because I tied it up! One week ago today I tied it up. It hasn't been untied since!"

The black truth began to loom before Mara's eyes. She sat straight up in bed, endeavoring to keep her breasts covered. She wished she were dressed, some scanty protection, at least, from this attack. "How low, Daddy! How mean and untrusting!"

"What are you talking about, Mara? I trusted him. He promised to put them on every morning and mumble a word or two to his God. I trusted him and he broke his promise."

Mara was shaking her head in disbelief. "Nothing he did could ever be as ugly as your way of finding it out. You will stop at nothing. I can see now why they're out to get you."

Leon's open palm shot out. It struck her on the cheek. The *tefilin* fell on her chest like a rock. She sat there, her face no longer her own. Her father's eyes looked like a disenchanted child's. He was crying. She worried about him now as she had never done before in her life. She could see death crouching in him. He was struggling to say something. It was hopeless. He let her watch the tears drop. She could not kiss him now, the poor man, because she was naked.

Some time later a meeting of the innermost circle was being held in the Lieb apartment. The participants naturally included Leon and Herzl Lieb, Reb Anschel Frankel, Max Brody, Sadie Stern, and the man whom Mara instantly recognized as the stranger she had witnessed escorting Murray Levine out of the building that dawn she and Sudah had returned early from Gold's. At the time she had experienced a pang of interest in this man. The thought had struck her that this was precisely the sort of son-in-law her parents would have debased themselves to acquire—orthodox yet modern, clearly a professional, handsome but not gaudy, with a good appetite for food and a sound instinct for when to dissipate his powers on a woman and when to harness them in pursuit of matters serious and manly. It was something about the way such men could despise you that had always drawn Mara to this type. Fortunately, her intelligence and sense of self-preservation warned her away. Besides, this sort was never naturally attracted to her. She was too outrageous. He was dressed in expensive jeans for the meeting this evening, and on his head he wore a small yarmulka with his Hebrew name skillfully worked in, crocheted for him by some woman, his wife perhaps. He was vain, that was obvious. His name was Paul Ashkenazi, a lawyer. Herzl described him this way: "Ashkenazi's tops, first class. What a head!" Within their circle, Paul Ashkenazi, the descendant of an honored line of rabbis and scholars, was hailed as one who had distinguished himself extraordinarily in the strangers' territory, who roamed at will there and was welcome, but who never forsook his source, returning daily for the nourishment of body and spirit. In fact, one of his specialties had become the defense of persons from his own background who had been victimized because of their stubborn piety in a secular world. Often he undertook such cases for nothing. With Leon Lieb, of course, it would not be necessary to forfeit the fee.

Everyone who had agreed to attend this meeting was now present. Only one other person had been invited and he had refused, bitterly refused, to participate. This was Victor Asher. Leon Lieb had called him personally. "Do yourself a favor," Leon had pleaded. "I'm not begging you to come for my sake but for your own!" But Victor could hardly reply, the rage was starting to boil up in him afresh. Over and over again, until he himself could no longer be certain even of his own innocence, for weeks and months now he had been forced to explain to probers from the government and the press how it had happened that his name, in the role of authorizing physician, had come to be affixed to certain requests for reimbursement from the government of great sums of money spent on the medical care of patients in his father-in-law's nursing homes. "I don't know, I just don't know," he had claimed at first, his eyes still bewildered. "I never okayed such a thing. I never even knew my name was there until you guys started telling me about it." It sounded so unconvincing. "How could you do this to me?" Victor cried out to Leon over the phone. Leon cleared his throat. "I'm telling you for the hundredth time, Victor, it wasn't me! It was my accountant, Levine. I didn't even know what was going on. I trusted him, that's all. In America they tell you a good executive delegates responsibilities. *Nu*, so I delegated. My mistake, God knows I'm paying for it, too. How can you even think I would agree to such a crazy idea? Would I ever risk damaging my own daughter? What's the matter with you, Victor? If I needed some doctors' signatures to falsify papers, I could buy them a dime a dozen. I don't take chances with my children, believe me. I have told them that you knew nothing about this, just like I knew nothing about it. It's all Levine's fault. This whole mess. Look, Victor, whether you like it or not, your name is involved. For your own benefit, come to this strategy meeting. I want you to meet Paul Ashkenazi." But Victor replied that the entire affair was a curse and an affliction. He would not enter their cabals. He would have nothing more to do with them.

They sat there awkwardly in a circle on some mismatched chairs Leon had pulled out from under the sheets Sudah had spread to protect the furniture. There was no table behind which they could conceal the vulnerable parts of their bodies. A yellow pad and pencil rested on the wrinkles in Sadie's lap. Paul Ashkenazi was pacing impatiently back and forth, puffing on a thin cigar. Each time he endeavored to begin, Reb Anschel Frankel would halt him with a broad raised palm. Herzl was whispering passionately into his father's ear, his mouth brushing the soft lobe, unloading into the dark hole where a tuft of gray hair sprouted. Every so often the father and son would pause, straighten up, and turn to send chilling wordless messages to the corner of the room where Sudah was engrossed in the application of a thin stripe of yellow paint diagonally across one of the gray canvases. Sudah was too busy to pay them any attention at all. This unusual situation frustrated Ashkenazi immensely. Angrily he flicked his ashes into the only available receptacle, which turned out to be the open upturned mouth of a marble chick, but a chick of such large and rough proportions that it seemed monstrous and insatiable. It was Sudah's half-finished sculpture. Max Brody had taken one look at it and cried out, "What is this, Leon? Idol worship in your house, God forbid?"

At last Leon stated the problem. He spoke in Yiddish, a language unknown to an Oriental Jew such as Sudah. Unfortunately, the younger generation of Western Jews, which included Herzl Lieb and Paul Ashkenazi, could barely understand it either. Leon explained that Herzl was not willing to commence their discussion within earshot of Sudah. Absolutely not. The fact was, plain and simple, that Herzl did not trust his own brother-in-law. A sad state of affairs within a family, but no one is perfect. Leon went even further and declared that Herzl suspected it was none other than Sudah himself who had sabotaged their Rosh Hashana demonstration by phoning in the fake bomb threat. Herzl strained to pick out the familiar words. He settled, instead, for nodding sorrowfully at his father's emphases. When Leon completed his statement, Reb Anschel Frankel unfolded to his full height and took a step or two toward Sudah, as if, without further wasteful delay, physically to eliminate the obstruction. Leon shook his head. No, it could not be solved that way. He placed a calming hand on Anschel's thigh. "Maybe we should converse in a different language," Leon suggested. But there was no foreign language common to all of them. "And certainly we could not speak French, even if we knew how," Leon went on, the mockery etching his voice, "for that is the native tongue of the artist himself, the language of his dead father and mother, may their memories be a blessing." He turned to cast the full glare of his disapproval on his son-in-law. The others turned, too. Their hostile stares bounced back at them. Sudah, his tongue between his teeth, was totally immersed in the route of that yellow stripe.

Leon rose, indicating to the others to follow. They filed behind him, past the kitchen, plates clotted with stale food strewn all over the table, along the counters and rising in piles in the sink, past the forbidden door to Mara's room, past Leon's study, which housed the Torah scroll that he had ransomed from a Pole a decade after the war and carried home triumphantly to singing, dancing, and celebration, past the sealed door to his bedroom with Rose, down the long hallway, to the room in which Herzl had spent his boyhood years. Well, it was at least safer than the living room, Herzl reflected, though he felt vaguely diminished at this broad display of the self he had been before he had acquired new purpose and seriousness in Israel. Rose had left the room virtually untouched. There was the narrow bed with the plaid spread, the simple student's desk behind which the yellowing magazine photos of his favorite baseball players were still taped, the wastepaper basket still dangling from the curtain rod, still containing the clumps of socks he used to toss in during his basketball days. The fingermarks blotting the ceiling bore witness to the hours he had spent perfecting his jump shot. Herzl grinned with boyish embarrassment, looking around furtively to assess the opinions of the others. Ashkenazi seemed thoroughly oblivious to these details. Enough time had been wasted. He insisted on getting on at once with the business at hand.

Paul Ashkenazi had one major point to deliver, and he hammered it in again and again. Henceforth, they were not to make a single statement to anyone. To no one, do you understand? Not a yes, not a no, not even a shrug, not a sigh. When pressed they must respond in this way only: "My lawyer has advised me to say nothing at this time." He pronounced these words slowly, syllable by syllable, as if he were instructing children. "I'm in charge from now on," said Ashkenazi. He brought his cigar up to the corner of his mouth and glowered at them from under knit brows. "Is that clear?" They all nodded. It was an overwhelming relief.

He pointed out that as yet no criminal charges had been brought against them. They were being investigated. All right, but the presumption was that they were innocent. This is America, don't forget. The topic of old-age homes is fashionable nowadays among the do-gooders. These things come and go. However, it will unfortunately be necessary, if merely for the sake of public relations, for Leon to testify at the hearing before the government committee that will soon convene to examine nursing-home abuses. Leon's face fell. "But, Paul," he cried, "try to understand my position. I'm a rabbi, after all. Think how it will look. I'll be sitting there in my yarmulka and they will be questioning me like a common criminal. It will be a regular circus, fun and games. It will be no good for the Jews, believe me. It will be a mockery of God's name."

Ashkenazi crumpled a piece of paper in his fist and shot it straight into Herzl's makeshift basket. "I'll handle it, Leon," he said, "don't worry. I'll be sitting right there by your side, whispering sweet nothings in your ear. If they turn this into a pogrom, I'll be ready. Let them just try!"

"It's no good, Paul. I have a family to protect. Already these reporters keep pestering me, asking me day and night if I talked to Teddy Schumacher at Mara's wedding about arranging that meeting with the governor. One of those little *pishers* even had the *chutzpah* to ask if I bribed Senator Schumacher. Put yourself in my shoes, Paul. The questions alone will destroy me. It won't matter what I say."

"Leon, I've already told you, leave it to me. How can you remember everyone you talked to at your own daughter's wedding? At such a time a father is naturally too excited and happy."

What could Leon do? His hands were tied. He had to put his faith in Ashkenazi. On the wall a picture of Herzl, chubby at age thirteen, was tilted. Leon tried to avoid his son's eyes. Ashkenazi frowned and glanced at his wristwatch. He had one further suggestion to offer. It would be advisable, he said in a commanding voice, for Leon and Rose to leave the country as soon as possible. Go somewhere, to a secluded place, but for God's sake not to Israel. It would be far better for the idiots to conclude that you have fled justice than for you to hang around and say the wrong thing. When should you return? A day before the hearing would not be a minute too soon.

They flew to Switzerland. A black limousine, with Reb Anschel Frankel in the driver's seat, met them at the airport. They were taken to Interlaken, sunglasses shadowing their eyes. From there they made their way by train to the Schreckhorn, a kosher hotel in the town of Grindelwald, in the Bernese Oberland. It was a cool summer in the cultivated mountains. The Jungfrau was shrouded by clouds. They spent their time between meals side by side on deck chairs, blankets over their laps, Rose knitting shawls for her daughters, Leon reading the *Moreh Nevuchim* of the Rambam. They spoke rarely, taking pains to avoid the subjects of Mara and the scandals. Instead, they remembered when the children were small. Once they took a slow walk down the mountain, following the path of a freezing little white river, running furiously. Leon pulled a melting chocolate bar out of his back pocket and dipped it in the water. In a second it was hard. They held hands on the way back, Reb Anschel striding twenty paces behind. Occasionally Leon would go off to Zurich, leaving Rose for a day or two and returning with gifts of jewelry and gold watches. The months passed. The High Holidays came and went. They waited for the mail. Rashi and Herzl wrote faithfully, but there was little news. One day Herzl reported that Sudah had found a job. Here it no longer mattered.

Sudah took this job in desperation. He had to get out of the house. At first he and Mara had rejoiced at the prospect of having the entire apartment to themselves. But then people began to move in. First Manny Fish with his girlfriend, Gila, who spent most of the morning in the bathroom applying her makeup, leaving behind a sour smell. Then Mark Bavli came with Mirabella and her howling child, Flora. Cookie Kalb arrived, sullen and hopeless, abandoned now by both her husband and her hairdresser. Luke Alfasi would spend nights there to escape the deadly battles with his mother. Strangers walked freely through the door, opened the refrigerator, curled up on the floor and went to sleep. Savage quarrels broke out, the wildest between Gila and Mibi over the use of the best bathroom and the baby's defeating wails. In the middle of one night Mibi grabbed her child and departed in a rage. Some days later the entire apartment started to stink like a ripe corpse. They began to find dead chickens everywhere, stuffed in drawers and crevices, behind books, under mattresses. This was Mibi's revenge, her farewell present. Herzl would arrive and beat on the walls and scream at Mara until his voice cracked. "Torture! Torture!" he cried. "What am I going to tell Daddy and Mommy?" The situation was unbearable. One day Mara said to him, "Tell them Sudah's got a job."

Sudah left for work gladly and stayed late. It was at an African gift shop called Tribal Treasures. His job was to restore the artifacts that arrived in crates, mending the broken nose of a mask here, brightening the paint on a shield there. He came back each night laden with gifts for everyone—blankets, tapestries, baskets, boxes hollowed out of dried vegetables, caftans, robes, skullcaps, sandals, gourds, carved stools, spears, beads, bone necklaces. One day he arrived home earlier than usual, empty-handed. "I was burned," he informed Mara. By this he meant he had been dismissed from his job. "Why? What happened?" Sudah explained that the boss was a crook and a cheat, a man who brazenly deceived his customers day in and day out, passing off garbage as art.

The Alps were robed in the first light snows of the coming winter, like royal children in fresh white undergarments. Side by side on their deck chairs, Rose and Leon understood that their respite here was now drawing to a close. Rose was knotting the fringes on a gray shawl for Rashi. She spoke to Leon without looking at him, as to herself. "Do you remember when I went to see Weisz before we left, to stock up on the pills?"

"What about it?"

"I didn't want to mention it to you then, but he told me during that session that he had gone—on his own initiative, mind you—to take a personal look at Sudah's painting. You know, the big gray one in the living room."

"Of course the big gray one. Is there any other?"

"Don't make jokes, Leon. He went one afternoon while Sudah was laying a green stripe down one of the canvases. Sudah didn't even notice him. Anyone could have walked in, for that matter, a burglar even. But Weisz just stepped in and stepped out. It took a minute altogether."

"Well, Weisz has a reputation for the fast diagnosis. *Nu,* so what did he say?"

"We are friends now, Leon, so I can tell you the truth. Weisz was very blunt. He said that Sudah's art failed to move him. It just did not move him at all."

Leon kissed the page he had been reading and closed his book. He turned to Rose. There was a distant look in his eyes.

He had already climbed down the mountain and sailed across the ocean. From the opposite shore he grinned his merchant's grin. He cupped his hands over his mouth and called out to Rose, "Does that mean he won't buy it?"

4 Fanny Gottlieb stretched herself out on the floor, the chill of the linoleum on her belly and breasts sending signals of doom to her heart. She put out her arm. In her fist she gripped the wire hanger she had untwisted, leaving only the hook at the end. Patiently she fished for the old shoebox. It had scraped its way to a distant corner under her bed. A thicket of dust eclipsed it. Jabbing fitfully, she nudged it at last and curved the hook over its limp cardboard side. She dragged the box out of hiding into the light. She blew away the clumps of dust. She took out the love letters from the great men. Why bother to glance at them? Her bones creaked as she raised herself from the floor. The crumbling letters left a powdery yellow trail behind her as she marched down the three flights of stairs to the Parklawn's cellar, past Russell Boomer, whose face was frozen into the shape of the "Hey, lady!" he had managed to cast out, into the boiler room, where she opened the iron door of the furnace and dumped them in. The words of Mr. Wells—he had called her "Titian's madonna"— rose up in bright-red flames paler than her hair had been that dim summer long ago.

It was a dark night and everyone in the building had loosened his grip on his soul in exchange for sleep. But Fanny was no longer afraid. Dora Popper had been buried that morning. Fanny and Julius Fleischer had asked to attend the funeral, but were turned down. "It would be too upsetting for you," said the chief aide. They did not even see the body being carted out. Fanny had known Dora was dying, but when it happened it was shocking and foul. Fanny could not bear it. She wanted to do something. She wanted to cut off all her hair with a slaughter knife. For weeks Dora had lain on the same stale sheets, rising with difficulty once a day to prevent bed sores. It was all in vain. One evening Fanny found an empty room with a freshly made bed. She led Dora to it and helped her friend's wasted body between the clean sheets. The next day Dora was given the medication for the person who had once occupied that bed. Blasts of diarrhea overwhelmed her. Two days later she died in her excrement, an unswallowed pill, like a tombstone, at the root of her tongue.

For weeks after, Fanny sat on the hard chair in her room, her liver-spotted hands folded in her lap, her extinguished eyes fixed on the wall opposite. Julius Fleischer insisted she come down once a day at least, to watch television. "Do it for me, Fanny." Obediently she sat at his side, her spirit sagging. Then one evening she saw a newscast about the upcoming hearing. When Julius escorted her back to her room, he sensed the change in her. She walked directly to her closet and pulled out her pink dress with the lace insets and the discolored patches from the vomit. She draped it over her chair. "What's this, Fanny? A party?" "It's my demonstration dress," she said, "I'm going to make a little stink!" Would Julius join her, to honor Dora? "Be realistic," he replied, "they wouldn't even let us go to the funeral." Fanny shook her head. "Are we children, Julius? If we want to go we can go. We're not in jail." Her eyes opened wide as she spoke these words, so astonished was she by the novelty and truth of her insight.

She spent the next few days appealing to others in the Parklawn. Very few would risk it. It was their conviction that the little comforts of their lives depended on keeping on the good side of the administration. In the end only she, Julius Fleischer, Henry Friedman, and Sylvia Upright climbed into the back of Russell Boomer's red pickup truck, their eyes smeared with the glare of the outdoors. Boomer roared up to the front of the hearing building, bumping his passengers mercilessly, leaped out of his seat, set up four folding chairs, and helped the old bones down. "Shove it up their asses, kids!" he yelled encouragingly. He disappeared in a puff of stinging fumes.

They sat quietly in their places, holding signs in their laps: REMEMBER DORA POPPER; PROTECT THE AGED—PROTECT YOURSELF. For each person who would bend down to listen, Fanny softly repeated the story of Dora Popper's death. "What do you call yourselves?" a reporter asked. "The Popper Gang," said Fanny. "The Last Gasp," said Julius Fleischer. "The Silver Stars," said Henry Friedman. "Silver, for the natural color of our hair—all our hair, my friend, what you see and what you don't see. It will happen to you, too, sonny, one of these days, so don't be so cocky! And star, as in *starb*. Ha, ha, ha." Sylvia Upright bared her lipstick-stained smile. "You're so clever, Henry!" she croaked in a voice that seemed to be coming from underground. She slapped Henry on the knee. Her claw, with its curled, red-lacquered fingernails, remained outstretched on his brown socialist corduroy pants for the rest of the morning. People scurried up and down the steps, some lugging cartons of documents, others striding past quickly and importantly. "You know why they don't come near us?" demanded Henry. "They're afraid they'll catch what we got, ha, ha, ha. Or maybe they just don't notice us. They think they're immune. That's even funnier!" It was an exhilarating, always changing spectacle. "We should come here to sit every day," said Julius. "It's better even than television." Only one other person remained outside with them throughout, pacing on padded shoes back and forth, eavesdropping on an internal conversation. He was a pale, almost transparent man of undetermined age. "Who's that?" Fanny asked Julius. "I don't know," Julius replied, "but he looks to me like he's already been where we're going." When Leon Lieb came up the steps with Rose dragging on his arm, followed by a procession that included Herzl and Rashi, Reb Anschel Frankel, Paul Ashkenazi, Sadie Stern, and a few others, the pacer at last came to a stop directly in front of the old people. "That's Rabbi Dr. Leon Lieb," he announced in a hollow voice. "I should know. I wrote his dissertation."

Several witnesses had already testified by the time Leon and his party entered the room, and the earnest young woman now before the audience suddenly lost track of what she had been saying and stared in open confusion, her passion stagnating in mid-air, as photographers flashed past her and as television cameras zoomed in on the new arrivals being ushered to their places in the front row. Leon removed his black felt hat with his right hand, exposing the blue velvet yarmulka with the gold trim, which contained on its silk underlining the stamped memento "Wedding reception in honor of Mr. and Mrs. Sudah Mizrahi." He smiled a flat, nervous smile, attended to Rose's comfort, and sat down himself. Senator Mack Frost, a personage who had skipped over old age, set a pinch of snuff in his anatomical snuff box, raised his hand sideways to his nostrils, inhaled deeply, and urged the woman to make haste and complete her statement. The startling point she had been saving for last now fell from her mouth like a deflated balloon. It was the revelation that a sudden order had come down from the state that inspections of nursing homes could no longer be carried out without prior warning. "There's no doubt about it," she said in a leaden voice, "it's a concession to pressures from certain specific interest groups—the owners, the bosses. It's nothing but a farce!" They were all craving to hear from Leon.

Leon took the oath, affirming rather than swearing, lest God's name be taken in vain. He read a statement he had prepared with the help of Paul Ashkenazi. He spoke of the ordeal into which he and his family had suddenly been plunged. It was a black dream from which he seemed unable to awake. It was eating him up alive, destroying the health of his wife, bringing chaos and strangeness into the lives of his children. They were modest people, they lived unpretentiously, as anyone who knew them would bear witness. Reports of their fabulous wealth, of their corrupt empire, were lies, lies pure and simple, spread by the press and by government officials bent on ruining him. He dared not speculate why. And all this in his beloved America, to whose shores he had arrived in flight from religious persecution, burning to do his share for the general good; a country in which he believed, in all innocence, that an orthodox Jew could make his way freely and thrive, unobstructed by the bigotry that had soured his life in the old world. He had flourished, true, though by no means to the preposterous extent that had been reported, and throughout he had tried to direct his energies not only for his own good but also for the good of others. In his nursing homes he had made every effort to promote the well-being of the aged and sick to whose service he had dedicated himself, struggling to accomplish this despite the constant ineptness of bureaucrats and the stumbling blocks they placed in his path. If he had petitioned government officials when something needed to be done, insisting on a hearing from them, pressing his case with all urgency and force before them, was this not the absolute right and privilege of each and every citizen of the United States? Was he not an American, after all, albeit a Jew who held fast to the traditions of his forefathers? Or must he forever resign himself to being a stranger in a strange land, a guest at the mercy of his host, an outsider knocking at the door? Never, never, at no time in his career, had he offered a single penny to any person in a position to grant him anything! The law of the land and the Torah forbade this, and to his own conscience it was abhorrent. "You may not take a bribe," the Torah commands, "because bribery will blind the clear-visioned and twist the words of the righteous." From this it may be learned that, in the case of bribery, it is as wrong to give as to receive. He was proud of his work, proud of the care he provided in his homes. He was gratified that as a consequence of his success, however limited, he was now able to extend charity wherever it was needed. He and his family had not sought to avoid this hearing, but, on the contrary, had been looking forward to it with genuine anticipation, in the hope that their name would be cleansed and their lives would begin anew.

As Leon's Yiddish-accented voice died out, an epidemic of coughing and shuffling erupted in the hall, and every pore seemed to open up with the relief and the disappointment that come when a tense speaker survives at the brink. Two men swooped down on either side of Senator Frost and began to whisper feverishly into the precious ear to which each staked a claim. The one on the left was Sanford Gross, the committee counsel, a tall, unusually skinny man with a hooked nose that propped up his glasses and a pointed Adam's apple that kept down his red polka-dotted bow tie. On the right was a dark and intense young man, the scamp politician who had started all this trouble for Leon and who was known in the Lieb household as the punk, the *putz*, the *pipik*, the *shmegeggie*, the twerp, the *vantz*, the *pisher*, the *farkockte tuches*, the *momzer*. A handsome man, thought Rashi. She stared at him with exaggerated disgust, suppressing the natural attraction she always felt to the enemy, the persecutor. The two men continued to squirt their counsel into the ears of the senator, whose heavy-veined lids were descending like a slow curtain over his bloodshot eyes. He took a sip of liquid. "By the way, Mr. Lieb," he said, as the whisperers still massaged his ears, "where'd you go, anyhow?"

His father's name, stripped of all titles, cut jaggedly into

Herzl's heart. He rose to protest, but at a sharp order from Ashkenazi, he was pushed back down unceremoniously by Reb Anschel Frankel. Leon conferred breath-to-breath with his lawyer. "To Switzerland, sir," he replied, "for the sake of my wife's health." Gross looked up from his whispering. He walked stiffly to his place on the dais, feeling each and every eye on the back of his neck, efficiently located the document he wanted, and waved it under Frost's chin. The senator slipped off his glasses and said, "Be my guest, Sandy."

Gross squeezed together his long nostrils, whose contents were visible to everyone in the first row. "To Switzerland, you say? For what purpose, if I might ask?" Gross had an irritating, high-pitched voice.

"As I said already, sir, for a rest."

"A rest? Purely for a rest? Did you conduct any business there at all?"

Paul Ashkenazi shot out of his seat. "Senator, Mr. Gross is using an old prosecutor's trick to lead my client into perjuring himself. No doubt he has in the back of his mind some obscure witness he can produce to testify that a business discussion did occur during the months my client was abroad. Maybe someone who asked my client in an idle way during dinner, 'How's business, Leon?' I know these tricks. I've been a prosecutor myself."

"Mr. Ashkenazi," said Frost, "we are merely trying to flush the facts out of the closet and spread them on the table. This is not a trial, after all."

Ashkenazi pounded his right fist into the mitt of his left palm. "Mr. Gross is trying to destroy my client's credibility at the outset. The situation in this room is already prejudicial enough; what with a biased press and a partisan audience filling every seat, the atmosphere here is blatantly unsympathetic to a fair hearing for my client."

"Mr. Ashkenazi, you are not letting us begin."

"Since it is obvious that there is little I can do to correct the situation, I feel that for the sake of my client—whose interests I am duty-bound to protect—I must at least expose that state of affairs as it exists. Why, for example, is State Senator Berlin up there on the dais, whispering in your ear? After all, he can hardly be called a disinterested party."

The corner of Frost's mouth budded into a smirk. "Would you like to come up here and join us on the dais, too, Mr. Ashkenazi?"

Ashkenazi shook his head gravely. His body was beginning to seat itself again. Frost slid his glasses down to the purplish bulb at the tip of his nose and fixed Ashkenazi over the flat gold rim. "I must warn you, Mr. Ashkenazi. Another outburst like this and I shall be obliged to request that you leave this room." He signaled Gross to continue. "Well, then, Mr. Lieb," said Gross, "did you get the rest you wanted?"

"My wife is feeling much better, thank God." Rose's cheeks were burning from the glare of this unwanted attention. She smiled ahead mechanically, but inside she was turning to ash.

"I'm glad to hear that," said Gross, "because your wife is obviously an important asset to your operation." He consulted one of his papers. "I read here that she worked for you for a time. As your dietitian. She was well paid, too." Leon was mute. "At the Parklawn," Gross pressed on, as if to refresh Leon's memory. "You are the owner of the Parklawn, are you not?"

"Correct." Leon's answer was spry and prompt.

"Maybe we should stop here and try to identify your holdings, Mr. Lieb. Can you help us out on this?"

"Certainly. The Parklawn, the Aishel, La Mahr, the Roseleon, and the Minnie Sweet Pavilion. That's all."

"That's all?" Gross found a piece of paper and brought it close to his face. In his grating voice he recited a long list consisting of about sixty names. When he finished he attempted a clumsy flourish. "What about those?" he demanded shrilly.

Leon shrugged. "What about them?"

"They're yours, aren't they?"

"No. It would be nice to own so many. I would be a very rich man then, wouldn't I? But unfortunately, they are not mine." Gross sighed. A hiss was swelling up in the room. "Have it your way, Mr. Lieb," Gross muttered. "We shall confine ourselves to an examination of the ones you confess to owning." Paul Ashkenazi stood up again, this time with a more subdued thrust. "*Confess,* Mr. Gross? Has it suddenly become a crime in America to own property?"

"Of course not," Gross replied. "I have nothing but respect for the honest capitalist. I shall be happy to confine myself to an investigation of the state of affairs at the Parklawn for the time being, if that's all right with you, Mr. Lieb?" Leon sighed.

"Fine," said Gross. "Your manager at this particular property, a Mr. Sidney Schneider, has been kind enough to hand over a few thousand documents, which I have enjoyed reading in my spare time. I wonder if you would take the trouble to help me explain some of the inconsistencies I have identified?"

In the lounge at the Parklawn Sid Schneider's eyes bulged at the queer sound of his own detached name, and his heart lurched against the woolen vest his wife had knitted him for warmth. He felt his stomach twisting ominously. He raised the volume of the television set, aggravating even further the old people who had been battling with him all morning to shut the thing off. Before she had departed against orders, Fanny had said, "At least watch it on the television. Out of respect for Dora." But it was their bingo day, the high point of their week, and they sat there with their wilted cards and piles of moist nickels and dimes, straining to hear the caller over the grunts erupting from that box.

Gross was talking about some money, a rather large sum, he

said. Where did it go? What happened to it? It seemed the record was lost.

"Mr. Gross, I am an American executive," Leon replied. "The details of my business I delegate to my subordinates. About such matters you will have to talk to my accountant."

"Mr. Murray Levine, you mean? I've been trying to get hold of him. Where is he, by the way?" Leon could not say. "In Switzerland, maybe?" inquired Gross.

Ashkenazi said evenly, "These are private, family funds, Mr. Gross. My client is under no obligation to report them to you."

"We are talking now about a sum of money totaling nearly a million dollars, Mr. Ashkenazi."

Leon placed a calming hand on his lawyer's shoulder. "Let me answer him, Pinya," he said in a fatherly way. After all, he had been present at the boy's circumcision and had even been honored with the reading of one of the blessings. Turning to Gross, Leon spoke, "I will tell you the truth, sir, I have been very disappointed in my accountant. I turned over the financial side of my business to him, no questions asked. I trusted him one hundred percent. Lately I have had reason to believe he has not been acting in such good faith."

Gross swallowed some water. He would deviate for a moment. "You know, Mr. Lieb," he said, "when we question a subordinate he tells us he was only following orders. When we get hold of the heavyweight himself, he tells us he didn't know what was going on, he handed the whole works over to his underlings. He was misled." Gross's voice was rising thinly. "We are a society with laws, Mr. Lieb! Somewhere responsibility has to be pinned down!" Ashkenazi was scratching audibly on his pad. "A Nazi?" he wrote. "Is he calling Leon a Nazi?" He stared at the words that scorched his page. He stared at Gross as at the lowest species of traitor.

Gross removed his glasses, misted them, polished them with the corner of his jacket, misted again, polished again, then hitched them back up on his Jewish nose. "I guess we have no choice but to trace that money ourselves," he said. "I'm sure you're as anxious to know where it has disappeared to as we are, Mr. Lieb. We'll get back to you on this, you can depend on us."

State Senator Berlin stood up abruptly to protest. "Mr. Gross, I think we should continue with this line of questioning. We are being far too gentle with this witness." Gross slit the dashing Berlin with a look of cold hatred. Frost assured Berlin that no one would be spared. "Not so long as there's juice in my pipettes," he growled. Berlin hunched back down, dejected. A sulker, Rashi mused, a spoiled brat. Gross began to expound on financial matters, to the boredom of everyone assembled, long numbers halting his long sentences. Finally he hit on something interesting. He noted that several large sums of money had been donated by Leon to a certain university in Israel, twenty-five, fifty, one hundred thousand dollars, nothing to sneeze at. These gifts occurred around the time that each of Leon's children respectively entered the school, and, oddly enough, at about the same time the government received requests for a suspiciously similar amount of money as reimbursement for medical care of the sick at the Parklawn. Yet there was no clear record of how the nursing home used that money. Could Mr. Lieb explain?

Leon was now experiencing nothing but disdain, even sympathy, for this poor prosecutor, armed with his fancy lawyer's degree, his lists, his order, his cerebral sarcasm, but bereft of all common sense, out of touch with the instinct necessary for survival; in a holocaust he would perish in a flash, like anything overly refined. Patiently he explained: "Mr. Gross, you should understand that running a nursing home is no bed of roses. Every day enormous sums go out for food, personnel, maintenance, equipment, doctors, drugs, and so on and so forth. The profit margin is very small, believe me. You're lucky if you squeak out a few cents. I'm not a bit surprised at the amounts of money you bring up. In my business, it's the nuts and bolts. Certainly I can't remember what exactly the money you mention went for. It's in the records somewhere, I'm sure. Go over them again. Seek and ye shall find, that's my advice to you."

A blush began to radiate from the tips of Gross's bow tie. A baby, thought Leon, just a kid. So easy to control. Leon was feeling quite calm now, paternal even. He wished that with a word or two he could so efficiently lay low his own Mara. On the other hand, he reflected, my Mara is a thousand times more exciting, more challenging, than this pickle. Gross was rambling on and on, obviously on the defensive in Leon's opinion, about the financial intricacies of the nursing homes, striving to demonstrate again and again, once and for all, how thoroughly he had mastered and assimilated the contents of the documents. He gave up at last, for even one who shunned embellishment and drama as much as he did could sense his audience leaving him. He turned in desperation to what he called matters of human interest.

He noted that there had been an avalanche of complaints, very serious complaints indeed. About patient care, cleanliness, the quality of food; about neglect, dehydration, mismanagement of drugs. He would be specific. He named a certain patient, a Mr. August Vesci, in his youth an acclaimed musician, a mandolinist, as it happened, left to die forgotten on a Parklawn commode. Gross was delicate. Besides, he could never have uttered the words "toilet bowl" within earshot of such a mob. Yet for some considerable time after the date on Mr. Vesci's death certificate the nursing home in question continued to collect the Social Security payments for this unfortunate gentleman. Does Mr. Lieb specialize in amassing dead souls?

Leon lifted his yarmulka slightly and shoved it a bit farther back on his head. This was the saddest part of his business, he intoned. Each and every one of us must die, we are all aware of that, but when you deal with old people day in and day out, you know that the end is soon, any minute, as a matter of fact. What can you do? "Our sages counsel us to live each day as if it were our last," Leon cried. "These words apply to the young as well as to the old, by the way. Every client's passing chips away at my heart, believe me. Naturally, I don't know the details of this poor man's end. I pray to God he is happy now. Let us all hope he is in the Garden of Eden, plucking peacefully on the strings of a golden harp." As for this allegation about continued Social Security payments, Leon sincerely doubted it. Of course, such things might happen on occasion, but when and if they do, they are purely unintentional, the result of an administrative error. Perhaps there was some confusing circumstance in this case. For example, perhaps the old man's room continued to be occupied in some sort of unofficial way. Leon raised his hands to demonstrate his helplessness here, and let them flop in resignation against his black-suited flanks.

A pang of shame and pity wrenched Mara as she squatted in front of the television set in the apartment and listened to her father defending himself in this way. Sudah watched transfixed all morning, but Mara could not bear it. She fled to the business of packing their belongings in cartons, once in a while finding herself drawn helplessly back to the spectacle. It was so squalid. More depressing than anything else was this voyeurism—this witnessing of the private act of a person defending himself. She had always felt that way. Why should anyone care to defend himself, anyhow? When accused, better just to give up, admit guilt, surrender, fade away. A person is nothing, after all, pathetic, puny, simply not worth defending, his lack of consequence most apparent when he stands up in his own behalf. She slipped out of the screen's grip—it was so wretched it nearly crushed her—only to be pulled back later against her will to hear Gross ranting about her brother, Herzl.

About the salary Herzl was earning as rabbi for the homes. "And is this what your average rabbi is pulling in these days?" Gross was demanding. He looked like a fish.

"I've also studied a thing or two in my time," Gross plunged on. "Did you think by some chance that I'm ignorant about these things, that I'm an *am-ha'aretz,* a boor? A rabbi is supposed to be a teacher first of all. That's one of the things I've learned. The best of rabbis accepts no compensation for his services. I, too, can quote the sages. The Torah should not be a spade to dig with, the wise men remind us. Materialism, profit, these things are for ordinary people, not the rabbi. *Torah l'shmah,* the study of Torah for its own sake. I'm sure you know what I mean, Mr. Lieb."

Paul Ashkenazi stood up. "I deplore your tactics, Mr. Gross." Ashkenazi cleared his throat. This was personal. "Your words reflect an attitude toward the orthodox Jew not so different from the attitude most human beings take toward their caveman origins. I'm sure you know what I mean, Mr. Gross."

"You are perverting the issue," said Gross.

"He's right," Sudah said.

"Yes," said Mara, "my father's a wise guy and a bandit. I'm saying this about my own father."

"No," Sudah replied, "Ashkenazi. Ashkenazi is right. It is old dirty story. New Jew screwing old Jew. And for what? For spot of honor in asshole of *goy.*" Sudah stuck out his tongue and lapped it about, making obscene licking noises.

Mara stared at this strange tongue. He surprised her lately, every day, new surprises on top of new. Here they were, making preparations at last to move into the loft. How long had they dreamed of this hour! Sudah had meticulously enumerated the equipment he would buy, the paints, the brushes, the canvases —he knew of a good wholesale outlet in New Jersey, he had said with pride—yet now when they were about to begin the life of art for which they had debased and ingratiated themselves, now he made no movement at all. Even the prospect of leaving this suffocating apartment, which he said he detested even more than she, aroused no enthusiasm in him. He had even offered to join the family at the hearing instead of hastening their own departure by spending the morning packing, as they had originally planned. But Leon had rejected this suggestion outright. And as far as Mara was concerned, it was just as well. She considered herself spared. "The two of you come along?" Leon had exclaimed. "Are you crazy? They'll take one look at you—at the way you dress, your hair—and they'll think I'm making fun of them. They'll think I consider this whole affair a joke. That's all I need!" That was the second time Leon had addressed them since his return from Switzerland. The first was just after he had stepped into the apartment and had come face to face with the African invasion, a host of glossy wooden sculptures of naked men bearing spears and naked women with breasts brushing their navels. At that time, too, Leon's words were spoken in a tone that absolutely precluded any appeal. "I'm going to my office now," he had said in a steady voice. "When I return tonight there will not be a single idol left in my house."

The last of their wedding gifts had gone as key money for the loft. Not a penny remained to pay for the extensive work that needed to be done on its interior. The loft consisted of one large room that ran the entire length of the third floor of what had once been a factory building, a sweatshop in fact. Two steep flights of stairs led up to it. A half inch of soot covered the rough plank floor. A facing of embossed tin, once thinly whitewashed but now almost black, had been hammered to the walls and the ceiling. Mara designated the front section, with its three huge windows and its floored-in elevator shaft, where she set up her old Parklawn typewriter, as their living quarters. The larger section, ending with the open toilet and sink in the rear corner and the barred windows opening to the fire escape, would be Sudah's studio. On the night of the hearing, their first night in the loft, they spread their quilts out on the floor, which seemed spongelike from the filth, at the foot of the great windows in front. Wide-eyed they lay there, rolling in the din from the streets, the songs of the drunks, the crepitations of the trucks, the horns, the flickering lights gone berserk. They dragged their quilts to the back, but the crying of cats on the fire escape would not abate. They opened the window and the demons sprang in. Pitch black they were, male and female, sinuous and ruthless. They stretched out at Mara's and Sudah's feet. Remembering from his boyhood the chants of the Arab children, Sudah gave them the names Bachunay and Chanda.

Sudah and the cats slept; beasts, all three, thought Mara. But in her mind the day's events continued to rattle like old bones, and she gnawed and gnawed at whatever meat still hung from them. The hearing had been grotesque enough. Her father plucked and naked up there—it had been torture. She had seen Fanny Gottlieb on television, too, celebrating Dora Popper. Was it possible that someone she had known, someone she had actually smelled and feared, was now dead? Dora, so smart, so tough, what a fraud you were, after all! And Sudah himself, trapping her into an act of treason against her father, baiting her, then turning around and exposing her himself—how could she forgive him? But bitterest of all had been the words that passed between her and Leon after his return from the hearing, accompanied only by Rose and Reb Anschel. She reviewed them again and again, shouting out what she should have said in a hollow voice that had no object. Rose had slipped straight into her bedroom muttering, "I'm going to lie down for a few minutes." All understood that she was not to be disturbed for at least the next twenty-four hours. Reb Anschel had begun immediately to carry their bags and cartons down to the car. Sudah strode up to Leon with his hand outstretched. *"Mazal tov, Aba,"* Sudah had said amiably, "you are star!" Leon continued flipping through his mail, pretending not to hear. "Sudah's talking to you, Daddy," said Mara.

"What am I supposed to say? Thank you? Was that a compliment in my ear or a spitball?"

"Don't be such a cynic. Sudah's with you down to the wire, believe it or not. You're two of a kind, you and Sudah. Mommy always said a girl ends up marrying a boy just like her father, no matter how hard she tries not to." Leon gave Sudah a curious once-over. He groaned.

"Well, we're going now, Daddy, goodbye. Thanks for the hospitality."

"Yes, all right. One good turn deserves another. When will I be invited over to see your big find?" Sudah waved to the thin air and left quickly, not wanting to be present for what was coming next.

"Not until it's all fixed up," Mara replied. "I'll need my ten thousand dollars now. The wedding money is gone. We're settling down, getting ourselves established. You promised. Will you send it out tomorrow?"

Leon smacked a fan of envelopes against the table. He and Mara were facing each other in the dining room, a well-leveled battleground. "Now?" He restrained himself behind a cage of teeth. "Now you have to ask for it? You couldn't pick a better time?"

Mara walked to the door. She paused with her hand on the knob. Her words squirmed out, ugly and wriggling, like worms. "You're right," she said, "now is a bad time. Forget I ever said anything. You couldn't very well ask the government for a refund on it now!" Her words pursued her, cackling down the hallway. Her hands were icy. Her heart was tolling in her chest. She should have controlled herself. In kindness she should have asked her father how he assessed the results of this grim day. She should have held a rag of sympathy out to him. But she could not.

Some nights later a heavy tread ascended the stairs to their loft. There was a knock at the door. Reb Anschel Frankel poked the tip of his red beard into the gloomy room. Mara saw the hurt and woeful look in his eye, turned up to the bare bulb dangling from a wire. "I will report to your father that you are living in a condemned gymnasium," said Reb Anschel. He handed Mara an envelope. She tore it open. As she was unfolding the letter from her mother, a pale green check fluttered face up to the floor. She couldn't find her glasses. She bent over and squinted. Here it was, her ten thousand hard-earned dollars. The check evaded her as she tried to pick it up. Without nails she was compelled to insert her soft fingertips under the paper to get it, but the dust and splinters on the floor made her hesitate. She trapped the check finally by dragging it along the floor, smudging the note her father had scrawled on the back, something about his washing his hands for good. Her mother's letter embarrassed her, as she knew it would, as had all Rose's letters penned in mushy agony at critical stages in Mara's development, reproach wrapped up in devotion. This one was addressed to Mara, and then, as an afterthought, to "and Sudah," in a different shade of blue-green ink. "We love you very much. Everything we have ever done in our lives has been for the sake of our children. This money we put aside to help you begin in life. Just enough to start you off, but not too much so that you would not think about the future. Plenty more is waiting for you, and it will be yours just as soon as you can show us you don't really need it. These are our values. Some people might disagree but there they are. I have convinced Daddy that you have grown more mature and responsible, and that you will use this money carefully and well. Please don't disappoint us." Mara recoiled from imagining the terrible meeting between her mother and father that brought forth this bloodstained check.

They drew on this money, day after day, for longer than a year, until it ran dry. They spent it on food for themselves and the cats and the guests, on clothing and rent and on all their heart's desires. At first they bought some necessities for the loft: a stove, a refrigerator, and an ancient cast-iron bathtub with claw feet so massive and heavy that four struggling men cursed an entire morning of their lives maneuvering it up the stairs. One day, after weeks of what had degenerated into shameless nagging by Mara, Sudah got some boards and built two walls to enclose the toilet and sink, a cubicle for privacy. It took him nearly a month to complete this job. The kitchen, without a sink of its own, was set up in the front end of the loft, and each night the scummy dishes were loaded into the tub, a tiresome distance away in the corner of the studio end. Roaches inhabited the pots and pans that hung from nails on the wall behind the stove.

They slept between their quilts, the merry floral ticking turning gray and greasy all over, though the floor itself became no cleaner. They owned no furniture at all until the day a van hired by Joe Gold pulled up in front of their building and two strangers dumped onto the sidewalk all the old pieces Sudah and Mara had collected during their aborted career as interior designers. The bamboo desk, the aqua armoire, the couch, the seatless rocker, the rattan chaise longue, the screeching piano stool, and last of all the burned round bed, its stuffing hanging out. "Like hemorrhoids," Sudah said. But Mara claimed these objects and convinced two drunks to carry them up the stairs. Sudah declared he no longer wanted to own things and would take no part in the enterprise. As a reward, the drunks were given the bed, which they dragged around for a few days and then forsook as unsuitable to the free life. Mara arranged and rearranged the furniture in the living quarters. She decorated the area with the African blankets, rugs, tapestries, and other accessories—Sudah's booty from his term at Tribal Treasures.

Rashi looked over the finished product and summed it up by quoting their mother in her better days, something Rose used to say when the children would dress up without washing: *"Oiben puts, inten shmuts;* fancy on top, filthy underneath." And on the day an anonymous note was slipped under the door Mara rushed out and bought some hand-painted Indian cloth and draped it across the three large front windows. It was a thank-you note: "Thank you, thank you, thank you for letting me look to my heart's content at your yummy pink bod every night. Skinny white girls with glasses and little tits, they turn me on. This letter is stained, but not with my tears."

Sudah's great gray unfinished painting was shoved up against the wall, its rough back mocking the large bare studio area. Mara's footsteps resounded in the empty space as she passed across the floor to and from the bathroom. The void grieved her, but Sudah would do nothing to fill it up. In addition to the neglected painting, the studio contained a litter for the cats and an old Persian rug that Rashi had rejected when its border of swastikas swirled into focus under her eyes. Each dawn Sudah sat down naked on this rug, in the lotus position, and commenced his yoga exercises. The cats lounged serenely at his side. One afternoon Chanda lifted her leg and expelled four kittens as Sudah stood on his head. She ate the afterbirth and licked up the blood until all that remained of her travail was a pale-pink stain on the rug. Two died at once. Sudah named them Plonie and Almonie. He wrapped their stunted corpses in newspaper, packed them in a small suitcase, and set it out in the street for a passer-by to steal. The other two, a male and a female, as black as their parents, were given to Rashi as a gift because Mara was of the opinion that little Naomi should be mistress of a pet. But to Rashi they were nothing but beasts; she had nothing in common with them. She did not cherish them. The male disappeared one night. Two weeks later he came limping painfully back—castrated. Rashi surmised that the poor creature had had the misfortune of crossing paths with the Cat Lady, a rich spinster with a passion for these sneaky animals, who used up her life prowling the city, enticing sassy cats with big swinging balls into her den and paying for their sterilization on humanitarian grounds. Mara bundled the spurned kittens into a basket and, with Naomi's plump hand clutching her sleeve, made her way back to the loft. It was a frosty evening and Sudah had put on a pair of loose white cotton drawstring pants. Naomi surveyed him coolly. "Sudah doing yogurt again," she commented. "Yeah, he's yogaling for a change," said Mara. Fasfusah, the female kitten, curled up in Sudah's lap and allowed him to stroke her black fur as he pored over his Sanskrit texts into the night. But the male paced the loft like a caged spirit ready to bolt. Sudah called him Mazhnoon, after the beggars of his childhood, for this cat, too, was bitter, distracted, crazy.

The space around Sudah's rug, which had at first awaited his art crop, now gradually became a storage center for all sorts of objects in transition. First Luke Alfasi, in a burst of therapeutic energy, divested his mother Luba of every single thing she owned in the hope of deflecting her gaze from the cluttered past to a clean future. Luba crouched naked in a corner of her son's rooms and howled and howled the loss of her life, until the white truck drove up again and the two indifferent men with their girlfriend carted her away. Her furniture, which had once been crammed into her Parklawn room, seemed to crowd the studio as well, though it was much larger. Mark Bavli, who was readying himself for a voyage to Barcelona with Mibi and Flora, brought over seven trunks stuffed with his papers. He had saved everything with an eye toward the convenience of his biographer, beginning with his earliest scribbles, his spelling tests, the notes he had passed to friends under the desk, his spitballs, his canceled checks, his fingernail parings, the hairs that had snagged in his comb, the hairs that had collected in his shower drain, used tissues and so on. Almost every person who passed through their loft, unrolling a sleeping bag on the floor for a night and sometimes for months, managed to leave an emblem of himself behind. Guy and Gevah, two handsome, blond Israelis, pacifists and artists like Sudah, remained with them for more than three months, smoking hashish with Mara and cracking sunflower seeds all day long. They left a bubble-gum machine, a lawn mower, a jukebox, thirty rubber truck tires which had been intended for a sculpture of some sort, and the rusted engine of a bus. Cases of dried-up cosmetics—rouge, powder, lipstick, mascara, eye shadow—constituted the re-mains of Manny Fish, who had taken shelter with them after a brutal quarrel with Gila. Calico, an escaped convict who slept with a knife under his pillow, one hand gripping the bone handle and the other holding down his woman, Ocilac, left cartons of small appliances—toasters, tape recorders, television and stereo sets, can openers, blenders, cameras, radios—and burlap sacks bumpy with thousands of beads piled high against the walls, like bags of sand in wartime. Only Spin, the lunatic drug dealer, departed without leaving a monument. On the contrary, he emptied the loft of fifty dollars and Sudah's gray painting.

Strangers roamed freely about. "It is all *hefker,*" Sudah said. "Right," said Mara, "open house. Come one, come all! Let in the vultures!" Sudah bought some lumber, and in a corner he built a platform on stilts, about five feet off the floor. Across the bare wooden planks on top he slept, and underneath he spread out his rug for yoga. "The shrine," Mara declared. She prostrated herself before it. Sudah ignored her mockery. "The holy of holies!" she cried. "But, of course, it's off limits to the likes of me, a mere unclean woman!" Once, on a rare night when they were alone, Sudah said to her, "I want to make love to you now." They had not been together for more than a month. They climbed up to the platform. They locked, Sudah behind Mara like two nesting S's. "Stop now," Sudah ordered, "look here." His arm reached over her flank. In his hand he held a magnifying mirror, which he adjusted to reflect the view between their legs. "What do you see?" "Your gigantic balls," Mara said. "Mine? You are sure they are not yours?" In fact they were resting tight and fist-like between their two bodies. "We are one, Mara. That is the root. We grow out from it, man and woman, like two stalks." He invited her to join him in the mystical discipline of yoga. He placed his dark hand on the snake coiled up at the base of her spine. "We shall wake up your *kundālinī*," he said, "and bring her up to your *sahasrāra*." His hand traveled slowly up her back and came to rest on her head, caressing it. "No!" she cried, wrenching herself free, "no, no, no! It's a cop-out! It's all bullshit!"

He became more and more austere, stripping away the frills of his existence. He ate only fruits, vegetables, grains, and nuts. He fasted often. Sometimes he would bake a loaf of bread, devoting an entire afternoon to this project. He lost a great deal of weight. He stopped smoking altogether, and frowned on Mara and her friends for their weakness and self-indulgence. His hair hung down in knots to his waist. He wore no leather at all and fashioned his own shoes out of a block of wood, a strip of rubber glued to the bottom for silence, and a peg with a wide head hammered in front to slip between his first and second toes. His clothing was loose, cut and sewn by him out of the thinnest white cotton. And one night he announced to Mara that he had made the decision to become celibate. "Terrific," she shot out. "And where does that put me?" Sudah acknowledged that he could understand her situation. He did not own her, he told her. He owned nothing. If her energy still came from sex, he, of course, released her to go out and quiet it. "Great," said Mara, "just great." Pockets of tears were filling up behind her eyes. Sudah had such admirable self-control, such endurance, and she had none. "And your art? What about that?" Her voice was quivering badly. This was a subject she had been unable to bring up before, fearful of what would come gushing out when she ventured to uncap it. "Art is ego," Sudah said. "I am killing ego." "Am I ego, too?" She began to cry now. She would have liked to melt into a smudge. Sudah held her and patted her back. He could stand there and pat my back forever, she thought—what stamina, goddamn him! "It's so obvious," she managed to say at last, her words snagging on her sobs, "it's just obvious. You don't love me. You don't love me. You just don't love me. That's all. That's all." She cried until she fell asleep along the border of his rug, curled up, every once in a while a sob springing her body loose. When she woke up again it was the next afternoon. Sudah had gone out. But every surface in the loft was covered with signs. And every sign had the same message: I Love You. I Love You. I Love You. I Love You. I Love You.

"I love you! I love you," Calico hooted, a shrill mimic. "He stayed up all night crapping out these signs, your old man. He's weird. He has too much willpower, that's his trap." "Style, it is style he possesses," said Ocilac in a husky voice and an accent that had no country. She read tarot cards for a fee. Her name used to be Sheila Salzman. Calico had been known as John Doe. Mara felt herself succumbing once again to Sudah's enchantment, but as for what he had written in the night, she did not believe a single word.

The days of that year and each dollar of the ten thousand eluded her. Mara could account for none of them. She slept half her hours away. Her waking time faded into the smoke of the hashish pipe. Like my mother, she thought, drugs and sleep. High on hash one night, she strode up and down the loft, her arms outstretched before her. "I am my mother! I am my mother!" she chanted. Calico grabbed her shoulders and shook her violently until she resigned herself to the tragedy of having her guts tear loose and float around in the chaos and void within her. "Don't freak out, kid!" he commanded. She became friendly with the woman who lived in the loft over theirs. Jana was her name, an artist who made meticulous constructions out of string. Jana brewed a pot of mint tea and set it on the low table between them. She brought her face so confidentially near that Mara could enter at will the craters that scarred it. "I hope you have no illusions about what's gone rotten," Jana said. Her breath smelled as if it came from a mouth that was seldom unsealed. "You invested in a man, you sank everything you had into him. You existed vicariously. You lived through your husband exactly like our legendary Jewish mothers live through their sons. You think you're something special because you sacrificed yourself for the *true* god, Art, but it's all idol worship in the end. It's self-immolation. It has always been the deadliest sin."

Rashi came more often now, to yoke herself somehow to her sister's suffering. She blamed herself for the marriage. Because she had wanted to prove to Leon that she could bring Mara home. Because she had panicked that Mara was no longer a virgin. "What's happening between you and Sudah?" Rashi asked finally, with difficulty, her eyes filmed with worry.

Mara grinned. "For goodness' sake, relax. We love each other now more than ever. We're just searching, growing in different directions. But our roots are joined, so don't worry."

Rashi shook her head. "Other people do yoga, I know," she said. "They meditate for an hour a day, maybe twenty minutes here, twenty minutes there. But from dawn until midnight, is that normal?"

"Sudah just likes to be complete, that's all. He'll be a great man someday, Rashi, a master. Just think of it as studying Gemara. Who were the boys Daddy used to admire most? The ones who sat and learned all day. They had a rebbe. Sudah has a guru. They sat in the *kollel* from sunrise till midnight. Soon Sudah will be going to an ashram, his kind of yeshiva. Then to India, his Jerusalem. Don't you see what I've done? I've gone and married Daddy's dreamboat!"

"But how will this all end?"

"In ten years he'll climb down into his grave. They'll bury him under six feet of dirt. Thirty days later he'll walk out alive and laughing."

"And what about you? How will you survive?"

"Look, I expected to be ignored by him while he became transported by his art. I wanted it, it would have been ecstasy for me. So now he's ignoring me for his yoga. What's the difference? Who am I to dictate to a man what he can ignore a woman over?" She walked away and switched on the radio. She wanted an end to these discussions. But over the passionate voices of some women she kept on. "I haven't exactly been standing still all this time, you know. While Sudah has been discovering his yoga, I've been discovering things about myself. Becoming stronger, becoming an independent woman. And then, of course, there's always my writing." It was a panel discussion that was being broadcast. The topic was Female Sexuality. "The full force of our sexuality has always terrified men," spoke a sincere voice. "If we are frozen, they are to blame. We must not be afraid to lose control, since self-control is their invention to restrain us! We must go out and experience anything and everyone, take our pleasure instead of give it!" Mara raised a clenched fist. "Right on!" she cried. "That's the voice of the fifth column within the feminist movement," Rashi said sadly.

Mara made some shadowy attempts to write that year. She began an epic called "Vashti," which took its inspiration from the chronicle in which a Persian queen was wiped out because she refused to obey the king's drunken command to present herself naked before his flatterers. Luke Alfasi extolled the first nine lines. "You are splendid, Mara," he said, crushing her against his undershirt, "a true revolutionary." The tenth line was never composed. She reread the second and third episodes of her virginity series. The first she could not even bear to touch, much less read, for her father's eyes had altered it utterly and the memory of how it had been used to blackmail Leon into promoting her marriage to Sudah still scalded her. One dawn, however, as their money was running low, she awoke with a strange alertness. She watched Sudah slip down from his platform, splash ice-cold water over his body, and start the day's rituals. Calico and Ocilac were asleep by their cartons, his hard arm flung across her chest like a bar. Mara wrapped herself in her dragon robe, walked barefoot to the elevator shaft, and sat down in front of the old black typewriter. She pressed her forehead against the keys. This was her pre-writing ceremony, as if the letters would magically combine and penetrate her skull. She thought about dying. She imagined how it would be if Sudah died. The sorrow, the burial, the healing, new men stepping up. Was it possible? It was a lavish indulgence, this reverie. She had had such fantasies before, about the death of her mother, her father, her brother, her sister, but this was the first time Sudah had ever starred in one. Refreshed, she raised her head and screwed the heels of her palms into her eyes until she was rewarded with a spectacle of bright floating sequins. She began to type.

### How I Lost It: The Definitive Version

When I reached the end of my nonage, my father told me it was time I went out into the world to seek my fortune. He whipped out a document which I had signed when I was still unable to hold a pen between two fat fingers. It was a lease, and the expiration date was looming. He gave me a purse stuffed with beads, and some advice. Be modest. Keep your eyes downcast so that people will not immediately notice that one is larger than the other. It is not necessary to announce for all the world that you have hairs sprouting from your nipples. Chew with your mouth closed. Do not herald your presence with your odor. Be certain your thighs do not irritate people by smacking against each other and unsmacking as you make your way from station to station. Stifle your body's noises. Remember that you are not lovable. However, you are ours, and despite everything, we love you.

He drove me to the train. "Goodbye, Father," I said. He tapped the stubble on his cheek. I kissed the spot. That was carfare. "Well, good luck to you," he said. He squeezed my thigh. There was a flash of light. Mother had been crouching on the floor in back, hiding. She waved the camera over her head. "Surprise!" she squealed. "I just knew this would be a moment to cherish!"

I had not been on the road for many days before I came to a street corner where some black musicians were entertaining the passers-by. A circle had formed around them. I elbowed my way to the front. The leader was an older man, with glistening skin drawn tightly across the muscles of his bare chest, and stiff bristles of gray hair shooting out like horns around his face. He fiddled casually on a beat-up instrument while his two younger assistants banged on homemade drums and sang turbulently. The music blazed up in me. I leaped into the center of the ring and began to dance, first slowly with my eyes closed, then faster and faster. The drummers squatted at my feet, setting the beat for me, which I could not disobey. I ripped off my shirt. My breasts were shaking like cream. The fiddler strode up behind me. His left hand gripped my shoulder. In his right hand he held his bow. He drew this bow across the front of my body, down bow, up bow, down bow. He was playing me. All three were laughing heartily, exposing great white teeth, clapping me on and ridiculing me at the same time. When it was all over, the onlookers turned away without a gesture. I lifted up the hem of my skirt, making my dress into a flimsy vessel, and glided from person to person, demanding the price of the entertainment. At night I followed the players back to their shabby hotel, where I slept on the floor alongside the leader's bed, for there was no snuggly rug on which he could warm his hooves when he set them down in the morning. I made myself useful during the day, too, dancing and collecting the coins. But one morning I woke up and noticed that my purse was empty. I said to the fiddler, "You stole my beads. Now that's just the limit!" Of course, he denied it. He blamed one of his assistants. Nevertheless, he gave me back my shirt, which he had hidden on the first day I had taken it off, and he released me.

Where could I go? Had I returned then to my father's house, he would have said to me, "So this, after all, is your fortune!" I traveled on, waiting for something good to befall me. Just as I was about to despair I came upon a sculpted garden where peacocks strutted up and down the stone pathways. In the distance I saw a white stucco house with a red tile roof. I crawled to the door like a dog and collapsed. When I woke up next, a middle-aged woman, tall, with blond hair pulled into a knot, was standing over me, her hands on her hips. She tightened the sash of her black satin dressing gown. She explained that she shared this house with a man, a German like herself, but he was away on business and would be returning someday. "Meanwhile, we must get ready for him," she said.

The rooms of this house followed each other, like beads on a string, all around a courtyard. Each room could be entered from the one adjacent to it, but only the last one opened into the courtyard itself. "When we complete a circuit of all the rooms," said the woman, "he will arrive." There was a room for every part of the body, including the superficial layer of the brain, one for each of the orifices, and in the final room the parts were united into a whole. The woman accompanied me from room to room, icily pointing out my assets and my defects, taking total charge of the preparations. My buttocks looked like dough that would never rise, she stated. They had no inner life. The back of my neck, on the other hand, was poignant and vulnerable. The length of time spent in each of the rooms depended on the improvements that were required. Six months with oils of myrrh and six months with sweet odors. Then on a night when I had abandoned all hope she said, "He's here!" She instructed me on how to enter the courtyard, on all fours, with my head hanging down and my eyes fixed on the space between my legs. I crept out. No living creature seemed to be taking any notice of me. I was growing faint and dizzy from the excess of my own body's smells. Then I felt someone stroke my back, as if I were a cat. After that someone gave me a hard kick from behind and knocked me over. I tried to let him see the nape of my neck, but this sight failed to soften him. It continued this way through the night, tenderness and destruction in no predictable pattern. In the morning he said to the woman, "And I have been gone for so long. Is this the best you could do?"

I don't know why I stayed there. It was a spell they had cast over me. I earned my keep by carrying armloads of firewood to the house from a shack two miles away. All day long I trudged back and forth, the rough logs tearing chunks of skin off my bones. At night I flattened myself against the wall as the two of them argued ferociously in German, pointing and snarling at me throughout. Then one evening I watched him slip into a tiny pink shed directly behind the house. He emerged with a cradle of logs in his arms. I confronted him. "You have turned me into a slave, but even my work was worth nothing. How could you do this to me?" He put a finger to the corner of his eye and tsked as he pretended to pat dry a mock tear. He tossed me a rag to cover myself and never bothered to look back at me as I struggled to part the briars and carve my way out.

I lowered my eyes to the dirt, whence came my help. Things could be found there, strips of tattered cloth with which I bound myself for warmth, rusty nails which I could peddle for seven cents a piece. On a lucky day I found a gray jacket with pads at the shoulder. I learned how to squat down behind a tree without dribbling on my loincloth when my bladder swelled up. I ate mushrooms and berries, rich people's garbage, cherries that had been trod upon and squashed. I slept where I could. Sometimes I would be kicked awake in the middle of a dream and heaved out into the darkness and cold. All day long I counted—windows, doors, lamp posts, benches, cars, trees, cats, the number of letters in a word, the number of words in a sentence, the sentences in a paragraph. An odd number meant that good luck would discover me. When an even number fell out, I would start the count all over again. Had my father recognized me in those days, how sorry he would have been. People called me trash, outcast, scum. They whispered hectically in each other's ear and rushed past. My best pickings were at the café frequented by the artists. They must have considered me akin to them. I became a regular at the fringe. Once I ventured to draw up a chair beside a painter with a waxed mustache. His ringed fingers flew up to his lips. "Dirt! Filth! She's filthy! Get her away from me!" he cried. Another time I was so hungry I stood by the table of a poet and waited. "Why do you hate yourself so much?" he asked me. "Why do you think you are something special?" Over and over again, the same monotonous questions. As he spoke he dropped crumbs into my mouth with two fingers of one hand, while the tall finger of his other hand was pushed up, up, high into my hole.

I was led by serpentine streets. I lost myself in black alleys. This was the Arab quarter. Women were nowhere to be seen. Men sat bunched around tables sipping sweet coffee, at ease with each other, picking each other's nose. They stared at me for days, nudging each other, consulting. I was a curiosity, a minor marvel. A group of old men approached me. Their leader spoke: "We have come to the conclusion that you are a female." I shrugged. "It is not safe for a female to walk up and down the highways alone like this. Are you somebody's daughter? We can help you. Come with us." They led me to an abandoned section of devastated stone houses, roofless and bleak. They stripped off my bandages, last of all my worn diaper. "We guessed right," said one of them. "Perhaps she is diseased," said another. "We shall purify ourselves afterward," the leader said. Then they raped me according to rank, the leader claiming the privilege of taking me while I was still screaming. When they were through, they examined each other's groin for fresh blotches and running sores. I searched for my poor spurned rags. I said to the leader, "I had always expected kindness from strangers." "Then you got what you deserved. You will thank me for this someday."

There was nothing left for me to do. I called my father. "Father," I wept, "they have called me kike. I have no money. Come get me now. And bring some underpants. The cotton kind that I wore when I was a girl. They were such a comfort."

The car roared right out of the empty night and pulled up alongside me. I climbed into the death seat. Inside, it was snug and private, and reeked of his farts. "You came so fast," I whispered, "thank you." "What is that rash you have all over you?" he asked. "From sleeping with the bedbugs," I replied. "I have been so miserable!" He took a tube of cream out of the glove compartment. "Over here it is worst," he said as he squeezed out thick white clots and smeared them across the plagued insides of my thighs. When he finished I buried my head in his lap. What a relief to be close at last to someone who cared for me. "Thank you," I murmured again. I cupped my hand over his bulge. There was something wrong with what we were doing, I knew, but I could not remember what it was. Then it occurred to me. The smell was alien. I raised my eyes from under a pleated forehead and dared to look closely at him and at our complicity. I saw his neck for the first time, a part he would expose only to the executioner. Then the craggy point of his chin, the droop of his lower lip, the bristles in his dark, moist nostrils, the pink lining of his eyelids, the ridge of his disapproving brows. This was not my father at all. It was a policeman. He threw a package at me. "Here's your underwear," he barked. I quickly pulled on a pair. They were the wrong kind, slimy and cold. "Now you're a little more decent," he said. He went on, "As for anything else, including the money, the message is as follows: 'Expect nothing from anybody until you have corrected your attitude.' "

"But when can I come home?"

"When you understand that the past is your own invention. We do not share your view of what has happened."

"But what shall I do in the meantime?"

"Fix your price, but make it negotiable." He had had enough of me. His pockets were crammed with many other messages to deliver to my father's other daughters. He jumped out of the car. He kicked the tire and disappeared through the gate of my father's estate.

I slid into the clammy driver's seat. Stretched out in front of me, the road was a glistening sheet of ice. To my left was a sheer drop of one hundred feet. Before me rose a massive wall of gray boulders, with tufts of weed and moss and folded-up notes stuffed in every cranny. And on my right were rolling hills of garbage—rotting food, the rusted entrails of machines, broken glass, worm-eaten furniture. In the rearview mirror I could see the spiked gates of my father's domain, locked and forbidding. I said to myself, "For once in your life you must take control of the wheel." I was glad to see that my attitude was already improving. I started the car. It began at once to skid wildly. I slammed the pedals down to the floor, one after the other, over and over again. I turned the wheel sharply to the right and then flung my arms across my eyes and waited in my own smell and blackness for death to take me over. Each millisecond in the second was italicized. The car spun around in mad circles and then took off through the air. I landed upside down in the muck. From that absurd position I did not wish to be rescued. But through my window, splattered with decayed tomatoes and eggs, I watched a car filled with children pull up beside my coffin. Seven little Chinese men tumbled out. They stationed themselves around my car, lifted it up out of the devastation, turned it over, and set it down on the road. I stepped out and extended my hand cordially but with dignity. "I hope I shall someday be in a position to repay your kindness," I said. The tallest and bulkiest in their group, the leader, I presumed, put out his hand in turn, pulled me to his body, jumped as high as he could, shot his tongue down my throat, and with his free hand snatched fistfuls of every bit of me, climbing up on my hips when he wanted something from the top. When he was through they installed me in their hovel, where I kept house for all seven while they set out each morning in their car, singing in chorus. They returned harmonizing at night, with bags of strange food and sometimes a gift for me, a better mop or a ruffled apron.

One afternoon while they were gone you came along disguised as the stranger I had been instructed to spurn. "What are you doing here?" you demanded. You clicked open your suitcase and spread out your wares across the well-swept threshold. You took up your pad and with your feather drew a picture of a pastry so tempting I could not resist. I pushed it all into my mouth and sucked it insatiably. It was delicious. The poison invaded me. I could not be roused. You stuffed me in a sack and slung it over your shoulder. When they asked, you told them I was dead. On the day that your trip ended, you dumped the contents of the sack outside my father's gate and rode triumphantly into his courtyard on your white donkey. My body hit the rocky ground. I gagged. The sodden piece of paper flew out of my mouth. My eyes opened. I was awake.

She got up and brushed a cockroach off her manuscript. Fasfusah was wailing under the table. The cat's belly was taut from hunger and pregnancy. Poor Fasfusah was pushing down desperately, wincing in agony, laboring in terror, without the elegance and knowledge her mother, Chanda, had flaunted. A week earlier Chanda and Bachunay had departed for good, leaping out the same iron-barred window through which they had claimed the privilege of entering on the night Mara and Sudah had moved into the loft. Not only was the cat food depleted, but there was no hope even from the garbage. They sensed the absence of a future in such poverty. Fasfusah and Mazhnoon remained, however, never daring again to go out into the world after their rejection by Rashi. Mazhnoon now circled his sister's struggle, calm for the first time. He waited with confidence. When the three kittens emerged, bloody and stunted, wet and matted, as black as black Bachunay, Mazh-noon closed in to carry out the obligations of the absent father. First he bit off the head of each one and spat it out. Then he snapped off the legs, crunching the soft bones between his teeth. Then he tore open the bellies and scooped out the guts, chewed them up and swallowed them down.

Sudah had found a suitable ashram in the mountains. It had been a summer camp in its previous incarnation, and the interior walls of the little rainbow-colored bungalows surrounding the lake chronicled the loves of the children who had wept there and longed for mother. The ashram was three hours away by bus. Their last pennies went for the fare. The morning he left, Sudah rolled his few possessions into his rug, bound it up with twine, tested and retested its weight on his back until he was completely satisfied with the feel and the look of it. Then he set his burden down on the floor and opened his arms to Mara. "You will come to visit me," he said. She nodded shyly into his neck. They had gone over it all before. The plan was for Sudah to remain in the ashram until he felt he could no longer benefit from what it offered. They would then sell the loft, split the money, fly off together to Europe, separate, and from there Sudah alone would embark on a pilgrimage to the banks of the Ganges. They were certainly destined to meet again. Meanwhile, Mara would acquire necessary experience in providing for herself. "When you come to visit," Sudah continued, "you must say you are a sister to me." Mara nodded again. They had discussed this detail before, too. His career at the ashram would not be advanced if his reputation as an ascetic were in any way blemished. Through the high front windows she watched him walk away from her down the street. He was so straight-backed and distant, how had she managed to draw him to her in the first place?

It took Mara a few months to realize that in order to survive she would need to find work. At first she considered turning for help to Rashi and Herzl. She even thought of debasing herself by approaching her father and tickling the soles of his feet. But these possibilities collapsed when the family was struck down by blow after blow. The indictments came unremittingly from the courts. First Teddy Schumacher was charged with accepting a bribe and using his influence unlawfully on Leon's behalf. Murray Levine, Sid Schneider, and Max Brody were accused of filing false reports and of defrauding the government of impressive sums of money. All three had pleaded guilty and were cooperating with the prosecution in exchange for lesser sentences or immunity. Each had agreed to testify against Leon. Leon Lieb himself, and his son Herzl, were indicted on charges of stealing over one million dollars from the government, and of violating public-health laws. Mara's troubles were frivolous in the face of such public calamity. She would have liked to succor her ruined family in some way, to put her own strength at the service of her mother at least, but Rashi recommended that she suppress her half-baked impulses. "I'll just call Mommy and tell her I love her," Mara had said. "Don't do it" was Rashi's advice. "They don't need to be reminded of their failures."

Leon now spent his days at home, no longer venturing out even to the synagogue for Sabbath-morning prayers. On his last visit to the genteel old *shul* he had built with his own money and supported over the years, he had been lashed by a fragment from the conversation of two octogenarians. "They should sentence him to one of his own homes, heh, heh, heh!" the blind one had shouted into the ear of his deaf bench mate. It was a fact that the community was now severing its ties with Leon, and whereas before he had always been greeted with pleasure and expectation, now even some of his gifts of charity were being returned to him without regret. The boards and organizations on which he served, usually in an honorary capacity in tribute to his beneficence, were now confidentially requesting that he quietly resign, at least until after the storm blew over. Sadie Stern ran the deserted office by herself these days. Reb Anschel Frankel, the fringes of his *talis* dangling over his waistband and a black velvet yarmulka on his head, kept a stony guard at the entrance to the apartment. Inside, Leon and Herzl conferred over piles of documents, their cheeks puffy and unshaven, like mourners. They seldom gazed directly at each other, and when by chance their eyes collided, Leon quickly averted his. Rose found their daytime presence in her space an added burden. She tried to confine herself to her bedroom, but the worst aspect of their intrusion was that it prevented her from eating as much and as often as she desired. Ultimately she abandoned all subterfuge and openly piled sweets onto her plate, occasionally even carrying them defiantly out into the dining room and chewing loudly in the presence of her husband, the contents of her mouth wet and on display. But sometimes she would dress herself in a skirt and blouse, draw on her stockings and pumps, efficiently invert her lips to spread her lipstick, sit down at the table, and, figuring with pencil and paper, help them sort out their financial status. "Cheer up, Leon, we'll continue to eat well," she would reassure him. "Trust your dietitian." Here was his old, capable, twinkling Rose again. It made Leon weak. At other times she would emerge in her nightgown, wringing her hands. "There's only one solution," she would cry. "You must apologize. Take out an ad in the newspapers. Buy time on television. Tell them you're sorry. Just get it over with and say you're sorry."

"For what? For what am I sorry?"

"For everything. For everything you've done. Just say you're sorry. Promise them you'll never do it again. It's the only solution, Leon, believe me, I know what I'm talking about."

One day, as Mara was switching from station to station on her radio, searching for good jazz, she heard a mechanical news voice casually link her father's name with the phrase "a broken man." She made the decision to ignore Rashi and visit that evening. She slipped into the dining room unnoticed. The bent backs of Leon and Herzl, as worn as targets, sent a pang of tenderness through her. From the rear the two men looked like brothers. With their elbows on the table and their palms stretching the skin of their cheeks upward, they were dolefully listening to Rose. Rose was speaking in complicated numbers, tapping her pencil for emphasis on the sheets of paper laid out like a feast before her. Her gaze climbed over the rhinestone-studded frame of her glasses, which had slid halfway down her nose. "Well, look who's here," said Rose, "our woman of the world! I was sure you would show up sooner or later. I said to your father, 'Our Mara always had a soft spot in her heart for criminals,' that's what I said." She took off her glasses and let them hang from the golden chain around her neck. Slowly she permitted her eyes to traverse the length of her daughter's shabby red velvet coat with the squared shoulders and the frayed silk gardenia at the lapel. "Thirty years ago I had a coat just like that one. It was junky even when it was new. I got rid of it as soon as I could afford something good. If I had only known!" Mara laughed and came up behind her mother. "You're so cute, Mommy, I just love you!" She threw her arms around Rose's neck and kissed the soft face.

"Humph!" said Rose. Leon counted out some bills and stacked them on the table. He pushed the wad toward Mara. "Make your mother happy," he said, "get yourself a new coat. Something normal. Things are hard enough as it is." Rose sniffed. "Well, I hear you've become an independent woman," she said. "I hear that the world's greatest artist has changed himself into the Holy Ghost and flown the coop!" Mara grinned. Rose plowed ahead. "I don't know how you stand for it. How could you allow him to degrade you in this way? Let him hug and kiss you one day, and the next day let him stamp you out like a roach—what am I saying?"—and here Rose's hand chided her mouth with a little slap—"he would *never* kill a roach, he told me so himself!" Rose's look was stern and triumphant. "Face it, Mara, he has used you. I never would have lowered myself as you've done."

"You don't understand, Mother," Mara said.

"Maybe not. To be honest, I never could understand what on earth you saw in him in the first place. To me he was so strange, he was a creature from outer space. All you knew about him were lies. How could you feel safe with someone so far from anything you've known? I could never figure out how you could ever let him touch you. People say he's handsome, but he never appealed to me at all."

"It's hard for each of us to understand the choices the other makes," said Mara.

Herzl stood up. "That's enough, Mommy." He walked up to Mara, placed his arm over her shoulder, and drew her to his side. "We worry about you all the time, Mara. You must forgive us."

"That's all right, Herzl." She brushed his cheek sadly. "How have you been?"

"If only you would come by and talk to us once in a while, tell us your plans, share your life with us, it would be such a relief," Herzl said.

Mara shrugged. "We're not hiding anything. What do you want to know?"

"Tell us the truth, Mara," said Leon. "Is he still Jewish?"

"Sudah has a Jewish soul. He can't be anything else."

"I just want to know if he's converted."

"Of course not. But why are we talking about me at such a time? You should concentrate on your own mess."

Herzl cleared his throat. "You are now a woman of some experience," he said. "You know by now that there are certain facts a person can predict simply by looking ahead a little bit. Why not take out insurance against a foreseeable disaster?

Suppose after you and Sudah have separated for a few years you meet another man and want to get married. These things happen, after all. Of course you will want a Jewish divorce." He glanced at her hopefully. "But how can Sudah give you the divorce if we can't find him? A Jewish divorce is not like a civil divorce. Both partners must be present, the husband to give, the wife to receive. But where would we begin to look for Sudah? In India there are millions of people. The Himalayas are full of caves."

"I've had more than my share of sermons in my lifetime," Mara said. "What's your point, Herzl?"

"Your brother is being too tactful," said Rose. "I'll tell it to you very plainly. You should get a divorce from that creep immediately. He doesn't have your best interests at heart. Herzl is prepared to help you in every way. Your family cares for you, Mara. If you have an ounce of self-protection left in your body, do it while you can."

Mara shook her head. "I'll always be married to Sudah. He'll be present in me even if he's thousands of miles away. Even if there are other men, Sudah will always be my true husband. Sudah's dybbuk has invaded me. I can never be free."

"Dybbuk, shmybbuk!" said Leon. "We are talking about real life now. One thing I've learned in business, and that is, if you've made a bad investment, you don't hang on to it to try to squeeze a little profit from it, a little self-justification. You give it up, forget it, chalk it up to experience—but you learn your lessons from it."

"Well, all things considered, Daddy, I wonder if I ought to take your business advice."

Leon began pacing the floor with his hands clasped behind his back. Mara's words left a sour smell in the air. She was cut by his gauntness, by how old and shrunken he had suddenly become. Once again she was afflicted by that newsman's description. "I'm going to tell you a little story that may hurt you a bit," Leon said, "but I think you'll thank me for it someday. About a week or so ago a certain upstate property was advertised for sale that looked as if it might have some potential as a nursing home. Naturally, I called up—I don't consider myself totally without a future, after all. Well, what do you think? It turns out to be the yoga camp of your friend, the *tzaddik*, the Messiah. After we talk a little business the time comes to *shmooze*. I ask them if they have there a certain so-and-so. 'Yes,' they tell me. 'So how is he doing?' I ask them. 'He is one of our best,' they say. Thanks very much, I think to myself, that's the first bit of *naches* I've gotten from that stinker. 'Do you know him?' they ask me. So I admit to them that I am an acquaintance of his wife. 'His wife?' they say. 'Oh, you must have in mind a different so-and-so. Our boy is not married.' 'Are you sure?' I ask. I could feel my blood pressure rising. 'Of course, of course,' they answer me, 'we are one hundred percent sure. Our so-and-so is not married and never has been.' " Leon halted in front of Mara, folded his arms across his chest, and waited. "Well?" he demanded.

"Well, what?" Mara smiled. "Did you buy the place, after all?"

"What about my little story, Mara? Very romantic, no?"

"I know all about it, Daddy. Sudah and I agreed beforehand that it would be better for him there if they didn't know he was married."

"You agreed to such a thing? You fell into such a trap? Why would you throw yourself away like nothing?"

Rose sighed. "Come here, Mara," she offered. Mara quickly perched on the edge of the table, taking refuge, as always, in her mother. Rose was inevitably the first to yield, the first to swerve from the family's hard line. No matter how firm her opposition, Mara could soften it. Hadn't Rose been the first to resign herself to the reality of Sudah after his stories had collapsed? Once Rose caved in, the rest of the family had no choice but to follow.

"Let me clean your glasses for you," Rose said. This was an old and comforting ritual between them, which they often enacted just before they were about to sink into one of their snug, womanly discussions. Rose breathed on the lenses and rubbed them industriously with the hem of her skirt. Mara stared at the familiar rings on the aging hands, the large pear-shaped diamond set in platinum and the golden marriage band with the Hebrew inscription from the Song of Songs, "I am to my beloved and my beloved is to me." "Glasses are so personal," Rose spoke. "I can't bear to touch the glasses of someone I don't love." That was what she always said at the start of these conversations. She finished her polishing and set the glasses on Mara's face. "You're such a pretty girl, Mara, it's really a great pity you can't see straight." She smoothed a strand of hair off Mara's forehead. "Do you remember how Sudah killed his parents before you were married?" said Rose. "Well, you'd better face it, darling. He's just done the same to you."

She sustained herself in the beginning by pawning the camera and lenses Sudah had selected with such exquisite care; next the television set they had acquired from Rashi for a small plastic bag of marijuana; the silver candlesticks her parents had given them; the diamond ring, pearl necklace, and gold watch Leon had bought for Mara when it became apparent that these conventional gifts from the groom's side would not be forthcoming; her gold wedding ring engraved with the sentence "A locked garden is my sister, my bride" from Solomon's Song; the dust-mantled set of *Shass*, whose binding Sudah had gravely inspected. The telephone, heat, and electric service were cut off. She stopped paying the rent. The landlord threatened to evict her. When she wrote to Sudah about her circumstances he admonished her to seek enjoyment from all her experiences and learn the correct lessons from them. Two black men crashed into her place one morning and began to remove the furniture. She pleaded with them to take their filthy hands off her armoire. The smaller of the two pushed her down to the floor, knocking off her glasses. Fine cobwebs soundlessly burst open in each lens. She dragged at his ankle. She sank her teeth into his calf. Just as he was about to descend on her with his fists, she remembered an old trick Sudah had taught her, a trick that had served him well during his imprisonment for pacifism. Her eyes narrowed to threads, her nostrils flared, her fingers began a weird dance in front of the diabolically contorted features of her face, ropes of saliva hung from the corners of her wide-open mouth, which was casting out bright-red screams like flaming tongues. The men fled, terrified by this woman's madness. In his next letter Sudah congratulated her on her amusing and quick-witted adaptation of King David's ruse. "Every man will want strong and sly woman," he assured her.

She became a waitress in a bar. The manager hired her at once because she was so lithe and her slanted eyes, released from the glasses she never replaced after the struggle in the loft, had a surprised and what he called a "bedroom" look about them. He had grandiose plans for her. He let her endure a taste of the waitress's servitude for a few long nights. Then he offered her her big opportunity to join the two girls clad in nylon fringes who danced nonstop on top of the mirrored bar. "I will make you a star." He leered. The pay was better, too. The first hour strained every muscle, but after that she was lifted up by her own sweet trances and reveries. Who could be watching her from out there? Was another cunning Sudah observing her, singling her out with the cool eye of a marksman? In the midst of her twitching she could still manage to converse with the dancer beside her, a dark girl named Ronit, an Israeli, as it happened, who during the day taught courses at a university on the psychology of women. "Why are we doing this?" Mara asked Ronit. "Look down," Ronit replied. In the mirror below her Mara saw her own crotch, the damp curly hair escaping from either side of the band of cloth. When a customer would pour beer over their feet and stick out his tongue to lick it off the space on the bar between their legs, Ronit would say, "The cocks are frisky tonight." The girls were untouchable, that was the house rule. Ronit taught Mara how to deliver a sharp kick to the chin of any violator. When Mara wrote to Sudah about her new employment, his response was, "It is holy to share yourself." Slivers of glass and small puddles glistened on the countertop. Nothing provoked more glee than the spectacle of a startled girl crashing down on her rump. Ronit instructed Mara on how deftly to avoid these traps. Mara could now pay the rent and buy what little food she needed. But mostly she subsisted on maraschino cherries, cocktail onions, pitted olives, pretzels, and peanuts. One stale dawn she said to Ronit, "I don't think I can stand much more of this." "What were you expecting?" Ronit asked. "I don't know," Mara replied, "but something, definitely something." She arrived at work later and later, and danced without spirit. The essential smile did not part her face. She spat on the head of a customer who was depositing wet kisses on the reflection in the counter between her legs. The manager said, "You drying up, Miz Rocky?" He fired her that night.

Through the steam from the two cups of tea she set down between them, Jana said to Mara, "But why did you spit on his head? You should have peed! You should have shit! Still, to spit is at least a beginning." Jana's nooses were strangling her from every side. Mara felt trapped in those spider webs. She waited for Jana to sip away at her vitality, but Jana only hovered over her and stroked. Jana declared her disappointment in Mara. "You let yourself swing up there like a piece of meat. How could you do it?" Mara glanced at Jana. "What choice did I have?" she asked with resignation. She did not want to explode all over Jana because it had been so long since she had had something hot in her belly. She rubbed her palms on the precious teacup. "I have to pay the rent, don't I? Where were you when those goons came to strip down my loft and dump me and every stick I own into the gutter? I'm not exactly the hottest property on today's job market, Jana!" It occurred to Jana then that she had it within her power to secure the perfect job for Mara. The women's cooperative art gallery, of which she was a member, needed an interesting-looking female to open and close the doors each day, to sit behind the desk and answer questions as viewers strolled through, to help coordinate the evening programs—lectures, films, poetry readings, etc. Would Mara be interested? It was far more than she could ever hope for, Jana reminded her. How could Mara refuse? Within the month the job was hers. Sudah expressed his skepticism. "Female art is dead end," he wrote her, "like female part."

The Coop, as it was called, was a storefront gallery on the ground floor of an old factory building in the neighborhood of Mara's loft. It consisted of two rooms: a large front room, in which the shows were exhibited, and a smaller back room, with metal folding chairs stacked against the wall, for the educational programs. Mara sat at a table directly beyond the door. "I am the first object on display," she joked in a letter to Sudah. But all in all it was a pleasant-enough job that required a minimum of exertion, and the atmosphere was congenial. She would acknowledge the presence of visitors and respond to their questions in a vague foreign accent and in the style of an insider. She answered the telephone. She mailed out circulars announcing upcoming events. She set up the chairs for the evening programs. If special equipment was needed, such as a screen or a slide projector, she would prepare it. During her first month on the job there was a showing of lucite sculpture by one of the members. The centerpiece was a fountain with a regulated flow of water controlled by electricity, and it was Mara's responsibility to make sure that the plug was firmly within the socket.

At the nearby cafés she was now recognized and greeted even by people who had never set foot in the Coop itself, for she was visible through the glass to every browser. She was new female blood on the scene, and the regulars wondered fleetingly about her, especially the men. "They're all interested in me, but they know I'm not available," she confided to Rashi. She was a mystery even to herself. She was not yet ready to disappoint anyone. People would squeeze closer together around a table to open up a space for her. A place was once or twice gladly made even for Rashi, who in these circles represented little more than a clue to her sister. Here it was Mara's turf. Mara introduced Rashi to the designer of record album jackets, the videotape artist, the poster artist, the fabric painter, the potter, the glass blower. Rashi sat in silence as Mara chatted familiarly with them, laughing and nodding often, and trading first names and nicknames like well-rubbed coins. "I suppose the real ones are too busy working," said Rashi after they left. Mara described an encounter with a "real one." She mentioned the well-known name of an artist, not yet old, who had in his youth been a shrewd original and who now, in his middle years, was very rich. Encircled by his court, he had descended on the blessed café in which she had been killing the time of night, Mara recalled, his face oily with fame and self-love. Oddly enough, several people had in the past noticed the resemblance between Mara and the women this particular artist preferred to paint—it was a matter of types— and a few had urged her to seek him out and become his model. What Mara did not talk to Rashi about was the glance that had locked her to this man. It was a special kind of communication, the kind that precedes language, the kind by which a man and a woman plainly show what they want from each other and what they know they can do and get, if circumstances should yield. It was what Sudah called "sex energy." Mara had been shaken for nights after that look had hooked her to this artist, and during the day she had waited in vain for him to stride into the Coop, casting about for her with his cruel and brooding eye.

Rashi gave Mara an account of the situation at home. "It's bad," she said, "very, very bad—in a quiet, fatalistic way. The screaming and yelling is over." The trial date for Leon and Herzl was approaching, and more and more evidence was being amassed against them as former associates scrounged for ways to be spared. Their mail was packed with letters of vilification, threats, stark and illiterate anti-Semitism. They had been forced to change their phone number. They were menaced and in hiding. How would it be possible to gather together an untainted jury of men and women in this blasted city? "But at least Mommy and Daddy feel better about you," Rashi said. "They think you're finally getting up on your own two feet now that you've taken this job."

"They're wrong, as usual," said Mara.

"Maybe. But now they have high hopes that you'll take Herzl up on his offer to help you get a divorce. At least a Jewish divorce."

"What I couldn't understand when I visited them, and what I still can't figure out, is how they can blithely go on giving me advice on what's best for me when it's obvious not only to me but to the whole damn world that they've screwed up their own affairs but good and turned their own lives into a super catastrophe. How can he go on preaching to me when he himself is such a celebrated sinner?"

"He still considers himself a righteous man," Rashi said

softly. "None of this has changed his opinion of himself. It's mellowed him, made him feel vulnerable, reminded him of his mortality, though he probably still feels an exception will be made in his case. As far as he's concerned, he's still smarter and more virtuous. People have always said unkind things about him. So what? He himself has simply never agreed, never collaborated as you and I do in the attempts of others to destroy us. That's why he was able to make it in the first place. He'll always believe in his natural right to wield authority, and even if the world strips him of it, he's not about to surrender it as far as his own family is concerned."

"Yeah, like the wretch who's humiliated every day by his supervisor in the factory. Then he comes home and spends the night beating the living daylights out of his wife."

"Anyway," said Rashi, "on this subject of divorce, I think they're right."

At a closed meeting of the Coop membership Jana criticized her sisters for their indifferent treatment of Mara. "We're worse than men because our own misfortunes as secretaries and slaves make it impossible for us to pretend we can't see what we're doing to her. We're cluttering her head with chores and trivia and details and nonsense the way a housewife's head is clogged with so much crap that even while she lies in bed with a man on top of her she composes grocery lists in her head. Any talent or creativity simply shrivels up from lack of nourishment and dies. We should know better. We should give Mara a chance." Several of the women were of the opinion that they had already done more than their share in promoting Mara's well-being. They noted that Mara was practically uneducated and totally untrained. Hundreds of better-qualified women would slice off a finger for a chance at the glamorous job Mara was lucky enough to have been handed on a silver platter. Mara was basically inefficient and disorganized, which forced the membership to put up with a variety of inconveniences, minor ones mostly, but irritating nonetheless. Jana insisted that it was natural for a person with such gifts as Mara possessed—did they know she was a writer and a poet?—to wilt from the dry and repetitious tasks she was assigned. One of the women wondered at the fervor of Jana's support of Mara. It was true that Mara was an attractive woman, but the antique clothing she favored was bizarre even on their landscape, and she seemed to consider herself above the vanity of using a deodorant. They knew she was suffering difficult personal changes— here Jana nodded emphatically—but this is precisely why women like themselves inevitably fail in business: because they set personal considerations above professional needs. Nevertheless, Jana's good will was valued by her colleagues, and so it was decided that Mara would be offered a chance to show her worth by devising and carrying out an original evening program of her own creation.

Mara opened with enthusiasm when Jana brought her the news. She let out a stream of charming, haunting ideas. But when she was alone later, all of them seemed pale and brittle. She sought out the suggestions of others. Sudah wrote from his ashram that she ought to form a committee to draft a law declaring that all makers of art—writers, composers, painters, whatever—must henceforth remain anonymous. Luke Alfasi proposed specialized poetry workshops for insane people, persons ninety years old or over, nursery children, lepers, psychiatrists, and so on, and although this idea beguiled Mara, she rejected it because the programs at the Coop were already limited to women exclusively. Rashi thought it would be nice to arrange a series of nine-month sessions for pregnant women, in which they would record in diaries or drawings the altered states of their bodies and souls. For Mara it was impossible to conceive of so extended a commitment. But one dull afternoon an idea began to crystallize in her mind. It came to her right there at her desk in the Coop, during one of the daily telephone conversations with her mother, a practice she had recently instituted as a gift to Rose, for since Mara's phone had been disconnected there was no other way to make contact and offer reassurance. As usual she sat with the receiver sandwiched between her uplifted shoulder and her ear, addressing envelopes, grunting every now and then while Rose did all the talking. When Rose's subject was not her medication and her depression or her overeating, it was their miserable legal entanglements. This time she was describing a peripheral sorrow— how it pained her that Leon's and Herzl's pictures were so often in the newspapers. What happened to these millions of photographs? Rose lamented. They were slivers of her dear ones' souls. Her own father, Rabbi Shlomo Isaac, may his memory be a blessing, after whom Rashi had been named, had never permitted his picture to be taken, for it was nothing but a graven image. Rose herself was extremely cautious about distributing photographs of her children, taking pains to extract in advance a promise from the recipient that they would be well preserved and cherished. It occurred to Mara then that while a person's face, his entire appearance, in short, was a thing that he himself owned, it was a part of himself that was visible firsthand only to others; it was a possession that could be stolen with impunity by any stranger in the form of a picture. She decided to organize a conference on the rights of the photographed. That very day she wrote up a proposal and presented it to the collective. It was ardently endorsed. Jana was exultant.

But when she set herself to the task of recruiting a suitable panel of female photographers, preparing the announcements and the circulars, and attending to all the other bothersome details, her excitement waned. She was clutched by panic at the prospect of standing up before an audience to introduce the program. She had no doubt she would be revealed as a fraud. The success of this enterprise would be her total responsibility. It was terrifying. At first the women inquired eagerly about the progress of the arrangements, but as it became clear that nothing was taking shape, they ceased to ask. Now when the members passed her desk at the Coop, Mara looked down and pretended to be busy. She felt ashamed and exposed, and moreover, she felt vexed at these unnatural women. She despised them. More and more now she was neglecting her other duties. It was obvious to everyone that Mara's days at the gallery were numbered.

It was the early spring of the third year of Mara's marriage to Sudah. In the warming weather Rashi would occasionally accompany Mara on her walk to work. They would go slowly, in silence, each holding on to one of Naomi's hands. On this particular day it was already half an hour after the time Mara was supposed to have opened the doors of the Coop. Suddenly, over the gap between them created by the child, Mara turned to her sister. "Guess what?" she said. Rashi held her breath. "I've just committed my first adultery," Mara announced.

*"Mazel tov."*

"Well, not exactly my first; my second, actually. I did one last night and one the night before, but I didn't speak to you yesterday."

"How did you do it?" Rashi blurted out. Mara laughed. "I mean, how did you manage to arrange it?" she hastily saved herself.

"It was all very easy, Rashi. I'll tell you in case you want to go out and try it for yourself someday." Mara beamed good-naturedly at her sister. "I went into a bar with this specific intention. I picked out a man who interested me. I walked up to him and said, 'There's sexual energy between us.' That's all I had to do. The next thing I knew, I was following him like a lamb to his room. We did it and that was that."

"Was it any good?"

"It was awful. The first one had an ugly body underneath his clothing. Whew! He screwed like a confirmed masturbator. The second was better, but still nothing much. My problem is, I'm used to the best. I'm spoiled. Sudah is first-class."

Rashi bent down to lift Naomi. She pressed her lips to the little girl's smooth forehead and sniffed the fragrant hair. Naomi did not know what to make of this insult of tenderness. She sensed that things were no longer orderly and predictable, and she began a steady, anxious whimpering. Rashi squeezed her in sympathy, to give comfort and take comfort, but this gesture served only to upset the child even more deeply. Against the background of Naomi's rising cries, Rashi was trying to talk to Mara about how sad it all was. "Well, it's just so sad, I can't tell you," Rashi was saying. "I can understand that you would go out and look for a man, but why should it be so sordid? At least there should be some warmth between you, some recognition. It's a terrible waste, really."

Mara's face hardened. "Look, this is a thing I need to do. I have to open myself to this experience. I've got to start somewhere. These two were pretty brutal, but good ones will come along."

Rashi was patting Naomi's stubborn back. "Who are these creatures?" she demanded, practically shouting to be heard over the child's wails. "They could be criminals! They could be sick! Do you protect yourself in any way? Do you take any precautions at all? What about birth control?"

"I follow the astrological method. By the moon and stars and planets. Don't worry, it works perfectly."

"By the planets, did you say? Are you crazy, Mara?"

With her free hand Rashi fumbled in her purse for her sunglasses. But the tears came down before she could adjust them properly over her eyes. Naomi stared with open mouth, struck dumb in mid-howl by the sight of her weeping mother, for here was Rashi claiming a privilege that Naomi prized as exclusively her own. Mara reached across to straighten the glasses on her sister's face. "You always put them on lopsided," Mara said affectionately. "It makes you look like a Picasso. There now, that's better."

Rashi was shaking her head, as if to knock out all the tears once and for all. "There's something else I wanted to tell you," Mara continued. "We've decided to go through with the divorce, Sudah and I. It's sort of a present from all of us to all of you. Sudah will be coming back in a few weeks, so we can do it then. Tell Herzl for me." Rashi was wiping her cheeks with the back of her hand. "But only a Jewish divorce," Mara said. "We don't feel ready to cut it off completely yet."

Rashi turned sharply to Mara. "What do you mean *we?*" she said bitterly. "*He!* He's the one who's not ready! He's not a fool like you. Where's his home? France? Israel? Egypt? India? Do you think for a moment he would be ready to give up the protection of an American wife?" She looked at Mara with dry anger. "And you know that what I say is the truth! You're deceiving yourself now, just as you've always done, to your endless harm!"

They parted at the door of the Coop, which had already been opened by one of the members. Rashi did not give Mara the news that she was pregnant, as she had planned to do during this walk. The child, Sarah, was already a separate and formed stranger on the day Mara first met her years later.

Arm in arm, nuzzling and bumping hips, they made their entrance into the rabbi's chamber. Herzl steered them in from behind, his eyes clouded with shame. Rabbi Levi Ashkenazi, the father of the lawyer Paul Ashkenazi, stared at them in astonishment, his wine-colored lips opening to encircle his teeth, stained by endless glasses of tea. He had never, over the many years he had engaged in the dark business of granting divorces, seen such a spectacle as this. His friend Leon Lieb was doubly cursed, at home and in the street. Herzl did nothing to betray the depths of his sympathy with the rabbi's outrage and bewilderment. This was not the time to stand foolishly on principle. There was a job to be done. Coming up the stairs, Sudah had pointedly reminded him that the medieval ban against polygamy of Rabbenu Gershom applied only to Western Jews. "To you, Herzl my brother, not to me," Sudah had said through a grin. Herzl's tongue and fists ached to smite, but he restrained them. Sudah's pivotal consent to this divorce was, at best, tenuous, a thing that still had to be flattered and coaxed. For the time being it would be wisest for Herzl to bow his head to every insult, to suppress all stirrings of self.

It was a somber, book-lined room filled with men. On opposite sides sat the two witnesses, unfriendly and blind to each other, Reb Anschel Frankel and Manny Fish. Why involve strangers? Already too many people had their noses in this, his private scandal. That was how Leon had reasoned when he had assigned this sensitive mission to these two men. Between the high windows draped in dusty maroon velvet was the portrait of Rabbi Shamai Ashkenazi, Rabbi Levi Ashkenazi's father and Paul's grandfather, the noted author of the definitive text, *The Agunah: A Blessing in Disguise,* a black-bearded visage with thick eyebrows that met over his nose as if to underline his imposing forehead. At a small table in the corner sat an old man with tags of skin hanging from his eyelids, like stalactites. This was the scribe, Reb Yudel Heller. In the presence of so many solemn and purposeful men, Mara was struck again by that familiar sense of herself shrinking into nothing more than a silly, helpless girl. It was as if she had trespassed in a restricted area where she had no right to be, a room filled with masked surgeons who were preparing themselves for the delicate operation they were about to perform on her body, and sharpening their scalpels.

Rabbi Ashkenazi requested that Mara step out into the

waiting room for a while, but Sudah held her hand tightly and would not release it. After consulting briefly with Herzl, however, the rabbi decided to waive this rule in this particular case. The main thing was to part this demonic man from this possessed woman, on paper if not in the flesh. Sudah and Mara sat side by side, weaving their fingers together, kissing intermittently. Such a display of intimate absorption in each other in this public place afflicted everyone. Sudah's long hair was tied back with string. On his head he wore the African skullcap, and his dark nipples were visible through the thin white cotton of his shirt. Mara was dressed in her workman's boots, above that three skirts of different lengths and a short threadbare velvet jacket fastened together with a rhinestone clip. Her hair had been cut so short it stood up from her scalp, like a disgraced woman's. Calico had hacked it off one night with his great bone-handled knife. Her front teeth were chipped. Her face was inflamed with an unwholesome rash that made its way down her neck and into the reaches of her clothing. There were lice in her quilt, she had explained to Herzl.

Rabbi Ashkenazi commenced the prescribed interrogation of the husband. "Do you, Sudah, son of Ezra, give this *get* of your own free will?" he asked. "Have you ever made a statement or a vow that would nullify this *get?*" On it went, and to each of these questions Sudah replied in the expected fashion, turning to smile at Mara from time to time and squeezing her hand. The old scribe then came slowly forward and presented Sudah with the parchment, the goose quill, and the bottle of specially prepared ink that could never be erased, in accordance with the biblical injunction that the husband himself write the *get*, the bill of divorcement. Sudah examined these objects with the interest of one who had formerly plied a related trade. He took his sweet time, setting Herzl's teeth on edge. At last he returned the tools to Reb Yudel, authorizing the scribe in the presence of the witnesses to prepare the document in his behalf. Reb Yudel dipped his quill into his bottle of black ink and put it to the parchment. Herzl watched the old man dip and bring his wizened face down until it almost rested on the table, dip and dip, until Herzl felt he would choke. It was crucial that there not be a single error in that text. Tragedy could ensue if even the thorn of the *yod*, the smallest of the letters, were in any way imperfect. Rabbi Levi Ashkenazi stared out the window with his hands clasped behind his back. Reb Anschel Frankel took a holy book down from a shelf and prayed. Manny Fish smoked cigarette after cigarette. This hour of terrible silence was punctuated by the staccato of Mara's giggles and their low, cooing whispers.

When at last the scroll was completed and the ink had dried, Reb Anschel and Manny reviewed it carefully and put their signatures to it. Rabbi Ashkenazi continued the formal questioning of the scribe, of the witnesses, and of Sudah. Then he turned to Mara. "Are you, Mara, daughter of Aryeh, accepting this *get* of your own free will?" he asked. "Yes," she said softly. He ordered her to remove all her rings so that nothing would come between her hands and their acceptance of the document, but of course her fingers were already bare, for every item of value had been pawned. "Stand so," said the rabbi. He set the couple face to face, with Mara's open palms turned upward in front of her to receive the *get.* "Now drop it in," the rabbi instructed Sudah, passing him the parchment, "and speak these words aloud to the woman."

"Behold you are cast out from me," Sudah said to Mara.

All the witnesses were in agreement that the divorce had been given. It was now in Mara's hands. "Place it under your arm," the rabbi said to Mara. "What for?" she demanded, as if suddenly and unexpectedly the anesthesia had worn off. "To show that you have received it," Herzl explained soothingly. Mara shrugged. "Okay. But I'm not so sure you guys will want it back after it's been in my armpit." "Please, Mara, don't make jokes," Herzl begged. Mara complied. "Now walk with it," said the rabbi. "What do you mean, 'walk with it'?" cried Mara. "Just do it, please," said Herzl, "it's only symbolic, the final sign before the witnesses that you have accepted it." "But that's too much," Mara protested, shaking her head obstinately, "that's just the limit. Why should I be the one to have to walk across this room with everybody's eyes on my ass? I'm Exhibit A, like Vashti, a freak! I just can't do it!" "I'll walk with you," said her brother. He put his arm across her shoulder, his hand on her biceps pressing the piece of parchment ever closer to her thin body, and together they walked to the door.

Sudah never returned to the ashram. He told Mara that its usefulness to his future had ended. He must now occupy himself with the preparations for his journey to India. He must get his papers in order and together they must seek out a buyer for the loft. Mara said that she, too, was ready. In front of their building, at the end of their slow and nostalgic walk back from the divorce, Mara found a wallet containing two hundred dollars as well as the owner's identification. Upstairs they split the money. "A good omen for a new life," she said.

She continued to live in the front part of the loft with Calico. "My John," she called him. Sudah reclaimed his platform and immersed himself again in his yoga. He fondled his celibacy like a treasure. Calico was a fierce and unpredictable lover. His uncircumcised penis never ceased to repel her. Sometimes he beat her with a strap. Sometimes he unsheathed his knife and pointed it at her, drawing his lips back over his gums. But when he held her, she could feel his desperation and his need, the death that was in him.

One morning in the early part of June, Leon Lieb stood alone in the urine smell of Mara's dark hallway and pushed the bell for her loft. There was no answer. He slumped against the wall and closed his eyes. A strange voice assaulted him. "Looking for something, old man?" Leon's hand closed instinctively around the lead pipe he had brought along for protection. "Does Mara Mizrahi live here?" he asked.

"Yup." It was a coarse-faced man with a turned-up snout. Alcohol fumes spread from his mouth.

"Do you think she's at home, maybe?"

"Yup."

"Would you please do me a favor and go and ask her to come down? I must talk to her."

"You one of her men? She probably up there with some guy right now." Leon slipped him a bill, if only to pay for his silence. Some minutes later Mara descended, hugging her torn silk dragon robe to herself.

"You look terrible," Leon said. "You look sick."

"Is that what you came here to tell me?" Mara turned, beginning her climb back up the stairs.

Leon seized her shoulder. "Wait, Mara'le, it's all right. You never were a neat child. When you were in school you ran as fast as the boys and every day you came home with your dress torn and hanging, one sock up and one sock down. Your teacher asked Mommy why you never pulled the other one up. I remember these things." Mara had heard this story before. She said nothing, on guard.

"Do you read the papers at all?" Leon continued. "Do you care to know what's happened to me? Answer me, Mara. I'm only asking you if you want to know. I'm not dumping my pack of troubles on you—what good would it do?"

"I'm listening, Daddy."

"It's that bloodsucker, Gross, the prosecutor, he's gone mad. What can I say? He's a leech, he won't let go. Just because his own father had an accent, do I have to suffer? I made a deal with that bum. I wouldn't wish such a deal on my worst enemy. I gave him everything he wanted. He held a knife to my throat. He said to me, 'You're guilty, right?' 'Yes, I'm guilty, I'm guilty,' I said to him. Thank God I wasn't under oath, but it wasn't a complete lie after all, for who among us is totally innocent? We have all sinned against God willingly and under compulsion, by hardening our hearts, knowingly and unknowingly." Leon thumped his chest with his fist as he enumerated these transgressions. He went on. "Then the torturer said to me, 'You can go to jail for ten years, you can die and rot there.' 'Fine,' I said, 'if it will make you happy, I'll sit in jail until the Messiah comes.' 'You'll tell us everything you know,' he said, 'you'll spill your guts out to us. If you're a good boy, maybe you'll get a lighter sentence, maybe not. We're not guaranteeing anything.' 'All right, all right,' I said, 'I'll cooperate, I'll do whatever you want—only leave my family in peace, leave my son, Herzl, alone!' And you know what that dog said to me then? He said, 'It's a deal. Why should we waste our time with your son, anyway? He's just a small-time operator. Besides, everything he did was at his father's orders.' And I had to sit through all that, Mara. It was the worst day of my life!" Leon glanced at his daughter. "Well, one of the worst," he said.

"You won't go to jail. You'll figure something out."

"I said to the rat, 'Gross,' I said, 'at least when I'm wiped out once and for all in that courtroom maybe you'll have the decency to stand up and admit that most of the things you've said about me and most of the things you've fed to the press about me were lies—*lies!* You should do this, Gross, not for my sake alone, but for your own, because God, unlike man, will always turn a kind ear to a master of repentance.' It's to my credit that at least I had the courage to say that. But I thank God that the charges against Herzl have been dismissed. Herzl is safe now. I've done this thing for my family."

"You did the right thing."

"My grandfather, Naftali Herz, the grand rabbi of Oświęcim, was known everywhere as a holy man. Yet he used to pray to God, 'How can I be a holy man if I love my own children more than I love other people's children?' Do you understand that, darling? I've always loved what is mine above all else. But that, too, is not what I came here to tell you." Mara waited, her arms locked across her chest.

"I came here to ask you to come home with me," Leon said. "No."

"Mara'le, tonight begins the holiday of Shavuos, when the Holy One, blessed be He, gave us the Torah and chose us from among all the other nations on this earth. Please come home."

"I can't, Daddy."

"We will be reading the Book of Ruth in *shul*. You were named after my mother, Naomi, may her memory be a blessing. 'Do not call me Naomi, call me Mara, for God has dealt very bitterly with me.' We will read these words tomorrow. Come home, Mara."

"No, Daddy, no."

"If not for my sake, then for Mommy's. It would do wonders for her. She's not well. Mara, I know you love your mother."

"No, I can't go with you, I'm sorry."

"But you see I'm begging you. How can you refuse me now?"

"It's impossible, Daddy." Mara turned unexpectedly. She ran up the stairs and slammed the door. Leon went out into the street. He stood on the sidewalk below her window. He picked up a fistful of pebbles and threw them against the glass. Mara lifted the curtain and looked down at her father. She let the cloth fall. The stones continued to rain on her window until an hour before dusk.

They sold the loft and divided the money. Mara sewed her share into the hems of her skirts, and wearing all three, she, with Sudah, boarded a plane for Paris, where they remained together for four days. Then Sudah said farewell and set off down the street with his thumb pointed in the direction of India.

Six months later Mara was living on the island of Forment-era, in a cave open on one side to the sea. That morning she had laid her yarrow sticks and consulted the *I Ching*. One of the formations showed a change from yin to yang. In Mara's text the interpretation was, "He allows himself to be drawn into returning."

She made her way up and down the rocky hills to the plaza. At the post office she was handed a letter from Sudah, which had been mailed to her not too many days after they had parted in Paris. Somehow it had followed her ragged trail doggedly from city to city and found her here among the herbs and the women garbed in black. She slipped his letter under her arm and began the long walk back to her cave. First she built a small fire of twigs. She ate some berries out of the palm of her hand and drank some water. She wrapped a cloth over her shoulders against the cold of evening. She squatted by the pale, low flames and she opened his letter.

My sister Mara,
I am now in Lyons. From Paris I walk all day, 60 kilometers maybe. Then I hitch ride in truck with Algerian man and boy, 80 kilometers. I walk some more. Then high society lady in bikini give me ride, 150 kilometers. Again I walk. American student give me lift in old bus, 80 kilometers. I wait and wait. Nobody stops for me. They all think I am hippie or Hindu. Nothing to do. I get small ride on motorcycle, about 40 kilometers. Then movie type drives out of his way for me, maybe 130 or 140 kilometers, and drops me in woods outside Lyons. I am so tired I go to sleep under a tree. In the morning I open my eyes. I look up. I see it is a cherry tree. So I have some.